SILENT THREAT

Book II of The Steeplewood Series

E R Major

Some secrets are more dangerous than desire.

Darby Williams believed she had finally found peace—married to ambitious young lawyer Blake Williams, building a future in Nashville, and ready to leave the pain behind. She had survived loss, betrayal, and danger—but the past refuses to let go. When a new threat emerges from old secrets, Darby must confront her deepest fears and the promises she's made—to her husband, to her family, and to herself. But keeping those promises may mean risking more than she is willing to lose.

Returning to their hometown of Steeplewood should offer comfort. Instead, Darby and Blake are pulled into a storm of old rivalries and buried secrets. Her half-brother's hostility runs deep, and one stolen kiss proves that danger isn't always from strangers.

As tension builds and threats close in, Darby must decide who to trust—and how much she's willing to sacrifice. Because silence can protect…or it can kill.

Table of Contents

He'd had the dream again last night. This time, it felt more like a divine vision. In the fantasy, Darby stood in a beautiful meadow with her back turned toward him. When he called her name, she turned to face him, her features illuminated by sunbeams. Her hands were resting on her stomach, rounded and swollen with their unborn child. The certainty of it lingered after he woke, heavy and unsettling, as if something had already been decided without asking either of them.

Outside, the early morning rain drummed steadily against their bedroom window, the occasional muted rumble of thunder breaking the quiet. Darby relaxed deeper into the comfort of their bed, a sigh slipping from her lips as Blake's warm kisses trailed down her throat, between her breasts, and lingered on her taut stomach. She ran her fingers through his dark-blonde hair, her body responding automatically to his touch.

Blake paused and looked up at her face. "Let's make a baby."

Lightning flashed, throwing sharp shadows across the

bedroom in the gray dawn. Darby sat up so fast that Blake nearly tumbled off the bed, her heart slamming hard enough to make her dizzy.

"Wow, honey. Where're you going?" he chuckled, crawling back toward her. "It was only thunder and lightning."

But to Darby, the storm did not feel harmless. It vibrated through her, lingering like a warning she could not explain.

He gently pinned her back to the mattress and kissed her again, slow and practiced, easing her resistance without addressing it. "It's Saturday and raining," he murmured. "Relax, honey."

She let herself go slack beneath him, not because she was calm, but because resisting meant explaining, and she did not yet have the words. "I smell coffee," she said quickly. "You want a cup?"

Blake smiled. "Darby, you were having a great time until I said the word *baby*. Now you're avoiding the discussion we're going to have anyway." He slid lower, kissing her abdomen again, his mouth lingering there.

Her breath hitched. "Okay, fine," she sighed. "We finally have a little calm in our lives, Blake. Let's enjoy it before adding the chaos of a baby, shall we?" Her smile stayed polite, thin.

"Bullshit." Still smiling, he tapped the end of her nose. "The master plan was for us to finish school, then start a family. You got your MBA almost two years ago. I completed law school and passed the bar. We decided to stay in Nashville for at least another two years." He rolled away and headed toward the bathroom. "Besides, we don't know how long it'll take for you to get pregnant. If the first baby arrived today, I'd be into my mid-thirties before junior starts school."

"First baby?" Darby muttered.

She sat up, pulled his faded T-shirt over her head, and went into the kitchen. The fabric smelled like him, clean and familiar, and it made her throat tighten unexpectedly.

He followed, swatting her playfully. "That's all you got out of what I said? Darby, you know perfectly well we agreed to have more than one child." He paused to check his tone. "I'd very much like to hear what you have to say about moving forward with our plans."

Darby watched with appreciation as he pulled on his gym clothes, carefully considering her reply. She poured two cups of coffee, her hands steady despite the tension buzzing under her skin. "Okay, cowboy, how about we have this conversation again in six months?"

He took a slow drink, then leaned down until his nose touched hers, his height and presence filling the small space. "I hear your point," he said evenly, "but consider this. You stop taking the pill, and we fuck like bunnies until there's a baby right here." His coffee-warmed hand spread across her stomach. His fingers kneaded her skin, and she felt warmth spread through her body immediately.

The *Law & Order* musical theme blared from his phone in the other room.

"That's your father's ringtone," she said. Thankful for the interruption, she felt relief and guilt cross her face.

"It's cool, right?" He did not look away. "I'll call him back."

As soon as his phone stopped ringing, hers started to. She picked it up from the counter and handed it to him. "Guess who?"

Blake rolled his eyes and answered. "Dad. Busy right now. What's up?"

Darby escaped to the shower. The water hit her skin hard, grounding her, giving her something immediate to focus on.

They'd had two pregnancy scares already, both blamed on stress. Darby wanted to be the mother of her husband's children. She just wasn't sure now was the right time, or whether the hesitation itself meant something she was afraid to name.

She was about to turn the water off when Blake opened the shower door and stepped in fully clothed. His chin trembled as he pulled her against him, his grip tight and desperate.

"Blake, what is it? What happened?" She rubbed her hands over his back and arms, feeling him shake.

He cleared his throat again and again, struggling for breath. "Dad said Grammy passed away this morning. I told him we'd head that way…sometime today." The word *sometime* broke apart as soon as it left his mouth.

"Oh, Blake, I'm so sorry." She held him tighter, pressing her face into his shoulder as his knees nearly buckled.

He lifted his face into the falling water and wept. The spray drummed against their skin, mingling with the tears, grief loud and inescapable in the small space they shared.

Darby awoke alone in bed at the Williams Farm guest house. The quiet pressed in on her, a sharp contrast to the constant hum of her usual life. In the hours leading up to the trip, she and Blake had rearranged schedules, delegated work, postponed meetings, and packed in a rush born of obligation rather than readiness. The drive from Nashville to Steeplewood had been long and tense, grief riding silently between them. Now they were here, and the stillness felt earned and undeserved all at once.

Lately, most of their life unfolded inside their modest Nashville condo, well located and carefully renovated after her surprise inheritance made it possible. Blake had taken on the remodeling himself, learning as he went, fixing what he broke, adapting without complaint. Darby had worked beside him, sanding, painting, holding boards in place. It was the way they functioned best, shoulder to shoulder, practical and productive. His resourcefulness and quiet competence were part of what had made her trust him with a future in the first place.

She reached for her phone and checked her messages. One stood out, sent earlier that morning. Omalita. Her former landlady, now married to her biological father, Winston Payne. The message was brief and cautiously casual. Colt and his wife were in town from Texas, if Darby felt like visiting.

Darby pushed herself out of bed and opened the front door. The smells hit her immediately. Freshly cut hay, sharp and green, layered with the heavier scent of livestock.

She sneezed, eyes watering, surprised by the sudden reaction. She had grown up on a farm only a few miles from here, but her body had changed. Nashville had softened her. Her immune system had learned a different rhythm.

She scanned the driveway. The silver BMW sat where Blake had left it, clean and out of place against the dirt and gravel. Once her mother-in-law's, now passed down to Blake, it felt like another marker of transition, another thing that belonged to someone else before it belonged to her.

She called Blake.

"Morning, sleepyhead," he answered, his voice easy and bright. "You ready for breakfast?"

"I called to see if you'd mind if I take the car into town."

"Of course, I don't mind. What's up?"

"I got a text from Omalita saying Colt and his wife are in town. You want to go with me?"

"Not really, babe." His attention drifted as he spoke, focused elsewhere. "I'm already on the backside of the farm checking the fence with Boyd, and I smell of horse." She could picture him easily, sitting tall on Shiloh, reins loose in his hands, content in a way that only the farm seemed to give him.

She sent a quick text to Colt while still holding the phone. "Okay. I'll head into town. Who knows when I'll have another opportunity to meet my new sister-in-law?"

"All right, cowgirl. Be careful. And Gramps wants us to eat at the main house while we're here."

The request did not surprise her. Benjamin Williams

had always preferred control, especially when it came wrapped in hospitality.

"I also heard from my baby sister this morning," Blake continued. "She should be here by dinnertime. Katie had to arrange for coverage before leaving Nashville."

"It's still hard for me to wrap my head around the fact that Katelyn is a nurse practitioner and married to one of my bosses," Darby said, stepping back inside. She caught her reflection in the bathroom mirror. Bare face. Hair pulled back. No effort made beyond necessity.

Blake laughed. "No one is more surprised by my sister's accomplishments than me, honey. Give my best to your family. They'll understand my absence. Love you."

The call ended, leaving the house quiet again.

Darby stood there for a moment longer than necessary, phone in hand, listening to the silence, aware that she was already moving toward something she could not quite name.

Colt Payne stood on the porch of the two-story Victorian as Darby parked in front of the house. He opened his arms the moment she stepped out of the car and lifted her off the ground when she reached him, both of them laughing in the familiar way that belonged only to shared history.

"There's my sister." He hugged her tight. "Climb any trees lately, little girl?"

Colt had been the one to rescue her from the first tree she ever climbed. Getting up had been easy. Getting down had terrified her. Even now, the memory tugged something loose in her chest.

Darby smiled, and Colt felt it then, the resemblance he had somehow missed before. Her eyes, brown shot through with gold, were unmistakably Payne eyes. His eyes.

"I can't wait for you to meet my wife. Blake couldn't come?" Colt's expression dipped briefly before he caught it, schooling his face as he guided her inside. Years of bedside manner, drilled into him by Laura, had begun to spill into the rest of his life.

"No, but he sends his regards," Darby said, explaining the sudden death of Geneva Williams.

"I'm very sorry," Colt said, his voice softening as he slid a comforting arm around her shoulders. "Please extend our condolences."

Darby had grown up next door to the Payne family, unaware that Colt and his brothers were also her half-siblings. The truth had come eighteen years too late to undo the damage it caused.

A red-haired woman stepped into view, tall and striking, her posture relaxed but confident.

"Hello," she said, offering her hand. "I'm Laura Payne, and you must be Darby. It's a pleasure to meet you."

"You too." Darby looked up at her clear blue eyes, bright and open, the kind of eyes that gave nothing away but honesty.

"And this," Colt said, patting Laura's rounded stomach, "is our son, Henry."

Darby smiled and gestured toward Laura's belly. "About that. Blake and I are thinking about starting a family, and I have some Payne-related questions." She didn't hedge. "Are there any traits I should be aware of?"

Later, seated beside Laura on the colorful front porch, the conversation grew quieter, more personal.

"I'm a nurse, and he's a doctor," Laura said easily. "Did that guarantee we took all the right precautions? No. But the good news is all the testing says we're on track for a healthy baby boy." She waved absently at a fly drifting too close.

"You'll have to stay for lunch," Colt said, returning with glasses of sweet tea. "Omalita's made enough food to feed an army. She and Dad should be back from church any minute." He chuckled. "Funny thing is, now Dad doesn't have an excuse to skip church anymore."

The sound of a vehicle pulling in broke the moment.

A black late-model pickup rolled to a stop behind the BMW. A breeze kicked up, carrying exhaust and heat across the porch. The two people inside the truck seemed to linger, talking longer than necessary.

"Hell," Colt muttered, louder than he meant to. He set his sweating glass on the side table, next to the fly swatter scarred from years of use. "I'm sorry, Darby. He and Melissa weren't supposed to be here until tonight."

Tyler Payne stepped out of the truck the way he did everything now. Deliberate. Controlled. A second later, Melissa followed, petite and cautious, her eyes scanning the yard. Tyler never looked away from Darby.

He walked with a cane, but there was no limp. The prosthetic leg stayed hidden beneath faded jeans and boots worn thin at the edges. His shoulders were broad, his arms hard, his body rebuilt with effort and anger. Brown hair. Brown eyes. And something darker underneath all of it.

Seven years since the forklift accident that took his leg. Seven years since Darby Hart married Blake Williams. The weight of both sat between them, live and crackling.

Colt stood. "Melissa Algood, this is our sister, Darby Williams."

"Nice to meet you," Melissa said, eyes dropping politely.

"Likewise," Darby replied. She dipped her head, never breaking eye contact with Tyler. Her body already felt tight, alert, braced.

Laura rose from her chair. "Melissa, why don't you help me set the table? Let these three catch up." She guided the other woman inside without waiting for an answer.

Darby took a step back. "I really have to get back—"

Tyler stepped in front of her.

His hand closed around the back of her neck, and he pulled her into him, his mouth crushing against hers, hard and uninvited.

"Tyler!" Colt hissed. "What the fuck are you doing?"

"That's where you're wrong, brother." Tyler didn't release her. His voice was flat, stripped bare. "I never did get to fuck her."

The crack of Darby's hand against his face echoed sharp and final.

"Oh, neighbor girl," Tyler said, his mouth twisting, "you like it rough now that you're a Williams and drive a shiny BMW?"

His grip tightened.

"Let her go," Colt growled, yanking at his shoulder. "Or I'll deck you myself."

Darby's eyes were ice. "I can take care of myself, Colt." She stared Tyler down. "I've felt sorry for you long enough. Try that again, and I'll put you down myself, Tyler. And you know I can."

Tyler had loved her once. He had asked her to marry him. He had put his life on the line for her. Then he had learned the truth. That she was his sister. Something in him had split wide open. With therapy, education, and distance, he had built a life out of the wreckage. But the anger stayed.

Slowly, he dropped his hand and stepped back.

His laugh followed her, low and ugly, as she walked away without looking back. Darby moved with rigid precision, climbed into the BMW, and drove off.

"You got a death wish, little brother?" Colt shoved him hard enough that Tyler had to plant his cane. "You'd better hope she doesn't tell Blake what you just pulled."

"Let the entitled son of a bitch try something," Tyler said. Whatever humor had been there burned out. He rested his fingers against the outline of the pistol in his pocket and watched her car disappear, his expression unreadable.

CHAPTER 2

Darby sought solace by taking a long drink straight from the cold wine bottle she'd found in the guest house refrigerator. It wasn't good wine. It was sharp and flat and too warm by the second swallow, but the alcohol content was high enough to do what she needed it to do. For the last few years, liquor on the Williams estate had been limited and quietly hidden, a concession made for Blake's grandmother, Geneva Williams, who had cycled through rehab three times and never missed an AA meeting. But Grammy was dead, and Darby needed something to take the edge off before she shattered.

She changed clothes without thinking, finished the bottle, and left the house at a jog, heading toward the main gate. The anger burned clean and hot. She was furious with herself for letting Tyler Payne run her off like prey, and furious with Blake for backing her into a corner with talk of babies, plans, and inevitability. Her phone vibrated against her thigh. Blake's name flashed on the screen. She ignored it.

"Fuck it," she muttered. "I can be busy too."

It was a quarter mile to the highway. That was the direction she chose.

Thirty minutes later, the blacktop had stripped the impulse bare. Her worn, fraying high-top sneakers slapped the pavement in a dull, repetitive rhythm that matched the pounding in her head. She hadn't eaten. The wine was catching up with her fast, souring in her stomach, dragging at her legs. For a moment, she considered lying down right there on the side of the road, letting the heat bake her into stillness. Instead, she turned around and jogged back toward the farm, jaw clenched in stubborn refusal.

A vehicle slowed beside her.

She glanced over and recognized one of the big red Williams Farm trucks immediately. The logo on the door was impossible to miss. She kept running as the tinted passenger window slid down.

"Darby, are you okay?"

She stopped. So did the truck.

The driver leaned across the cab. Jonathan Hawkins. Hawk. One of the farmhands, one of the security detail. Reliable. Observant. Too damn professional.

"Hey, Hawk," she said, forcing a breath. "Give a girl a ride?"

"Hop in, Ms. Williams," he said, eyes fixed carefully on her forehead as she climbed into the seat. He was fairly certain she had no idea her nipples were hard enough to show through her sweat-soaked shirt, or that the shorts clinging to her hips left very little to the imagination. Darby Hart Williams was built solid and strong, a woman who filled space whether she meant to or not.

"Does anybody know you're out here?" Hawk asked once she buckled her seatbelt and he eased the truck forward.

"Gee, Hawk," she snapped, "didn't know I needed permission to run on a public highway."

Sweat-dark strands of her long chestnut hair clung to her neck and jaw. The attitude was sharp, defensive, and completely out of character.

He kept his voice even. "There are hundreds of acres on the farm where you could run. There's even a treadmill at the bunkhouse. Somewhere you'd be safe."

She turned and glared at him. Admitting weakness was unthinkable, especially to Hawk, whose opinion mattered more than she wanted to admit. She hadn't eaten all day. She hadn't had a drink in weeks. The combination was catching up with her fast.

Hawk pulled the truck to a stop in front of the guest house.

Blake stood outside, waiting. Thumbs hooked casually in the front pockets of his jeans, dirt still clinging to the cuffs. Calm. Controlled.

"Okay, Ms. Williams," Hawk said. "Here you go."

"Thanks for the ride." Darby jumped out, waved once in Blake's direction, and disappeared into the house, heading straight for the bathroom.

Hawk stayed put. He knew what was coming.

Blake approached the driver's side as the window lowered. He moved with quiet confidence, the kind that didn't need to announce itself.

"Explain," Blake said.

"I found her running down the highway near the main gate," Hawk replied. "Don't know how long she was out there. Gave her a ride back."

"That's it?"

"That's all I know. I'll check the cameras when I get back to the AV room."

"Thanks. Keep me informed."

Blake turned and went inside as Hawk drove away.

"Darby." Blake knocked once on the bathroom door. "Are you all right?"

"I am now." Her voice came muffled through the wood, followed by the sound of running water.

He waited, then turned the knob. The door was unlocked.

Darby stood at the sink, splashing water over her face. Droplets slid down her neck, darkening the collar of her shirt.

"I got concerned when you didn't answer my call," Blake said. He leaned against the doorframe, arms crossed, the easy strength of years of martial arts evident in his stance. The worry in his eyes was harder to hide.

She tugged her phone from her damp pocket and glanced at the screen. "Sorry about that."

"You're not even looking at me."

She sighed and lifted her gaze to meet his in the mirror.

Blake didn't blink. "Everything go okay in town?"

"Tyler and his girlfriend showed up just as I was leaving. Colt was surprised. Said they weren't supposed to arrive until tonight."

"That's it?" His tone sharpened. "No drama?"

"Blake, stop looking for trouble. I can take care of myself." She turned too fast and had to grab the towel bar to steady herself.

He straightened immediately. "Based on the facts, I disagree. There's an empty wine bottle in the trash. You're wearing clothes that would fit a six-year-old. No underwear. And you were running on a public highway. None of that sounds like you."

"Yup." She tried for breezy and failed. "Now tell me about Grammy's service."

"Bad redirect, honey." His voice softened but didn't bend. "We'll talk when you're ready. Right now, we're going to sober you up. Gramps has been asking for you."

His phone chimed. Blake checked the screen, stepped into the hall, and closed the door quietly behind him as he took Hawk's call.

She stayed where she was, hands braced on the sink, staring at her reflection. The adrenaline ebbed, leaving behind the raw ache of everything she hadn't outrun.

Darby pulled herself together and managed to look presentable despite the alcohol pulling gently at her eyelids. The kitchen staff had already begun preparing for the evening, no doubt determined to outdo themselves by incorporating the preserved delicacies from Geneva Williams' gardens. Darby had always preferred heirloom tomato bisque to prime cuts of beef, no matter how perfectly cooked. Comfort mattered more than indulgence tonight.

Blake had stopped questioning her earlier behavior, but she knew him too well to believe the matter was settled. He did not retreat. He advanced, quietly and methodically, until he reached whatever truth or outcome he believed was owed to him. Still, guilt crept in at the thought of making Ben wait, especially under the circumstances. Benjamin Franklin Williams, attorney and politician, was wealthy and formidable, but he had also been a steady voice of reason during some of the most unstable years of her life.

"There's my beautiful granddaughter-in-law."

Ben stood dressed in black, shoulders squared, grief etched into the lines of his face. Time and sun had weathered him, but his posture remained unbent. When he saw her, something softened. He opened his arms, and she moved into them without hesitation.

"Oh, Ben. I'm so very sorry." She rested her forehead against his chest, the faint scent of jasmine rising from her skin. He inhaled deeply before speaking.

"Now, kitten, we are not going to get mired in sadness. Geneva wouldn't want that, and neither do I."

He settled into one of the commanding high-back leather chairs near the cold marble fireplace and pulled her onto his lap with practiced ease. Blake crossed the room and sat at the white baby grand piano near the wall of French doors. He began to play softly, a melody Darby didn't recognize. He rarely played these days unless Geneva had asked him to. Grammy had begun teaching him when he was four, insisting on discipline and precision. This, Darby realized, was his goodbye.

"Blake mentioned you visited your brother Colt and his new wife this morning," Ben said. "I hope it was pleasant. He and Wyatt used to pick up work here when they were younger. Good hands. Reliable."

"It was good to see him," Darby said. "They're expecting their first child. I had questions about the Payne family genetics. The timing worked out."

"Any particular reason for the concern?" Ben asked mildly.

"Your grandson wants us to start a family," she said. "He's reminded me more than once that it's part of our plan. An obligation, really."

She rose and crossed the room to the ornate liquor cart. It had been returned to its place now that Geneva was gone. The sight of it made something twist low in her stomach.

Ben joined her, pouring wine carefully into a tall glass, mindful of her earlier excess. He glanced toward the piano and caught Blake's subtle look of disapproval. Ben poured himself a shot of bourbon without hesitation.

"Let's step out onto the veranda while we wait for the others," Ben said, attempting to guide her away.

"Sounds lovely," she replied, topping off her glass before following him past the piano.

"Is more wine wise, my love?" Blake asked, the notes under his fingers suddenly sharper.

Darby did not answer. She kept walking.

Ben noticed. He noticed everything.

Outside, he set both drinks on the small table between them and lowered himself into a chair. "You and Blake are quarreling," he said calmly. "Tell me about it. I need something else to think about besides my dead wife."

He felt no guilt in the manipulation. He had built careers on it.

"Forgive me, Ben. I'm being selfish." Darby dropped her head. The sun warmed her face, and for a moment she longed for the sleep she had denied herself earlier.

"No," Ben said gently. "You're being young. Now talk to me. Give me something else to focus on."

She hesitated, then spoke. "Your grandson has decided it's time for us to have a baby." She exhaled. "We finally have some calm, Ben. I want to enjoy it before adding a child. And now he wants to know what happened while I was in town."

"What did happen?" Ben asked, studying his glass instead of her face, a tactic he'd perfected long ago.

"Tyler kissed me." Her hand shook as she reached for the wine.

Ben took the glass from her hand and set it back down. "You mean a brotherly peck?" He gently swirled the contents of his glass.

"No. Hard. On the mouth." She looked down at her hands, neatly folded on her lap.

Ben's jaw tightened, though his voice remained steady. "How did you respond?"

"I slapped him and left." Her words were firm as she raised her chin to meet his eyes.

Silence settled between them. Darby felt lighter having said it. Ben weighed his next move carefully, choosing guilt over reassurance.

"This will eat at you until you tell Blake," he said. "What are you afraid of?"

"That Blake will confront him. Blake thinks he's invincible, but Tyler carries a gun. Has for years. I don't think he'd hesitate if he felt threatened. And even if no one dies, Blake could ruin his life if he hurts Tyler. I'll wait until Tyler leaves town, or until we're back in Nashville. Distance will keep Blake from overreacting."

She pressed her palm briefly to her forehead.

Ben chuckled softly. "I was worse at his age. Much worse." He leaned back. "Now, about that great-grandchild."

"Not you too," she groaned.

"I agree with your husband," Ben said plainly. "Let's move this along. I can afford whatever help you need. Since you'll be in Nashville a few more years, I might even buy nearby property and let Reece take over here."

The idea animated him. His wife was gone, but the promise of another generation steadied him.

"What if it's a girl?" Darby asked quietly.

"Doesn't matter," Ben said. "The child will be a Williams."

Later, Ben advised Blake to be patient and let Darby come to him. He reminded his grandson that leadership required restraint and that legacy depended on care, not force. Blake suspected grief and bourbon had softened his grandfather's delivery, but the lesson was familiar. Do not show weakness. Think like a leader. Become one.

"I'll never understand what our son sees in that woman,"

Josephine Williams said, her arms crossed tight against her chest as they drove back toward town.

Reece kept his eyes on the road, the dashboard lights casting soft shadows across the car's interior. He smiled to himself, a small private thing. "JoJo, I believe you're the one who predicted their marriage wouldn't last six weeks. Look where they are now. They love each other. Pure and simple. Besides, I'm not sure Blake would have made it through school without her. He's happy. Be happy for them."

"Well," she huffed, shifting in her seat. "He wasn't happy tonight."

"Of course not," Reece said evenly. "His grandmother, my mother, is gone. When Katelyn was born, I swear that girl cried every day for the first two years of her life. Blake's Grammy stepped in and took him often just to give you a break." He paused, tightening his grip on the steering wheel. "This isn't exactly gala time, JoJo."

"I didn't mean any disrespect," Josephine said quickly. She glanced at the time on her expensive wristwatch. "And why in God's name does your father insist on calling her *kitten*? It sounds ridiculous. Like something out of a 1950s movie."

"Pops says it's because Darby clearly has nine lives," Reece replied, a quiet chuckle slipping out. "I'm inclined to agree."

"You would," she scoffed, turning her face toward the window.

"Careful," Reece said mildly. "You're starting to sound jealous of the girl."

Josephine didn't answer. She was grateful for the darkness that hid the sharp look she sent his way.

Reece was just as grateful that she couldn't see the brief sneer that crossed his face before he smoothed it away and kept driving.

CHAPTER 3

Ben Williams had not slept well. That much was expected, given the recent death of his wife, but it was not grief alone that kept him awake. It was his conversation with Darby. The way she had spoken. What she had not said. By morning, he had sorted his thoughts into something usable. He had several objectives for the day, and he had finally settled on the order in which to handle them.

Darby was right. Blake would storm into town to defend his wife's honor and could very well get himself shot in the process. Ben didn't particularly care if he himself got shot, but no one was going to insult his beautiful granddaughter-in-law and walk away uncorrected. Certainly not her renegade half-brother. People pitied Tyler Payne because he had lost a leg in a reckless, emotionally charged accident after learning the woman he loved was not only his half-sister, but was also marrying Blake Williams. Sympathy, Ben believed, had been allowed to excuse too much.

He pushed the sports car harder than necessary, enjoying the rush. His tall frame had never quite fit the

Porsche the way it should have, but he knew he looked damn good driving it. He was tired of being treated like an old man. With Geneva gone, he could already picture the procession of casseroles and sympathetic smiles. He had no intention of shrinking quietly into that role. He still had teeth.

The colorful Victorian came into view. Ben slowed, noting the black *Ford* pickup parked out front with Knox County plates. He walked past it deliberately, then picked up speed and knocked hard on the bright blue front door.

"Well, good morning, Ben," Colt Payne said, stepping onto the porch and shaking his hand. Colt had always respected Benjamin Williams. "I'm sorry to hear about Ms. Geneva. She was good to Wyatt and me when we worked out at the farm."

"I appreciate that, Colt," Ben said. "We missed you boys when you grew up and moved on. But I've watched you do well, and I never doubted you would."

Colt nodded. "So what brings you by this morning, sir?"

"I'm here to see Tyler," Ben said. "He around?"

"As a matter of fact, he and Melissa are getting ready to head back to Knoxville. You just caught him." Colt smiled faintly. "Ty," he called over his shoulder. "You've got company."

Tyler appeared in the doorway, a petite blonde woman hovering just behind him. Ben assumed this was Melissa. He acknowledged her with a brief nod.

"Mr. Williams," Tyler said, stepping onto the porch. "What can I do for you?" His expression was slack, guarded.

"Well, Tyler," Ben said evenly, "you can keep your hands and everything else to yourself where Darby Williams is concerned. If you see her on the street, I suggest you turn around and walk the other way. I need your assurance that what happened yesterday will not happen again."

His voice was calm, almost gentle.

"That might be fucking awkward," Tyler said, folding his arms across his chest, his mouth twisting, "seeing as she's my *sister*."

Ben's left uppercut landed clean under Tyler's chin, snapping his head back and dropping him hard onto the porch.

"Tyler!" the blonde woman screamed, rushing to his side. "What did you do that for, you crazy old man?"

"Why don't you ask him what he said and did yesterday to his *sister*?" Ben said, stressing the word the same way Tyler had. "He should be grateful she told me instead of her husband. I don't know how much longer that luck will hold. For his sake, I suggest you get him out of town quickly. You haven't seen crazy until Blake Williams finds out."

Ben turned and walked back toward his car.

"Good to see you, Ben," Colt called, unable to hide his grin.

"You too," Ben replied. "Next time you're in town, we'll catch a bass or two."

"I'd like that," Colt said sincerely, lifting a hand in farewell.

Ben drove off.

Colt turned back to Tyler, who was sitting upright now, rubbing his jaw. "He tried to warn you. You chose to be an asshole. You deserved that. I wish I'd done it myself yesterday. Grow up and move on." He didn't bother to offer a hand. Colt went inside and shut the door.

Ben parked at the family law office and stayed put. He wasn't sure whether Reece would come in, but Ben intended to remain nearby until he was certain Tyler Payne had left town. He pulled out his phone and checked the signal. The cheap tracker he'd planted in the truck's fender well was transmitting. It might fall off before Knoxville, but it would last long enough to tell him what he needed to know.

Condolences were already pouring in. A public memorial would be held on Saturday at the Methodist church. A private burial of sorts would follow at Williams Farm, where Geneva's ashes would be spread alongside his when the time came. Ben had delayed the memorial intentionally, keeping his family close under the guise of grief. He felt no shame in it. In a town this size, death was both personal and social, and Benjamin Williams had never wasted an opportunity to manage either.

Blake smiled in the quiet of the morning as he felt her fingers trail across his ribcage, her palm coming to rest warm and flat against his chest. When she pressed a soft kiss to his shoulder, the contact sent a spark straight to his core. He could feel her breasts molded against his back, the friction of her hardened nipples telegraphing her intent.

She tucked her knees into the small of his back, anchoring him to her.

"Good morning, beautiful," he rumbled, his voice thick with the husk of sleep and rising desire. "Is there something on your mind?"

"Yes," she whispered. Her hand began a slow, playful descent. "I want to remind you that you cannot bully me into submission, Blake. However... I want to finish our discussion regarding a baby."

Blake's breath hitched. He tried to roll over to face her, his heart hammering, but she held him firm, the sudden tension in her body pinning him in place.

"Hear me out, husband," she commanded softly.

He stilled, the air leaving his lungs in a rush. "As you wish, my love."

It was a rare, exquisite torture to submit to her like this. He felt his pulse thrumming in his ears as she laid out the terms: the appointment in Nashville, the preliminary testing, the systematic plan to stop her birth control.

Again, he tried to turn, desperate to see her eyes, but she threw a pale, ivory thigh over his hip, using her weight to keep him trapped. "Wait, I'm not finished," she warned. "You will not freak out during the process. We do this with patience. When it happens, Blake, it happens."

She lingered for a moment, letting the weight of her words sink in before she slowly slid her leg back and loosened her grip.

"Now?" he asked, his voice strained.

"Now," she agreed.

He flipped in one fluid, whirling motion, his body

blanketing hers as he hauled her into his arms. He rained a feverish trail of kisses across her jaw, her brow, and her mouth.

"Do you agree?" she managed to squeak out, breathless beneath him.

"Yes. God, *yes.*" The word was a jagged growl of relief, thick with the kind of hunger only she could provoke. "I've been spiraling, terrified you'd clawed it all back——that you'd decided you didn't want a family with me."

He didn't just move; he claimed the space between her thighs, his hands heavy and worshipful as he pinned her legs wide. His gaze was dark, fixed on her with a predatory sort of devotion that made her blood hum.

"I want to watch you shatter," he rasped, his thumb brushing her lower lip. "I want to feel you tighten and gasp my name until you cum so hard you can't see straight. And the second you find your breath? I'm going to make you do it all over again."

Darby let out a shaky, delighted laugh, her fingers tangling in his hair. "Blake...we aren't making a baby today."

"God, I love you," he groaned, his mouth finding the sensitive skin beneath her ear. "I promise I'll be a great father to our children. I'll give you everything."

His touch was already working her into a frenzy; his movements deliberate and commanding.

"Yes, Blake," she whispered, arching into him. "I believe you will."

Ben checked the tracker and saw that Tyler Payne was well

clear of the area. Satisfied, he dialed Darby's cell.

"Hey, Ben. What's up?" Her voice sounded breathless, warm.

"You all right, girl?" he asked.

"I am fantastic," she said.

"Hey, Gramps." Blake cut in. "Boyd said you got dressed up and took the *Porsche* out this morning. You okay?"

"I'm fine, boy. I'm at the office in town working my ass off. If you see your father, tell him to get down here. And if you see your mother, tell her to call me. I've got a job for her. Put that pretty wife of yours back on the phone."

"Yes, sir. I live to serve," Blake said, laughing.

"Don't be a smartass." Ben's voice boomed. "Let me talk to Darby."

"I'm back, Ben," she said as Blake's laughter carried faintly in the background.

"Kitten, Tyler Payne is over an hour out of town. Talk to your husband."

"You're positive?"

"Absolutely. I paid Tyler a visit this morning and told him to stay away from you. He got smart. I knocked him on his ass, and that was the end of it."

"Oh, Ben, you didn't."

The breathiness in her voice made him pause.

"Don't worry about it. Felt damn good. Now talk to your husband." Ben ended the call.

Blake wrapped his arms around her from behind, still riding the high of the morning and the promise it carried. "So what are you and Gramps conspiring about today?"

"I need to tell you the rest of what happened when I went to see Colt." Her voice went careful, almost shy. For a moment, she wished her side of the family felt as steady as his.

Blake's body stiffened. "This is about Tyler, isn't it?"

"Yes." She told him everything. Tyler's sudden appearance. Colt's confusion. Ben stepping in. Blake's jaw tightened as she spoke, his breath heavy with restrained anger.

"Well," he said finally, voice tight, "that explains your behavior. Why didn't you tell me when I asked?"

"Because I could have simply called Colt. But seeing him and meeting his wife felt normal. Good, even. Until it wasn't." Her throat tightened. "Blake, our children will share DNA with these people. I can't change that I'm a bastard. A hybrid Payne."

"I wish you wouldn't talk about yourself that way," he said quietly.

"I was afraid you'd confront Tyler."

"Darling." He turned her by the shoulders, forcing her to meet his eyes. "I'm your husband. It's my job to protect you. We've had this conversation."

"Ty was my best friend growing up," she said. "I missed things. Red flags. But I never would have married him. If I hadn't fallen in love with you, I would've left Steeplewood forever. And let's be honest. You and Tyler are both dangerous men."

His eyes darkened. "You're not asking me to back off. You're choosing him over me."

"That's not true."

"That's how it feels. Tyler Payne stopped being your childhood playmate long before you noticed. He even used my sister's generosity to spy on us in high school."

"I get it. You don't trust him."

"No. I don't trust him around you." The silence between them thickened, airless.

"Ben told me Tyler's gone," she said softly. "I didn't know he was going to confront him. Apparently, Tyler mouthed off, and Gramps knocked him flat."

Blake's anger broke into a short laugh. "Oh hell. Tyler Payne didn't expect Ben Williams." He shook his head. "Jesus. Now I've got to keep an eye on both of you." He smiled without humor. "Never underestimate a Williams." He started dressing.

"Not to worry, cowboy. I'm done with the Paynes. And I'm done sharing secrets with Benjamin Williams."

Blake followed her, pulling his shirt over his head. "Avoid the Paynes, yes. But Gramps adores you. And you and I don't keep secrets."

"I was going to tell you. I was waiting for the right time." She stepped into the shower, assuming the conversation was over.

"And was that time dependent on Tyler leaving town?" His voice cut through the sound of the water.

"That, or us being back in Nashville." She met his eyes through the clear glass.

He studied her for a long moment. "I don't accept that, Darby. It makes me question your motives." He turned and left before she could answer.

The front door slammed. The sound traveled through

the house, through her chest. She stood still as the water beat against her shoulders, hot and relentless, unable to rinse away the hollow ache spreading inside her.

She braced her palms against the tile, head bowed, breath catching on sobs she refused to release. She hated fighting with him. Hated the look he gave her just before he walked away. That mix of restraint and hurt. Like he wanted to protect her and punish her at the same time.

She had meant what she said. She had been waiting for the right time. But Blake Williams lived in a world where problems were met head-on, where silence felt like a weapon, and hesitation looked like guilt.

She shut off the water and stepped out, grabbing a towel but barely using it. The house felt too large without him. His absence hung heavy in the air. In the mirror, her reflection startled her. Red eyes. Pale skin. A woman caught between confession and collapse.

She dressed slowly, hands shaking as she picked up her phone. For a moment, she considered calling him. Apologizing. Explaining. She didn't. He needed space.

By the time she reached the kitchen, the stove clock read twelve minutes since he'd left.

Twelve minutes, and the day that had begun with love and certainty already felt split clean down the middle.

The rhythmic thud of Blake's boots echoed through the sprawling two-story main house as he entered. The first-floor master suite alone was the size of the guest house he and Darby occupied. Five additional bedrooms lined the second floor, and the open living and dining area felt less like a home than a carefully curated hotel lobby. Ben and Geneva had built it after they married, convinced they would fill it with children. Instead, it had produced only one son. To the family, it was simply Benjamin Williams' stronghold.

"Hey, brother," Katelyn called over her shoulder as she dismantled a whiskey and cheese basket that had just arrived. She worked at one end of the massive white oak dining table, custom-built on site to fit the room. "Nice of you to show up."

"Hey, Katie. Love you too." He walked past her, grinning despite himself. "I'm looking for food before I head to the barn to shovel shit. Care to switch places?"

"Nah. I'm good." She didn't look up. "My boo bear says the office is falling apart without Darby directing traffic. Apparently, Greg Turner and Richard Nealy literally ran into each other outside Adam's door. Adam laughed so hard that they threatened to kick his ass, which terrified the new *Playgirl*-looking receptionist Greg hired. She quit on the spot."

Blake laughed. "Do not tell Darby." One of the kitchen staff handed him a plate and a cup of coffee. "The sooner she gets pregnant and quits Turner, Nealy & Taylor, the better. And boo bear? Does Adam know you call him that?"

"You're starting a family?" Kate ignored his question entirely.

"Yes. But my overthinking wife wants us to see an OB first. Testing. Planning. All that." He sighed heavily. "Before she gives up the pill."

"That's smart," she said. "You want a healthy child, right?"

"Of course." He took a sip of the hot coffee. "I agreed to her conditions. Which is to say, I would've agreed to anything to get things moving."

"Then why the jab at the engineering firm?"

Blake stopped eating. "Because Greg Turner has a thing for my wife. He hasn't made a move yet, but he will."

"You know, I used to think you were imagining that," Katelyn said slowly. "But since being with Adam, I'm starting to think you're right."

His fork froze midair. "Why?"

"There's a look," she said. "The way Greg watches her when she doesn't notice. Writers call it *hungry eyes*."

"Exactly." Blake set his plate aside. "Darby thinks I'm overreacting. I doubt Greg will want her once she's pregnant."

"Please tell me that's not the only reason you want a baby," Kate said carefully.

"Of course not." His voice came out louder than intended. He resumed eating. "You ever think about having one?"

"Yes," she said. "But I don't know if I'm the motherly type. Adam says he's fine either way." She frowned, sorting another basket.

"You'd be great," Blake said. "You were such a pain growing up, you'd recognize every warning sign." He grinned. "Payback, right?"

She hurled a wedge of cheese at him. He dodged it and bolted for the door.

Darby returned a call from the TNT office, her voice calm and professional as she fielded questions. The partners were finally hiring an office manager. She'd carried that role for six months like an anchor she never asked for. Soon she'd have an excuse to step away. Motherhood would leave no room for late nights and endless crises. But as the thought settled, another followed. Maybe Blake wanted a baby now, not for them, but for himself.

"Darby," Blake called as he entered the guest house.

She ended the call. "I talked to the TNT office. Would you mind if I took the car to Nashville? I could be back by Friday. The memorial service isn't until Saturday."

Blake crossed his arms. The silence stretched until she shifted beneath it.

"I would mind very much," he said finally. "We agreed to stay. Besides, Dad called. He needs you at the office. Connie and Adele are drowning. Deadlines don't pause for grief."

"Of course I'll stay if I'm needed." She turned toward the hall. "I'll change."

He caught her in seconds.

"I need you here," he said, hands settling at her waist. "I need your support. Body and mind." His voice tightened. "It hurts that you'd rather run back to that office than stand with me. You didn't trust me about Tyler, and now this?"

"Blake, I never—"

He cut her off, pulling the keys from his jeans and tossing them onto the table. They clattered loudly. "Here. Do whatever makes you happy."

He left without another word, the door slamming hard enough to shake the room.

The house fell silent again.

Hawk dropped Darby off in town. She could have driven herself—she had her own set of keys to the BMW—but parking near the law office was nearly impossible. Inside, she slipped easily into the familiar rhythm of being directed, assigned, and managed. Her role narrowed to tasks and schedules, and decisions made by others. The priority of the day was confirming Wednesday's meeting regarding the Williams Land Development project. A representative from TNT Engineering was coming from Nashville. She silently hoped it would be Adam Taylor. If it were Greg Turner, Blake's simmering jealousy would flare again, and she still couldn't fully understand why it bothered him so deeply.

Late in the afternoon, Reece sent her to the courthouse. She ran the last filing through with seconds to spare, breathless but relieved. The feeling lasted until she returned to the office.

The parking lot was empty.

Every car was gone.

Unease crept up her spine as she tried the door. Locked. She knocked, then pounded harder, heart climbing into her throat. No one answered. Her purse and phone were inside. She had been left behind. Forgotten.

High heels made the long walk back to the farm impossible. After a moment's hesitation, she turned toward the house of her biological father, Winston Payne.

The Williams family had just sat down to an early dinner when Blake walked into the main house, dust clinging to his boots and streaking the polished wood floor.

"Does anyone know where Darby is?" His voice cut through the low murmur of conversation. "Our car's still at the guest house."

Ben's chair scraped back sharply. He and Reece stood at the same time.

"Damn," Ben muttered. "We forgot Darby."

"I'll go," Reece said quickly. "I'm the one who sent her to the courthouse."

Blake's face flushed red. "You stranded my wife after asking for her help?" His finger jabbed the air between them.

His phone rang. He answered without looking away. "I'll handle it, Hawk." A pause. His jaw flexed. "Thanks."

He ended the call hard. "Darby's on her way up the drive," he said flatly. "Colt Payne is bringing her."

He reached the front door just as the bell rang and flung it open.

Darby stood on the porch, the cool evening air lifting her hair.

"Honey, this was unintentional," Blake said quickly, reaching for her.

She stepped back.

"I need a key to the office," she said, brittle politeness edging her voice. "My purse and phone are locked inside."

"I'll take care of it," he said. "Tell Colt he can leave."

"No." Her tone was firm. "Please give me the key. Colt offered to take me back."

"Not happening." His voice softened, but his body stayed rigid.

He moved forward and said something to her brother that she couldn't hear. Colt gave her a small apologetic wave, turned the car, and drove off.

"Honey, again, it was unintentional," Blake said. "I don't appreciate it either, but we're dealing with extraordinary circumstances. Grammy—"

"I understand the situation," Darby said evenly. "But I want a key. I want my things. And I need some space. I don't want to argue."

Pain flickered across his face before he masked it. "Have dinner with me," he said. "Then I'll go get your things."

She turned, but he caught her wrist.

"Don't," she said quietly, trying to pull free.

"Not going to happen," he said, low and immovable. "I will never let you go."

"I know you're grieving," she said carefully. "I'm factoring that in. But I'm not your enemy."

He pulled her into him, controlled, careful. "You're right. You're not." His voice cracked. "I should've gone with you to see Colt. It's my fault you didn't tell me about Tyler. I've wanted to punch that bastard for years." His kiss came hard, then softened, then deepened again. Darby felt herself give, the way she always did when he touched her like this.

Reece appeared, pale and uncomfortable. "Darby, please don't punish Blake. This was my mistake. I'm going to get your things." He left without waiting.

"Go eat," she said, cupping Blake's face. "I'm not hungry."

Her stomach growled loudly.

Blake laughed. "Let's eat. Then I'll take you back to the guest house, strip you out of those clothes, and make love to every inch of you."

She rolled her eyes, smiling despite herself. "Fine."

"That's my girl." He swatted her playfully. "Thank you for staying."

"I didn't realize how much it mattered," she admitted.

"My world revolves around you," he said, serious again. "Even when it doesn't look like it. I'm selfish where you're concerned. I always will be."

Blake woke suddenly before dawn and reached for her. The space beside him was cold.

"Darby?" His voice cracked.

She appeared in the doorway, backlit by pale morning light. "What's wrong?"

"Come here," he whispered, hands shaking.

She crossed the room quickly. He pulled her against him, clinging, his body trembling beneath hers.

"I'm here," she murmured, cheek pressed to his chest. "I'm not going anywhere."

A sob caught in his throat. "Please don't leave me."

"I could never," she said, stroking his hair. "Everything's going to be all right. I love you."

"I love you, too."

Steeplewood was haunted ground for Blake. Every version of his past lived here—rumors, fear, longing. Loving Darby had never been simple. He'd nearly lost her more than once. The man she believed was her father had almost destroyed her. Blake still carried guilt from the night he'd walked away in young pride, a decision that led to a beating so brutal it nearly killed her.

Then came the staged robbery. The gun. Her body falling. Blood on tile.

She survived, but the truth that followed changed everything. Winston Payne. A lineage that complicated all of them. Blake hadn't hesitated. He married her fast, desperate to protect what he loved.

They ran to Nashville. School, work, therapy. Over time, the nightmares had faded.

Until tonight.

This one had been worse. In it, Darby wasn't missing.

She was dead.

Blake sat in the dark, chest heaving, refusing to tell her. His grandmother's death had cracked something old open, and fear had slipped back into him like poison. He would not burden Darby with it. She carried enough ghosts of her own.

Darby rested her hand on Blake's thigh beneath the dining table, a quiet, grounding touch after the night they'd survived. She knew the dream would linger with him for days, maybe longer, and until it loosened its grip, he would hold just as tightly to her. She didn't mind. She understood the bargain.

Morning had brought a thin but welcome thread of hope. An email from Nashville confirmed an opening with their preferred OB/GYN in three weeks. Blake kept glancing her way, flashing crooked smiles full of promise, the kind that made it clear he considered the baby-making phase officially underway.

"Good grief," Katelyn groaned. "The two of you are nauseating. Stop acting like you just invented sex."

Blake leaned back in his chair, unapologetic. "We didn't invent it. We perfected it. You're welcome."

Darby squeezed his thigh, cheeks warm as she fought a laugh. His humor was armor, polished and practiced, but she could still feel the fractures underneath from the nightmare that had shaken him. To everyone else, Blake Williams was in control and confident. Only she knew how much of him lived in the quiet spaces between fear and devotion. And he loved her for seeing it.

"So," Blake said, his tone sharpening just slightly, "Darby's staying close with me today. I'll be keeping track of her whereabouts myself. What's on the agenda for the rest of you?"

Ben and Reece both flinched, the comment landing where the memory of the courthouse mishap was still tender. Josephine ignored it completely, eyes fixed on her plate.

His sister laughed outright. She no longer worried about her family's approval, and neither did Blake. Whatever tension lingered in the room, it bent around the simple truth neither of them bothered to hide anymore.

CHAPTER 4

Greg Turner eased his *Audi* into the parking lot of the Steeplewood law office as the last of the dawn burned off the sky. Benjamin Williams liked his meetings early. Greg had learned not to complain. Admire him, fear him. Both came naturally when dealing with the patriarch.

The drive from Nashville had been quiet, long enough for the tension to settle deep in his gut. The Williams Land Development project was a monster. Profitable, yes, but demanding in a way that wore a man down. As chief engineer, Greg had carried the weight from the beginning. Pressure was part of the job. That did not mean it ever stopped grinding.

The partnership between Williams Inc. and Turner, Nealy, and Taylor had been lucrative. On paper, it was just business. For Greg, there was one complication he never mentioned.

Darby.

He still remembered her as the determined young girl who answered phones at TNT. Part-time. Bright smile.

Disarming. He had noticed that first. Then everything else.

She was no girl now. She was Darby Williams, MBA, interim office manager. Blake Williams' wife.

Beautiful and untouchable.

Greg knew it. He told himself he respected the boundary. But the truth lingered, curling in the corners of his thoughts. Darby was an obsession, and obsessions always surfaced eventually.

His partners were in Nashville today, interviewing candidates for the office manager role. The truth was that the engineering firm had never run better than when Darby stepped in. Efficient. Calm. Unshakeable. If it were up to Greg, they would keep throwing money at her until she stayed.

But Darby Williams did not need their money.

She was married to Blake Williams.

A third-generation attorney. Ruthless when necessary. Blake had cut his way through Nashville's most competitive entertainment firm and outperformed men twice his age. When he passed the bar, he negotiated an unheard-of arrangement to stay as a senior associate for two more years.

Blake was ambitious. Connected. Dangerous when crossed.

And Greg was fairly certain Blake knew. Not everything. Just enough. The glances. The pauses. The way Blake's stare lingered just a second too long.

Even Adam Taylor had noticed. Had warned him, joking in tone but not in meaning.

Still, Greg could not shake it. Darby had been the best

thing that ever happened to his firm. And the one woman he could never have.

Which made her irresistible.

The meeting was a final review of Phase Two for Williams Land Development. Unfortunate timing, given Geneva Williams' recent passing. TNT had made an obligatory donation in her name. Adam would attend the memorial.

"Morning, boss." Darby smiled at him from behind one of the borrowed paralegal desks. Her lipstick was a vivid fuchsia.

Greg paused. Took in the sight of her blouse and the lace beneath it. The vivid color matched her lips.

Surreal did not begin to cover it.

"Quite a change from Nashville," he said, positioning himself just enough to see more than he should. He filed the image away without shame.

"Glad you could join us today, Turner." Blake's voice came from the hallway.

Greg flinched.

Blake stood in the doorway, calm and unreadable. "We have a tight agenda." He gestured toward the conference room where Ben and Reece were already seated.

The door shut behind them.

"Does he always look at you like that?" Adele Carter asked quietly.

"Like what?" Darby asked, genuinely confused.

"First of all down your blouse and then like he wants to eat you alive. Good thing Blake didn't see it." Adele answered.

Darby smiled politely. "I'm sure it's nothing. TNT has strict policies."

The phone rang. Adele answered. The moment passed.

Darby knew Blake had warned her about Greg more than once. Others had mentioned it too. But Greg had never crossed a line. Unlike some clients. She knew how to shut those men down.

Midway through the meeting, Blake's phone vibrated.

"I apologize, gentlemen," Blake said evenly. "I need to review something." He quietly read the private text from Adele, the office manager.

When the conference room door opened later, his face gave nothing away.

"I'll walk you out, Turner."

The steel in his voice was unmistakable.

They cleared the corner of the building.

Blake slammed Greg into the brick wall.

The impact knocked the air from the other man's lungs. Blake struck him twice, sharp and precise, then wrapped a hand around Greg's throat and squeezed until panic took over.

"You stay away from my wife," Blake growled. "You breathe her name, and I finish this."

He slammed Greg's head back again. Pulled him upright by the collar.

"You are removed from every Williams project. Now and forever. You tell your partners why, or I will. If you test me, I will bury you. Professionally and personally. Do you understand?"

Greg nodded, gasping.

Blake shoved him hard. Greg stumbled toward his car, blood dripping freely from his nose.

"Blake." Reece stood nearby, pale and rigid.

"That was me protecting my wife," Blake said flatly.

"You could have killed him."

"Don't lecture me."

Reece exhaled slowly. "Darby attracts men, son. Some want to protect her. Some want to possess her. You want both." He uncoiled a hose and rinsed the blood from the brick wall. Calm. Methodical. "You need to get control of this before someone else sees it."

Blake said nothing. He turned and walked away, leaving his father standing alone, unsettled.

Later that evening, Blake and Darby sprawled across the familiar four-poster bed in his childhood bedroom, stripped down to nothing but their underwear. They had his parents' house to themselves for the night, free to accept deliveries earlier in the evening. His parents had decided to stay at the farm, giving Josephine full rein to begin remodeling the first-floor master suite. Ben had issued only one directive—get rid of all the dark crap and fake flowers. Josephine had attacked the task with ruthless precision.

Now the quiet belonged to them.

Blake lay on his side, one arm curled protectively around her, his hand resting low on her hip, thumb brushing the edge of lace. His expression was relaxed, but there was still something sharp behind his eyes—the leftover heat from a long day, tempered only by her presence.

"Did everything go okay in the meeting with Greg today?" Darby asked, unaware of what had actually taken place.

Blake shook his head, scrolling through photos on his phone. "No. I was very specific two weeks ago about details I wanted included, and none of them were addressed. So I refused to sign off. Official approval requires three signatures—mine, Gramps and Dad's."

Her eyes widened. "How did Ben and Reece take that?"

"They're not thrilled," he said evenly. "But I reminded them who dropped the ball. TNT has until Friday to deliver corrected plans and secure all three signatures. After that, it's ten grand a day in penalties."

"Oof. Adam and Richard aren't going to like that. Greg's got a reputation for perfection."

"Well, he fucked up this time." Blake set the phone aside and pulled her closer.

"I love it when you take charge, cowboy," she murmured.

His phone rang.

Blake groaned and rolled his eyes before answering. "Blake Williams."

Darby lay beside him, idly scrolling through messages while Blake listened, one hand still resting possessively on her backside.

"No," he said firmly. "Chelsea Lambert will not be coming to Steeplewood. I don't care who her new client is. My family is in mourning. We're conducting only essential business. If she shows up anyway, I will refuse to work with her going forward."

He paused, jaw tightening. "Yes, I saw the photo. No, I will not approve the chair until I sit in it Monday—even if it claims to accommodate tall people."

Blake stood at a solid six-foot-two.

"Thank you," he said. "Good evening."

He hung up and leaned down, kissing the small of Darby's back. "I owe you an apology. I was rough about your office earlier. I could've handled that better."

She smiled over her shoulder. "Under the circumstances, apology accepted." Then she tilted her head. "Isn't Chelsea Lambert the agent who aggressively wants to sleep with you?"

"That's Chelsea," he said dryly. "She wants everyone. Are you jealous?"

His finger slid beneath the waistband of her panties.

Darby flipped onto her back. "You ever fuck her?"

His brows shot up. "No."

"You planning to?"

"No, ma'am. I do not cheat."

"Then I'm not jealous." She traced the waistband of his briefs the way he had done to her.

"I am a very lucky man."

Blake moved with a sudden, predatory grace, snapping her wrists together and hauling them over her head. He pinned them against the headboard with a single, massive hand, settling his full weight between her thighs. His body was a solid wall of heat, his heavy frame anchoring her to the mattress.

His mouth hovered just inches from hers, his scent— clean soap and raw, male hunger—filling her senses. "I get to live out fantasies I used to have about you in this room," he rasped, the vibration of his voice echoing in her own chest. "Fantasies that kept me awake and aching for you."

"Were they naughty?" Darby whispered. Her lashes fluttered, her gaze smoldering as it swept down the hard, familiar lines of his torso before snapping back to his dark, blown-out pupils.

His smile didn't just turn dangerous; it turned wicked. "Girlfriend, the things I used to do to you in my dreams would have scorched the sheets. I spent years in this room jacking off until my hand was cramped and my head was spinning, just picturing exactly how you'd feel under me."

He dropped his head, his tongue trailing a wet, scorching path down the sensitive cord of her neck. He nipped at the skin there, a possessive bite that marked her as his. "I'd close my eyes and imagine you tightening around me," he growled against her skin, "gasping and screaming my name just like you're about to do now."

Beneath him, Darby arched, her hips wiggling in a desperate search for friction. She felt his dick getting hard, thick, heavy, straining against his briefs and pressing against her soft thigh.

"Did I like it?" she breathed, her voice breaking as she felt the sheer, staggering scale of his need.

"In my head? You were a goddamn masterpiece," he groaned, shifting to bury his face in the swell of her breast, his teeth grazing her nipple through the thin fabric. "You were so responsive it nearly wrecked me. You begged for every inch of it. You begged until you couldn't speak."

Darby's breath came in ragged gasps, her body primed and screaming for him to take the lead. She looked up at him, her eyes defiant and hungry, seeing the husband who worshipped her and the man who wanted to consume her.

"Well then, boyfriend," she challenged, her voice a low, sultry dare. "Stop talking and make me beg."

<h1>CHAPTER 5</h1>

Blake tossed their college-worn overnight bags into the back seat and slid behind the wheel of the BMW. Instead of starting the engine, he gripped the steering wheel and turned to stare at his wife.

Darby frowned, leaning toward him. "What?"

"I don't even know what to call what we did in the middle of the night, honey."

Her grin came quickly. She tugged at her clothes as if trying to hide a memory, but failing.

"Woman," he said reverently, "that was the most erotic experience of my life." His eyes lingered on her as if she were brand new.

"You were the one speaking in tongues," she grinned.

"That wasn't tongues. That was me losing my grip on reality. I couldn't believe what was happening."

"It was your fantasy, cowboy. You're telling me you weren't pleased?"

"If I were any more pleased, they'd be chiseling my headstone right now."

She snorted. "Well, you did pass out on the floor

afterward." She flipped down the sun visor and peered into the little mirror.

"I was exhausted!" His voice cracked in mock outrage.

Darby tilted the visor to check her hair. "Blake, I'm just making sure, I did what you asked, right?"

"To perfection," he said solemnly.

"Good. Then buy me breakfast down at the City Diner."

He laughed. "That's all it takes to win your heart? A couple of eggs?"

"Honey, I don't want eggs. I want a cathead biscuit handmade by Maedean Buley herself. And if you don't step on it, they'll be gone."

"I'll buy you the whole damn diner if that's what it takes." He slipped the car into drive and eased onto the street.

"Just a biscuit," she said, snapping the visor shut, "and maybe a cup of that brown sludge they dare to call coffee."

"Yes, ma'am." He grinned as he steered toward the diner.

Blake and Darby watched their breakfasts grow cold as they stood by a wobbly, worn table in the diner, shaking hands with everyone who offered condolences for the death of Genevia Williams. Many of them had lengthy stories to share regarding his grandmother's kindness. Most of the tales began with the words, *I remember this one time…*

The few sips of strong coffee Darby had managed were already turning to acid in her stomach when Robert

Badcock slouched through the door. His red hoodie looked as though he had slept in it multiple times, but it was the way his eyes darted, dull and restless, that made her grip the mug tighter. His name did not exactly appear high on the list of favorites in Steeplewood, despite his wealthy family having owned a large farm and the town's only insurance agency for many years. His older brother, Morgan Jr, and his wife now managed that same office and apparently had little to do with his younger brother, Robert.

"Well, if it ain't one of the high-and-mighty Williams clan, sittin' here with his bastard beauty queen wife. Y'all remember, don't ya? The one he married cause he thought she was pregnant, back when Calvin Holder put a bullet in her at the Napier's farm store. Surprised that place is still in business. Between her gettin' shot and her half-brother, Tyler, crushed under that forklift he wrecked, must've cost the Napier's a fortune." Robert's voice cut through the diner, his eyes locked on Blake.

"That's enough, Badcock." Blake's reply was low, steady. The room had gone still.

"Let it go, Blake. Don't take the bait. Grammy would be embarrassed if you got into a fight." Darby's hand gently squeezing his forearm.

"You're right, cowgirl. We'll pay up and leave," Blake said, though his jaw tightened.

"Damn, Williams," Robert sneered, leaning back in his chair. "Y'all think you're better than everybody else. How much longer 'til she finally has that kid anyway? What's it been like six, seven years now?"

"That's it." Blake slammed a fist down hard on the wobbly table, moving fast toward Badcock. Darby reached and missed in an effort to stop him.

Robert grinned, like he'd been waiting a lifetime for this moment.

Maedean Buley came charging out of the kitchen, wiping her hands on her already dirty apron and blocking Blake's intended path. "You get out of my diner, Robbie Badcock, and don't ever come back. Go on now." She waved her black but flour-covered hand toward the door. "Go on and git out of here, or I'll call the cops."

As luck would have it, Sheriff Vechel Locke walked through the diner's front door expecting his daily free cup of coffee and fried egg sandwich. The morning light followed him in, glinting off the silver badge pinned to his broad chest.

"What's going on here, Maedean?" His deep drawl rolled through the room like a slow river, unhurried but carrying weight. His massive fists came to rest on his hips, and one hand lingered close to the polished revolver he wore, more habit than threat, but everyone noticed.

Maedean's short posture and stance were firm. "Robert Badcock is causing a ruckus and cussin' in my diner. I told him to leave and not come back and the sooner the better."

"Rob," Sheriff Locke said, his tone deceptively mild, "you and I need to step outside for a conversation." He held the exit door open, his gaze steady, kind, but leaving no room for argument.

With an evil grin, Badcock turned toward Blake. His eyes glinted like he knew a secret. "Another time, young master. Another time. Give my regards to your grandfather." His voice had a kind of mock respect that made the hairs rise on Darby's neck. Then Robert followed the Sheriff out, boots dragging just enough to make a point.

The bell above the door jangled closed. For a beat, no one spoke. The low murmur of the ceiling fan filled the silence. Then, slowly, conversations resumed, cautious at first, then swelling back to the usual din of silverware and gossip.

Blake exhaled and reached for his wallet, pulling a few bills free. "Let me pay for what we ordered," he said, even though the plates were untouched.

Maedean waved him off with a dismissive flick of her towel. "Madeline Green already paid y'all's tab. Said it was the least she could do for the grandson of the woman who was always kind to her."

He blinked. "Madeline Green? Where is she? I want to thank her."

Blake scanned the diner, booths filled with familiar faces pretending not to watch him, the hiss of bacon from the griddle, the sharp scent of coffee, but Madeline was gone. He tucked his wallet away, a frown pulling at the corner of his mouth. There was always something about Madeline, the way she could appear and vanish like smoke.

Maedean nodded toward the back hallway that led to the kitchen door. "She slipped out while the Sheriff was talking to Robert. Looked like she didn't want to be seen."

He left an overly generous tip for the young waitress, who looked barely sixteen and eight months pregnant at most. She smiled shyly as she cleared the table, and Blake felt a flicker of pity. She should've been in a classroom, passing notes and dreaming about prom, not working double shifts in a diner that smelled of grease and regret.

Darby's cell phone rang as Blake drove them down the street toward the law office. She held it up for Blake to see before answering and put the caller on speakerphone. "Morning, Winston."

"You and Blake alright, daughter?" Winston asked. Darby cringed; she didn't like it when he referred to her as *daughter*, even though the title was biologically correct.

"We're fine, Winston," Blake answered on her behalf.

"Did Robert Badcock refer to my only daughter as a *bastard beauty queen* this morning down at the diner?" Irritation evident in his tone of voice.

"He did," she exhaled. "But everything is under control. Maedean and Sheriff Locke took care of it. We have to go to the office now, Winston. Blake has an early appointment with one of the development engineers."

"Alright, kids, but you let me know if Badcock gives you any more trouble," Winston said.

"We'll do that, Winston. Thanks for the concern." She ended the call. "I hate it when he tries to act like a father." Darby wrinkled her nose and felt her husband's warm hand on her thigh as he pulled the vehicle into the law office lot. They were the first to arrive.

Blake put the car in park and killed the motor. "He's got a lot to make up for, Darby."

"Can't be done." She shook her head, and he watched as her eyes slowly misted with regret. "At least he's stopped bringing up the subject of adopting me." She cringed.

"Come here, honey." Blake pulled her to him, his hand on the nape of her neck and his forehead resting against hers. "Always remember. You're a Williams, now and forever. You are mine, and I am yours. And someday, in the not-too-distant future, we'll have a family of our own."

Connie and Adele, the two paralegals, were the next to arrive. Blake and Darby were busy making out in the BMW's front seat and did not notice the two women as they walked past the car.

"Well, I see nothing has changed with those two," Connie said, her tone casting a light coating of jealousy mixed with sarcasm.

"You know," Adele paused to look back over her shoulder as Connie unlocked the solid office door. "You'd think after all these years they'd be chaffed raw by now." Both women laughed as they entered the building and flipped on the buzzing fluorescent lights.

Blake's hands were intertwined in Darby's beautiful, long hair as he repeatedly possessed her sweet and firm mouth. He was thinking of returning with her to his former bedroom when the tapping on the driver's glass interrupted his plans. He slowly lowered the electric device.

"What's up, Dad?" He stared into the eyes of Reece Williams.

"You two realize it's legal for you to do that stuff in private now, right?" he asked.

"And the last time you made out in public with your wife was?" Blake countered, which Reece met with silence.

"Uh," Blake said, shifting the topic. "Madeline Green

paid for our breakfast this morning down at the City Diner. Not that we got to eat any of it." He gave a rueful half-smile. "Maedean said she told her it was because Grammy was always kind to her. She was gone before I could thank her."

Reece nodded slowly, taking a sip of coffee from his travel mug. "That sounds like your grandmother, all right. She never could stand by and let someone drown, even when folks said they'd brought it on themselves."

"What do you mean?" Darby asked, leaning forward slightly to look in his direction.

Reece glanced at her, then back to Blake. "Madeline isn't from this area. She came here with her husband, Nate Green, when he left the Army. Then her husband died years back in an accident on the Badcock farm. There was an insurance settlement afterward, but that only goes so far. Badcock Insurance has a fine reputation, at least on paper, but the owner…" He trailed off, lips tightening. "Let's just say Morgan Badcock Senior had a habit of finding opportunity in other people's misfortune. Don't think there were a lot of tears shed at his funeral."

Blake frowned. "You're saying he took advantage of her?"

Reece nodded once. "That's the rumor. She had a baby to raise, a mortgage hanging over her head, and apparently no one else to turn to. A lot of the town shunned her after that, but not Genevia Williams. Your grandmother didn't care what the gossip was."

"How sad," Darby murmured. Her eyes softened, a mist gathering there. "People can be cruel."

Reece's expression hardened again, shutting the moment down. "Small-town gossip feeds on tragedy. Best not to put much stock in it," he said with a quiet finality. "Now, enough about all that. Your grandfather will be here any minute, and Adam Taylor's bringing the corrected plans. We need this deal finalized before noon."

"After I review the plans and they meet the requested specifications, I will sign, but not until then. This is business, Dad. The future of Williams Development depends on each step being concise and well-defined. I refuse to let incompetence slide, and I think Gramps will agree," Blake said.

"Oh, you two missed last night's latest Ben Williams proclamation. He's promised the Lexus and your grandmother's diamond earrings to the female who bears the next Williams heir." He paused as if in deep thought. "I think your mother is actually considering it. Those heirloom diamonds are worth a small fortune."

The sound of Blake's laughter followed Reece all the way to the door and inside the office building.

CHAPTER 6

A month after the scripted memorial services, Blake quietly helped Darby toss an empty birth control pack into the trash. Weeks later, on a Friday evening, he came home later than usual.

"Darby," he called softly as he stepped inside, setting down his briefcase. "Something smells incredible. Can't believe you had time to cook."

"You're late." She appeared from the bedroom in a sheer slip that caught the light and clung to her in all the right places.

"Traffic was a mess downtown," he said, though his eyes never left her. He tossed his jacket neatly on a chair in the living room. "But none of that matters. You're breathtaking." His voice dipped low as his silk tie joined the jacket. He couldn't take his eyes off of her. "Please tell me I'm about to get lucky."

"Maybe." She brushed past him with a smile, hips swaying deliberately.

He followed, reaching, but stopped when he noticed a colorful gift bag on the counter. The curling ribbons shimmered under the Edison lights. He touched them lightly. "What's this?"

"The appetizer," she teased, slipping something into the kitchen's oven. "Open it."

Inside was a single item. He pulled it out, recognition dawning. His grin spread slow and wide. "A pregnancy test?" His voice trembled with hope.

Darby leaned against the counter, eyes glinting beneath her lashes. "I'm late. I thought it was time to check."

Blake swallowed hard. "Darling, you're exactly twelve days late. I've been keeping track." His hands closed over her waist, drawing her close. She flushed. "And I love that you still blush when we talk about it." He kissed her temple, then her mouth, before tugging her gently toward the bathroom.

She hesitated. "I can't do this with you standing there."

"Yes, you can," he whispered, brushing his thumb across her lips. "I don't want to miss any of this."

Moments later, the test was done. She laid it carefully on top of the box by the sink. She washed her hands, then they stood together, fingers laced, eyes fixed on the tiny window on the device.

"How long?" he asked, hope rising in his chest.

"Sixty seconds."

"No leaving." His grip tightened. "We'll wait here."

The silence stretched. Then his chest heaved. "Darby, it's positive." His voice cracked, rough and reverent. For a heartbeat, the world stilled. Then he swept her into his arms, spinning her until she laughed through tears.

"You're pregnant. We're having a baby."

He carried her to the bed and set her down as though she were something sacred. His lips moved slowly over her forehead, cheeks, the hollow of her throat, the tips of her fingers, before tracing lower, savoring every inch of her. She shivered, arching toward him, her breath catching when his mouth lingered against her skin. His remaining clothes disappeared, and he was less careful now about where they landed.

"Blake…" Her voice was a plea.

He slid over her, kissing her deeply before pressing into her with aching care. Her body welcomed him, warm and yielding, her thighs parting to draw him closer. Her hands massaged his shoulders as she instantly tightened around him.

"This isn't the wild thing I thought I wanted when I walked in the door," he murmured against her ear, "but it's everything I need."

Her back arched, her nails digging into his shoulders as she moved with him. He matched her rhythm, slow at first, then deeper, more urgent as their breath tangled.

"God, I love you, woman," he groaned, and the words broke into a shudder as he spilled into her, their bodies shaking with release.

They clung together afterward, damp and trembling, his forehead pressed to hers. They whispered of promises and possibilities for their family's future. He kissed her lazily, reverently, until sleep pulled him under. When he woke, the bed was still warm, but her side was empty.

"Darby!" he sat up so quickly his head spun. He hated waking up without her beside him.

"In the kitchen," she replied.

Blake joined her at the sink and wrapped his arms around her nude and warm body from behind. His woman.

She was staring at a baking dish that held their now unrecognizable dinner. "I'll throw this in the trash. No need to break the garbage disposal."

"Don't toss it, honey. I'll eat it. I know how you hate to waste food." He pulled her sex tousled hair to one side and kissed her neck.

"I'll fix you something else, Blake. This is some kind of weird jerky now."

He picked her up and sat her down on the countertop.

"Oh, this is hygienic," she said, sarcasm evident.

"Hey, I happen to know a beautiful girl who has had some good times on that counter in the past." He spread her legs to bring himself closer to her. His hands were on her hips. His lips softly captured her mouth as if for the first time. Blake reluctantly backed away. "I'll fix something while God and you work on making that boy of ours."

"Blake, we just found out I'm pregnant. We do not know the sex."

"It's a boy, darling." He scraped the overcooked food into the trash and opened the refrigerator.

"How can you possibly know that for sure?" she questioned.

"Because I have a big dick and men with big dicks produce more male heirs."

"You read this information in a medical journal?" she challenged with a wide grin.

"No." He paused momentarily. "When I was like 13, Gramps caught me taking a leak behind one of the sheds on the farm. Even then, I was well-endowed. Anyway, he told me to be proud of it because men with big dicks produced more boys. And Gramps would not lie, not about dicks anyway." He put a container in the microwave and set the cook time. "Let's call my folks," he suggested as he rejoined her at the counter. Gently spreading her thighs again and kissing her neck.

"Can't it wait, cowboy?"

"Damn it, Darby. I'm happy. I want the whole world to know." He spread his arms wide to demonstrate his point.

"Blake," her hands rested on his chest. "Can't tonight just be about us?" Her shoulders slumped slightly.

He swallowed hard before answering. "Of course, honey. I'm sorry. You're right, this is about us and our future."

The morning sickness was tenacious. Darby, who had scarcely been ill a day in their years together, now found herself undone by it. Blake would kneel beside her, holding her hair back as she retched into the toilet, until at last they learned to keep a plastic clip on the vanity for those moments. Once, in frustration, she threatened to cut off her long hair, and he begged her not to. Their mornings began an hour earlier now, to reach work on time. He urged her to quit her job, but she met his pleading with quiet refusal.

She lost weight, and her complexion became pale. Blake was filled with worry and anxiety. He felt both physically and emotionally drained, and could only guess at how his dehydrated wife was feeling. Their OB/GYN was cautious and encouraging, but Blake found himself sitting beside his wife in an outpatient clinic as a nurse hung a bag of fluids from an IV pole and inserted a needle into Darby's arm. He held her opposite hand while they quietly watched a *McConaughey* romcom on a small monitor. Both were lost in their own thoughts.

Blake also held the bag of fluids at head height when she had to visit the restroom halfway through the process, which the nurse said was a good sign. Darby's face had flushed red to her ears. She grew weary of sharing her bodily functions with others, especially her husband.

"How are things going, son?" Reece asked later over the phone.

"Darby's not as pale now, and her cheeks no longer have that hollow look. She keeps apologizing for inconveniencing me. I've tried to reassure her that it's not an inconvenience but a privilege. I don't know what else to do, Dad."

"Blake, you and Darby have been living on an extended honeymoon for the last few years. But pregnancy and childbirth can be an extremely revealing experience for some individuals. My advice is that you be patient with her and yourself."

"Darby doesn't like asking for help or admitting that she might need it. She also tends to punish herself when she feels guilty."

"Son, maybe you two should consider counseling before the baby gets here. Absolutely nothing wrong with it, especially in this day and age."

"I've suggested that already, but Darby has yet to agree."

"I wish I could tell you that it gets easier from here on out, but that would be a lie, son."

A few weeks later, Darby awoke and didn't have to rush to the bathroom. She lay quietly in bed, hoping not to disturb her husband, but he was already awake, waiting for a call to duty.

"You all right, Darby?" His hand, lightly, touched her side.

"Believe it or not, I think I am." She sat up slowly on the side of the bed without any ill effects. Blake rushed to her side but left a clear path in case she had to race to the bathroom. "So far, so good," she said. "I'm going to take a shower. Go back to bed, cowboy. I'll be fine."

"No." He slowly picked her up and carried her into the shower. He stripped her nightshirt off over her head, put the clip in her hair, and washed them both.

"Thank you for taking care of me, Blake. I had no idea how it would be."

"I didn't know either, Darby, but we're in this together. Thank you for agreeing to be my baby's momma," he said, kissing her softly and then drying her with a towel before giving her some privacy to get dressed.

Blake had been correct. It was a boy. They were both overjoyed by the confirmation, and he immediately presented her with a possible name for their son: Eli Benjamin Williams.

"Eli," she repeated the name, liking the sound of it. "How did you come up with it?"

"Simple. It's the first three letters of your middle name, Darby Eli-zabeth. This way, our son will be named after both of us. I thought of it years ago when I first found out your full name and thought that if we ever had a son, we should name him Eli."

"Blake, we were still in high school when you came up with this name?"

"Now that you mention it, yes, we were."

Tears slid slowly down her face. "And you were already naming our children? That's the most beautiful thing I've ever heard." She went into his arms.

"Oh, Darby, you are so pregnant." Grinning, he held her against him.

"I know. My hormones are all over the place," she agreed.

"Do you think we could put those hormones to use in the bedroom? It's been a while, and I miss being intimate with you, but if you're not comfortable with the idea, I'll understand."

"Blake, everything you do and say is intimate. The only reason it hasn't been happening is that I was afraid I might throw up on you, which would definitely put a damper on things."

"Make love. Swing from a chandelier. Whatever you want, honey. I'm your man."

"Yes, you are," she said, taking him by the hand and leading him into their bedroom.

The Saturday morning broke with a soft, golden sunrise over Nashville. Darby was feeling much better and had plans at the spa with Miguel Garcia, the friend she often called her big brother. To Blake, the title seemed more genuine than anything her half-siblings had ever offered. After all, his wife carried the uneasy legacy of being the only child born from Winston Payne's affair with Malina Hart, a fact that set her apart before she had even drawn her first breath.

The urban neighborhood scent of expensive coffee and stale vehicle exhaust claimed Blake's senses as he tossed his gym bag into the back seat of the BMW. He had long since grown accustomed to the echoes of vehicular traffic, both near and far, punctuated by overhead air transportation and the daily events unfolding downtown Nashville.

The dojo pulsed with unusual energy, the parking lot already buzzing with arrivals. Security waved Blake into an open parking space, and he slipped his membership tag from the console, tossing it onto the dashboard. The cost of belonging here was steep, but Darby had been the one to insist they keep it, "worthwhile," she'd called it, despite her usual frugality. Normally, he would've biked over when the weather allowed. But today was different. Today was the competition he'd registered for three months earlier, the one he hadn't told another soul about.

Inside, the air smelled of sweat and disinfectant, mats squeaking under quick feet. He was focused and allowed himself absolutely no distractions. When the match began, Blake moved with quiet ferocity, each strike and counter precise, calculated. He felt the shock of contact in his bones, heard the elite crowd's sharp intake of breath with every takedown. One by one, his opponents fell away until only he remained, chest heaving, victorious.

The aftermath blurred: cameras flashing, reporters pressing forward, his pre-approved photo and bio suddenly everywhere, handed out like currency by the proud gym owner who'd clearly expected this all along. A formal invitation arrived on the spot; New York, three months, an international competition. He turned it down. Darby would be too far along by then.

Maybe he should have asked her to be here. But he had been afraid he wouldn't be able to maintain his focus with her in the room. This was his victory, yes, but it was also something he'd wanted to show her, something to hand down to the son they'd begun to imagine.

An hour later, showered, muscles still humming with adrenaline, Blake pushed through the condo door with his customary call: "Darby?" He tossed his gym bag into the corner just as she ran to him. Social media had beaten him home. She already knew. Blake barely had time to close the door before Darby barreled into him, arms winding around his waist. Her cheeks were flushed, eyes bright with pride and outrage.

"You!" She smacked his chest with the flat of her hand before squeezing him tighter. "You went and won a whole damn tournament and didn't bother to mention you were even competing?"

Blake grinned down at her, sheepishly. "I was going to tell you… after. I didn't want to fail in front of the most important person in my life."

Her lips parted, torn between a smile and a scold. "Do you have any idea how terrifying it was to open my feed and see you in competition mode. My heart about stopped."

He tilted his head, amused. "I know it looked intense, but maybe you're exaggerating just a little."

"No, I'm not," she insisted, poking his ribs. "And don't think you're off the hook just because you look all shiny and smug right now. You scared me. You thrilled me. You, God, Blake, you made me so proud." Her voice caught on the last word, the fight draining from her expression.

He gathered her closer, resting his forehead against hers. "I'll take proud. Proud I can live with."

Darby pulled back just enough to search his face, then let out a long sigh. "Fine. But next time, Williams, I'm there in the front row, no excuses."

"Yes, Ma'am," he murmured, kissing her temple.

They walked into Garcia's restaurant to celebrate his victory as though stepping onto a runway, and the room responded in kind. Conversations stuttered, then hushed, cell phones lifting to capture the couple in pixels and flashes. Blake's white chinos were sharp against the sheen of polished hardwood; his black dress shirt open just enough to whisper of rebellion. On his wrist, a gold watch, his grandfather's legacy, caught every stray beam of light and flung it back at the crowd. Darby was radiant at his side, her black mini skirt hugging her curves, her white crop top glimmering with each turn beneath the chandeliers. Her long, smooth ponytail swayed like a metronome of confidence, and her magenta lips smiled with effortless poise. They didn't just look good. They looked untouchable.

The hostess nearly stumbled over herself to escort them to the chef's table, whispering apologies as though they were royalty. Blake smoothly removed the wine glass from Darby's setting, his gesture protective and possessive all at once.

She tilted her head, full lashes fluttering. "A sip of wine will not hurt the baby, handsome."

"Guess we'll never know," he murmured, voice carrying just enough for the nearest tables to smile. "Because it's not happening."

The air around them seemed to hum with amusement, admiration, and envy. Blake's earlier victory dominated local media and beyond:

Nashville's Blackbelt Attorney: Blake Williams Takes Top Honors at Prestigious Tournament.

And then the applause rose as the handsome Eduardo Garcia appeared, sweeping from the kitchen like a showman stepping onto stage. His chef's whites gleamed, his smile as practiced as if it were sincere. Eduardo had his own syndicated cooking show and, more recently, his first part in a popular movie.

"Ladies and gentlemen, welcome," he called, arms wide. "You honor Garcia's with your presence."

His eyes found Blake and Darby, and with a flourish, he

joined them at the table, kissing Darby's cheek and fist-bumping Blake. A tall security guard in a sleek black chef's coat stationed himself behind them, completing the tableau.

For Darby, it was dazzling and overwhelming at once, this glittering circle of admiration from her found family, from strangers, from the city itself.

"I didn't know the star was working tonight," Blake teased.

"Keeps me humble," Eduardo mumbled. "But what about you? Brother, why didn't you tell me? A victory like yours deserves a parade."

"Don't feel bad," Darby's pout was deliberate. "I didn't know either."

When Blake changed the subject and revealed that they were expecting a son, Eduardo seized the moment. Standing tall, his glass raised. "Ladies and gentlemen, attention, please!" The chandeliers scattered firelight over every lifted face. "Join me in celebrating the most wonderful news of all: Blake and Darby Williams are expecting a son!"

The room erupted, champagne corks popping, flutes lifted, applause ringing like a symphony. Diners surged to their feet, cameras flashing in a dazzling storm. Darby dabbed tears from her eyes, radiant under the golden light, her emotions laid bare in the glittering public gaze.

Blake, with a grin meant for her alone, cupped her face and kissed her boldly, shamelessly, as the crowd's roar swelled around them, like the encore of a grand performance. For that shimmering instant, they weren't just two people in love. They were celebrities.

CHAPTER 7

Josephine Williams' intimate family-only birthday party had grown to 125 guests for a catered outdoor event at Williams Farm. Three giant, opulent white tents already dotted the landscape. Darby *had not* been looking forward to it all week. On the other hand, her husband had bought a new shirt for the event. Blake immediately left for the horse barn upon their early morning arrival at the farm's guest house.

"I thought I'd go riding with you today." Darby tried to follow.

"Honey, I don't think that's a good idea." He spun around and brushed his fingers lightly across her stomach. "I don't like the thought of you and our unborn son bouncing around on the back of a horse."

"Blake, I'll be riding the aging Winnie. I can probably walk faster than she can."

"That's another thing. I plan on giving Shiloh a good run once he warms up. You won't be able to keep up."

"Just say you want to go by yourself, Blake." Her voice was firm, and her lips were pressed tight.

"Darby, it's unwise for you to take unnecessary risks." He pointed a finger in the direction of her abdomen as if making a valid point.

Disappointed, she spun angrily around and headed in the opposite direction. He gently caught her around the waist and pulled her against his chest.

"Pout all you want to, girl, but you're starting to thicken up, and before you know it, we'll be a family." He turned her to face him and grinned down at her attempt at a stoic expression. "That look is not going to work this time, Darby." He ran his hands across her shoulders and down her back to cup her denim-clad butt cheeks in his hands. "Now give me a kiss," he softly demanded.

She gave him a quick peck on his chin and tried to escape his grasp, but he gently tightened his hold. His dark chuckle caused a delighted chill to run down her spine and her nipples to harden.

"You are a sassy little hellcat sometimes, but you will not get your way this time." His lips crashed into hers, demanding submission. "We'll continue this conversation later." He swatted her behind only enough to make a point, as his sister, Katelyn, pulled up in her polished car.

"Good grief. Don't you two ever stop mauling one another?" she asked.

The sound of Darby's giggle assured him that all was right with the world.

"Hey, baby sis, what's up?" Blake grinned in Kate's direction.

"I thought I'd see if Darby wanted to ride into town with me to pick up the birthday cakes."

"That sounds good," Darby said, opening the passenger door and climbing inside. "Since I'm not allowed to ride a horse, I might as well *ride* somewhere." Blake gave her a quick grin as the car sped away. He'd give her something to ride later.

"Trouble in paradise?" Kate smirked as she turned the car onto the main highway toward Steeplewood.

"Your brother will not let me ride Winnie today because he thinks it's risky now that I'm pregnant." Darby crossed her arms across her chest.

"Sounds a little overprotective at this stage, but I'm sure he has your best interest at heart," Kate offered.

"I think he wanted to go riding alone."

"Could be that too," Kate said as both females laughed like teenagers.

The grocery store parking lot was already busy on a Saturday morning, and they had to park at the far end.

"We'll go in and make sure everything is ready and see which door the bakery people want us to pull up to and load the car." Kate headed out ahead of Darby.

"Well, if it ain't the lucky Mrs. Williams." The voice behind her froze Darby mid-step, a lazy drawl soaked in arrogance and, no doubt, alcohol. She didn't need to turn to know—it could only be Robert Badcock. Still, she pivoted slowly, fixing her gaze on the man slouched in the doorway, the ever-present red hoodie sagging off his frame.

His eyes were glassy, but focused. There was a sharpness lurking beneath the haze, the kind that made the hair rise on the back of her neck. The stench of alcohol clung to him, but so did the smug certainty that he'd gotten her attention.

She steadied her breathing, her tone flat. "What do you want, Badcock?"

His savage grin widened. He didn't answer right away. He just let the silence stretch, as if to say that he could take all the time he liked. "Oh, just making conversation with the privileged. Saw on the internet where your momma got herself put away for a long time for her part in hiring the Holder brothers to put you down."

Darby remained silent.

"Also heard you finally got yourself knocked up for real this time. After all, what's one more bastard on the Williams family tree? I figure maybe old Ben did you himself since rumor is that pretty boy husband of yours likes to have his dick sucked by men," Badcock wheezed a laugh.

The move was so fast that Robert Badcock never saw it coming. The sharp toe of Darby's red boot slammed straight into his crotch, folding him with a strangled groan. Before he could even register the pain, her palm shot upward, the crack of breaking cartilage ringing out as blood gushed from his nose. He hit the pavement hard, gasping, eyes wide with fear.

Darby's pulse surged. She knew how to inflict pain, having learned that early in life from her childhood peppered by abuse. Not to mention the self-defense class Blake had made her take. She pivoted, ready to drive her boot into his chest and finish it—

And then the ground vanished beneath her.

"Enough, Darby," Hawk's voice rumbled, low and dangerous, as he hauled her over his shoulder like she weighed nothing. She thrashed once, furious, but his grip was iron.

Out of the corner of her eye, she saw Eric Youngman sprinting toward Kate. Hawk didn't hesitate. He tore across the lot and all but flung Darby into the cab of a red Williams Farm truck. In one fluid motion, he slid behind the wheel, slammed the door, and the tires shrieked as the truck shot forward, carrying them away.

"Buckle up," Hawk yelled. "What the hell happened back there?"

"He pissed me off." Darby calmly fastened the seat belt around her.

"Are you hurt?" He eased up slightly on the gas long enough to click his own seatbelt into place.

Darby shook her head. "Nope. Felt pretty good actually."

"Well, remind me never to *piss* you off," Hawk laughed, and she joined in.

"How'd you and Eric get there so fast?"

"We'd just left the farm store down the street when Kate sent out an SOS."

Minutes later, Hawk stopped the truck in front of the farm bunkhouse. "I'll run you up to the guest house in a minute or two. I've got to secure something here first." He jumped out of the truck and came around to open her door for her, but she was already jumping down from the tall vehicle. "Please be careful, Darby." He pushed the door closed.

"It's not that far, Hawk. I can walk."

"I don't think so, Mrs. Williams." He opened the door to the rustic-looking building and motioned her inside.

"Oh, all right." She walked in and headed straight down the hallway to the kitchen, while he turned into the AV control room. He had to notify the crew that she was safe. There were numerous security measures in place on a property that housed both livestock and people worth millions.

Hawk rounded the corner just as she turned up the whiskey Ben kept there and took a long drag from the bottle. "Darby!" He vaulted across the room, jerking the bottle from her hand as she lowered it.

She coughed and sputtered as the alcohol burned her throat and took her breath.

Hawk pounded her on the back. "Are you all right? Breathe, damn it."

"What the fuck is going on here?!" Blake Williams' voice roared through the entire bunkhouse. He stood in the middle of the kitchen, back straight, eyes angry, jaw clenched, and fists clenching and unclenching at his sides. Boyd, the farm foreman, and Reece Williams stood silently behind him in the doorway.

Hawk backed cautiously away from Darby, who was now breathing on her own as she reached for a paper towel and blew her nose. John Hawkins respected Blake and knew that he was more intelligent than his grandfather and father combined, and definitely more than twice as dangerous.

"Blake, calm down. I got strangled, and Hawk was trying to help me," Darby said, her tone even and completely rational.

But Blake was anything but calm, especially after spying the bottle sitting on the counter and putting two and two together. "Goddamn it!" he took one step toward her and stopped. "You get angry with me because I thought it was too risky for you to ride a horse because you're pregnant, so you get into a street fight in town? Then come back here and have a shot of whiskey? Did I leave anything out?" he yelled.

"Blake, I am not on trial here." She stomped her right foot in his direction as if challenging him.

"Not yet," he screamed.

They heard the bunkhouse door slam closed. "Got the grocery store security tape." Eric Youngman called down the hall as he headed into the control room, waving something in his hand. "I'd have been here faster, but I had to help Kate with the birthday cakes." He was pushing buttons on the console. "Excuse me for saying so, but Blake, you should see the video Kate shot on her phone. It has audio," Eric said, concentrating on the central monitor over the console.

"All right," Blake agreed. "Load it up." His voice sounded less harsh, but his eyes were still locked with hers.

Hawk crept silently out of the room and followed Reece and Boyd down the hallway as they retreated into the AV room. She overheard Boyd say that Ben would be coming through the door at any minute.

"Well, you boys have a good time. I'm going to the house," Darby said. She tried to walk past her husband, but his arm shot out to stop her, and he pulled her against his chest.

"Are you hurt?" Blake asked her, his tone of voice much calmer now.

"No, Blake, I'm perfectly fine. Thanks for asking." Her slender arms encircled his waist.

He chuckled. "Girl, you are a handful and a half, but I'm afraid to let you out of my sight right now. So, let's watch some films. We'll discuss your actions later."

"Are you going to spank me?" With whisky-scented breath, and standing on tiptoes, her lips softly touched his.

"Damn it, woman." He growled into her ear before his mouth took hers, and he practically carried her to the AV room.

"Darby Williams?" Ben announced his presence upon entering the bunkhouse. "Where you at, girl?" The bulletproof glass rattled when he slammed the door behind him.

"In here, Ben." She said from the room where Eric was about to hit *play* from the keyboard.

Ben entered the room in his perpetual mud-caked work boots, wearing a dirty cowboy hat pushed back on his head. Darby felt she was seeing her husband's image 50 years in the future.

"Kitten, did you beat up Robert Badcock in a parking lot in town?"

"Yes, sir, I did. Would have done more, but Hawk made

me stop," she said, her back straight and a defiant look on her face as Blake held her securely anchored to his side.

The room was silent for two beats until Ben erupted in a loud belly laugh. "Damn, girl, you may be more Williams than the rest of us." Ben held his hand up for a high five, and Darby jumped to meet it.

"Well, Gramps, then your *kitten* came down here and had herself a shot of your expensive whiskey straight out of the bottle." Blake's hand popped her on the behind.

Hawk suppressed the flicker of irritation he felt at Blake openly disciplining his wife and stared out the tinted one-way glass surrounding the room.

"I don't imagine a shot of good whiskey will hurt *my* great-grandson. It might help make a man out of him. Now let's see this film. We've got guests arriving in a few hours and lots to get done." Ben's eyes twinkled.

Eric Youngman reversed the play order. First, they watched the silent film from the grocery store, which showed Badcock approaching Darby, her attacking him, and Hawk removing her from the scene. Robert Badcock lay on the pavement for over five minutes before he managed to get to his feet and limp away. At no time did another person appear on the screen. Then Eric played the footage recorded by Kate's phone, which included audio. The entire room tensed when Badcock insinuated that Ben had impregnated Darby himself, since the rumor was that her husband liked to have *his dick sucked by men.*

Blake gently grasped her shoulders and turned her to face him. "You kicked his ass because of me, didn't you?"

"Yes," She nodded while looking down at the floor.

"But you asked me not to confront him when he called you a *bastard beauty queen.* Why the double standard, honey?"

"You have a black belt, Blake. If you hurt someone, then you could end up doing time."

"She's not wrong, son," Reece agreed, his appreciation for his daughter-in-law apparent in his tone of voice.

Cell phones erupted as Darby and Blake stared into one another's eyes. Boyd and Hawk were issuing orders to other workers on the farm who were prepping the grounds for the evening's birthday event. Reece was holding his phone at a distance from his ear as Josephine Williams' angry voice could be overheard coming from the other end. He left the room for the outdoors for privacy. Ben had moved to the TV room, where his one-sided conversation was a series of "I see. Are you positive? When?"

Everyone pretended not to notice when Blake cupped Darby's face in his hands and kissed her tenderly. "You want to go home? Back to Nashville?" he asked.

"Yes, please." She stepped into his embrace, resting her forehead on his chest.

Hawk felt an emptiness and longing that he quickly suppressed. Not here. Not now. Certainly not over this woman.

"Afraid that's not possible." Ben charged back into the room.

"I agree." Reece quickly followed, shoving his cellphone back into his pocket. He had turned Josephine's anger over to their daughter, Katelyn. Let her explain what happened. His focus was on damage control.

"A limping and bloody-faced Robert Badcock showed up at the sheriff's office to try and file charges against Darby," Ben said, slapping a hand down hard on the control console. Eric flinched with concern for the delicate electronics.

"You two kids have to look good and be in complete control tonight. I'm talking about award-winning performances." Reece motioned in the direction of the couple. "Darby will look guilty if you're not present."

"But I am guilty," Darby admitted.

"No!" Every male voice sounded at once as all eyes turned to stare at her.

"Damn, that's intimidating." She backed away.

"Son, it's time to put that attorney stuff to use and prep your wife for tonight. You know the drill." Reece pointed in Blake's direction.

"Yes, sir." Blake grasped Darby's hand. "Let's go, honey. We have work to do and a short time to accomplish it." He led her outside and lifted her into the passenger seat of an available farm truck.

"Blake, I'm sorry you had to be reminded of what that terrible man tried to do to you when you were only 14 years old." She said on the short ride.

"Not your fault, honey. Dad's right about small-town gossip. It just never dies."

Darby's cell phone rang as soon as they entered the guest house. "It's Winston." She rolled her eyes. "I might as well get this over with."

Blake held his hand out, and she gladly relinquished the

phone. "Winston, this is Blake. Darby's not available at the moment. What can I do for you?" There was a pause in the conversation. "He said that, huh? Well, Winston, you know what a blowhard Robbie Badcock is." He kept talking as she rushed for the restroom and closed the door. Staring at herself in the vanity mirror, the reality of what she had done stared back at her.

He eased the truck off the gravel, parking midway down the overgrown access road behind the property. Hopefully, the vehicle's modern blue hue would help it blend into the trees. Usually, he'd have sent his associate. She was better at jobs like this, precise and invisible, but she was out of town on business. Robbie had become a liability, and the truck's driver needed to act fast.

He pulled on the disposable gloves before entering through the unlocked back door of the Badcock property. Not much ever changed around here. Inside, Robert was snoring loudly from a leather recliner that had once belonged to Morgan Badcock Senior, the ever-present open bottle of gin on the side table. The once elegant room smelled of body odor and congealed takeout, a stench that mocked its faded stateliness.

The wooden front door was wide open, with only the full-view New Orleans-style storm door between an intruder and discovery. It was unlocked as well. Typical.

Robbie's face looked like hell. The William's girl, or someone, had certainly done a number on him. Not that he hadn't deserved what he got, but he had caught the attention of the Williams family one too many times, and that was unacceptable.

The intruder pulled the over-the-counter bottle of sleeping pills from his pocket and emptied the contents into the gin bottle. Sooner or later, Robert would wake up long enough to finish off the gin, and when he did, he'd finish himself. He dropped the empty pill bottle purposefully on the floor by the recliner, then slipped silently out the way he came.

CHAPTER 8

Blake woke alone in bed with bright sunlight filling the room. "Darby?" he called out without receiving a reply. Glancing at the bedside clock, he saw it was nearly noon. He had fallen into bed with his wife in his arms around two in the morning after the party had been declared a roaring success. He, Ben, and Reece had managed to take turns being at Darby's side during the festivities. Even Adam Taylor had stepped in to allow Blake to dance with Katelyn. Rising from the bed, he wandered into the empty living area.

"Where are you, you little hellcat?" He pulled the front door open and stood in the opening in all his naked glory as the sun warmed his skin. It had been a long time since he'd strolled in hidden parts of the farm in nothing but his underwear and boots. One had to be conscious of sunburn and snakes.

Halfway across the grassy meadow between the cottage and the bunkhouse stood his wife, talking to John Hawkins. The entire right side of Blake's face twitched briefly. At least ten feet were between them, but Hawk acted like a schoolboy with his first crush. His head was partially bowed, leaning in her direction as his feet shifted timidly. Darby wasn't helping the situation, innocently standing there wearing a pink sundress with a matching bow in the back of her chestnut-colored hair like she was on her way to Sunday school or a church picnic.

"Darby!" Blake yelled loudly. She abruptly turned, waved back at Hawk, and started walking swiftly in Blake's direction. Her hips swayed in rhythm with the movement of her breasts. Hawk turned and sprinted toward the bunkhouse. The closer she got, the more Blake could hear her girlish giggles.

"Blake, are you alright?" she asked, eyes wide and bright.

That's when he remembered that he was standing in the doorway naked and was now getting hard as he watched her approach. He started laughing. "Get in here, hellcat. I have about five minutes to run through the shower and get us to the main house for brunch."

Josephine Williams was still annoyed with her daughter-in-law's actions. She had put on a great performance the night before at her own party, even avoiding alcohol to make sure she stayed mentally sharp under the circumstances. But she was about to make up for that today, because Ben was preparing mimosas in honor of her birthday.

Blake gave Darby a stern look.

"Don't worry, *daddy*. I'm not having any." Darby teased him.

"Damn right you're not, but to show support, I won't

have one either." He looked smug.

"But you don't like mimosas," Katelyn said.

"Trader." Blake rolled his eyes at his sister, who laughed along with Darby.

"I'm glad everyone is in a good mood this morning after a late night," Adam Taylor said. But those moods were about to change. Ben, Reece, and Blake's cell phones all alarmed simultaneously.

"Fuck." Blake tossed his napkin on the table as all three men stood and headed toward the door. "Got an emergency at the bunkhouse, pretty girl," he said, and they were gone.

"Does this happen often?" Adam asked, frowning.

"No, but it's never good when it does," Kate replied, seemingly unphased.

The three men returned twenty minutes later. Their loud, distinctly male voices matched their perplexed expressions. The silent but well-paid kitchen staff brought out fresh food.

"Darby," Blake kissed her temple before taking his seat. "I don't think you've touched a bite of food, and I know you didn't have more than a dinky piece of cake yesterday." He exchanged his fresh plate for her cold one, then began eating it immediately.

"Not true," Ben grinned. "You left out the shot of whiskey."

Blake glared first at his grandfather and then at his wife. "Are you two conspiring behind my back again?"

Ben laughed, easing the tension in the room.

"Blake, I'm worried about what's going on," Darby said,

pushing her plate away. She was also experiencing a nagging lower backache today. She guessed it had to do with her extracurricular activities the day before and the late night that had followed.

"Please eat, Darby." He pointed first at her, then at the heaping plate of food, and then back at her again.

"So, is everything under control, or should we plan to spend the night in the bomb shelter?" Kate asked and watched as her husband's eyebrows shot skyward.

"You have an actual bomb shelter?" Adam Taylor refused a third cup of coffee with the wave of his hand.

"Bomb, tornado, basement, whatever you want to call it," Kate answered, both her voice and temperament neutral in response to his question.

Ben cleared his throat, getting everyone's attention. Darby put her fork down. Blake picked it up and silently placed it back into her hand. She sighed and took a bite of eggs.

"According to reliable sources, Robert Badcock's sister, Terry, drove in early this morning from Louisville to ask her brother *not* to press charges against Darby. She claims to have received an anonymous phone call yesterday. My guess is that person was probably Omalita Payne. The woman can't seem to mind her own business." He paused. "Anyway, Terry arrived at their parents' home to find the front door wide open and Robert unconscious in a recliner," Ben said.

Darby choked on her eggs, coughing hard enough to draw every eye at the table. She grabbed her napkin, spitting into it as Blake immediately pushed his chair back and rubbed her back with anxious circles, his other hand steadying her shoulder.

"Easy, hellcat. Breathe." His voice was low, worried.

Darby managed to get a sip of water, eyes watering, but trying for a reassuring smile for her husband's sake.

From the other end of the table came a sharp, exasperated sigh. Josephine Williams set down her fork with deliberate clatter. "Good heavens, Blake. She's pregnant, not dying. You'd think the woman had swallowed a chicken bone the way you fuss." Her eyes swept the table, daring someone to disagree, then rolled skyward with dramatic flair.

Ben stabbed his steak without comment, but his jaw flexed. Reece's hand tightened around his coffee cup. Even Adam Taylor paused mid-bite, eyes flicking between Josephine and Blake.

Blake, however, stayed focused on Darby, his hand still soothing her back. Darby dabbed her eyes with a clean corner of her napkin, cheeks flushing, not from coughing but from Josephine's barb.

A brittle silence hung over the table until Kate finally broke it by asking Reece to please pass the biscuits.

"What happened to Badcock?" Adam refocused the conversation.

"No one knows at this point. Badcock is still unconscious. The sheriff's office and the state police are at his place now, taking photos, dusting for prints, and searching for evidence of a crime." Reece answered while pouring himself a shot.

"So, can we go home?" Darby still wasn't eating. Her

hands were neatly clasped on her lap, her gaze downcast.

"Absolutely." Ben tried to sound reassuring. "But you need to take the long way and avoid going through town. You, too, Katelyn." Both siblings nodded in agreement.

Darby was strangely quiet on the drive to Nashville and afterward. They had packed their refrigerator full of party and breakfast leftovers that his mother had insisted they take. Blake was changing clothes to go for a run when his cellphone rang.

"What's up, Dad? Really? Nothing at all?" He paused. "Well, I guess time will tell. Thanks." Blake ended the call and glanced at Darby.

"They finally flushed enough alcohol out of Robert Badcock and he woke up this afternoon. Says he can't remember a thing about what happened. The police don't know much yet. His place is tucked away at the end of the street, with lots of old oaks in the way. None of the neighbors saw anything unusual."

Blake sat in the chair nearest to the sofa where she sat curled up, knees drawn close. He leaned forward, elbows on his knees, and took a slow, deliberate breath. "Darby," he began softly, "we need to talk about something serious."

Her eyes flicked up, then away. "Blake, I know what I did embarrassed your family. Especially your mother. I ruined her party. I've apologized. I don't know what else to do." She squeezed her eyes shut and lifted her hands helplessly before they fell back into her lap.

He reached over and covered one of her hands, his thumb tracing gentle circles against her skin. "Honey, it's not about embarrassment. It's about control, how we react when things go sideways. Believe me, I know how difficult that can be." His tone was steady but kind. "When you didn't keep walking, you put yourself, our baby, and Kate in danger, which means that the rest of the family and our team were also pulled into that danger. Having money and power makes the target on our backs bigger."

Her chin trembled, and she tried to look away again. Blake slid to the edge of his seat, catching her gaze and using his fingers to tilt her chin up. "Hey," he murmured. "Please don't cry. I'm not angry. This isn't a punishment, sweetheart. It's just a conversation." He brushed his thumb along her cheekbone, wiping away a tear before it could fall. "Mother was frustrated, sure, but mostly she's worried. You didn't know if Robert Badcock had a weapon."

"I was pretty sure he wasn't getting up anytime soon after I busted his balls and broke his nose," she said, trying not to smile, though one corner of her mouth betrayed her.

He huffed a quiet laugh, proud of her, the tension easing. "Yeah, well, that's the other thing. Hawk said when he pulled you away, it looked like you were going in for the kill. A kick to the crotch is one thing, Darby, but a bootheel to the sternum…you could've killed him."

Her breath hitched, guilt flashing across her face.

Blake reached forward, took both her hands in his, and brought them to his lips. "I know you were defending me," he said, voice low. "But promise me something, okay? Next time, you walk away. You let me handle it."

She nodded, and he leaned in until his forehead rested against hers. For a long, quiet moment, neither of them moved, just the steady rhythm of their breathing and the warmth between them.

His thumbs brushed the backs of her hands, a slow rhythm meant to calm and anchor them.

Darby swallowed hard. "You make it sound so simple," she whispered. "Walk away. Be calm."

He smiled faintly. "Sweetheart, I've had to learn it the hard way, and sometimes I have failed." His hand moved to cradle her jaw, his thumb tracing the curve just below her ear.

Her lashes fluttered, eyes glimmering with tears she refused to let fall. "I hate that I scared you," she admitted softly. "And I hate that I put everyone else in danger."

"You reminded me what it feels like to lose control over someone you love." He leaned closer, pressing a gentle kiss to her temple. "But I've got you. We're okay."

Darby let out a shaky laugh that broke halfway into a sigh. She shifted closer until her knees brushed his, then slid from the sofa onto his lap, curling against his chest. His arms came around her instinctively, strong and sure, his chin resting on top of her head.

"I don't deserve you sometimes," she murmured into his neck.

Smiling against her hair, he said, "You're not getting rid of me, but remind me not to piss you off, hellcat."

Darby snorted, the laugh easing the last of the heaviness.

He tilted her chin up again, eyes searching hers before his lips found hers, slow, tender, and full of apology and promise. The kiss deepened only slightly, more about reassurance than desire; his hand splayed across her back as if to remind her she was safe, loved, and forgiven. When he finally pulled back, their foreheads stayed touching.

"Oh." She suddenly giggled, her face bright, a hand flying instinctively to her stomach.

Blake's head snapped up. "You okay, babe?"

Darby's eyes shimmered, wide and amazed. "I think I felt the baby move." Her smile spread slow, lighting her face with something pure and wordless.

Blake froze, half afraid to breathe. "Are you serious?"

She nodded, still laughing softly in disbelief. "It was like, like a flutter, deep inside. Like butterfly wings."

"Can I?" he asked. His voice had dropped to a whisper, reverent.

She guided his hand, pressing his palm to the gentle curve of her belly. Her skin was warm beneath his touch, and he felt the faint rhythm of her heartbeat through it. His eyes misted.

"I don't know if you can. It's more internal right now," she said, shifting slightly, angling his hand to where she'd felt it. "Wait. Oh, there it is again."

He held his breath, every muscle still, his fingers splayed in awe. Seconds passed. Then he exhaled slowly. "Nothing," he murmured, trying to hide his disappointment with a smile. "Guess he's shy today."

She caught his chin between her fingers, turning his face back to hers. "He's not shy. He knows his daddy is here."

That did him in. He laughed through the emotion thickening his throat and pulled her gently, tighter into his arms. Their hands stayed over her stomach, resting between them like a promise. For a long moment they just breathed, her head against his chest, his palm steady on the life they'd made together.

When she finally looked up, her voice was a whisper. "He's real now, isn't he?"

Blake nodded, his smile trembling. "Yeah. He's real." He bent to kiss her, a soft brush of lips that lingered with gratitude and awe. "And he's already got you giggling and me crying. Guess he's a Williams."

Darby laughed again, this time through happy tears, as baby Eli's first flutters faded into stillness between them.

For a different man and woman in Steeplewood, the conversation wasn't so euphoric.

"Are you sure you used the whole bottle?" the woman asked, eyes flat, as she leaned on the blue truck's fender.

"Of course I'm sure, bitch." He snapped, offended at the slightest doubt. He was the boss here. "If Terry hadn't shown up and called an ambulance, this would've been finished. Once they flushed the shit from his system—"

She inclined her head. "There's another way. It'll take longer, but it steers suspicion away from you."

He studied her, jaw working. "I'm listening."

She folded her hands and leaned closer, voice low. "We build a smear people will swallow. Don't rush it. Make the facts line up slowly. People trust patterns. Give them one they'll believe."

A loud TV murmured the evening news down the block—mundane, useful cover. He let the silence stretch, weighing risk against the patience it would demand. Finally, he nodded. "We'll do it your way. But it cannot fail."

By midweek, the high-octane drama of the farm had settled into a low hum of normalcy, though the air remained thick with things left unsaid. Blake stopped at the dojo on his way home, his movements fueled by a restless, jagged energy he couldn't seem to sweat out. He pushed himself until his muscles screamed and his lungs burned, seeking the kind of exhaustion that would finally quiet his mind. But even as he showered and headed back to the condo, the edge lingered, a cold premonition he couldn't name.

"Darby!"

His voice echoed through the hallway as he kicked off his shoes. He didn't have to wait long. She emerged from the bedroom, a vision of unapologetic heat in nothing but her bra and panties. She wore a smile that was pure mischief, her eyes dancing with the light of a woman who knew exactly what she was doing to him.

Blake's grin broke wide, his exhaustion vanishing in a surge of primal heat. "Now that's the kind of welcome I like. Are you dinner, dessert—or both?"

"Oh, Blake." She laughed, a bright, melodic sound as she tried to squirm out of his reach. He caught her easily, his large hands anchoring her hips and pulling her flush against his gym-heated skin. "I was just trying on clothes. I had to officially retire a skirt this morning—it was snug, and it fit perfectly just last week."

"The boy's growing, honey. Exactly what he's supposed to do." He held her close, his head dipping to the hollow of her neck until she melted against him, her sighs vibrating against his chest. "This weekend, we're going shopping. Anything you want, anything you need. My treat." He tilted her face up, his mouth finding hers in a kiss that was slow, deep, and meant to claim every inch of her.

"Miguel's taking me in a couple of weeks," she whispered against his lips, her hands sliding under his shirt to find the damp heat of his back. "To a boutique he knows—maternity wear and some high-end baby things."

Blake nipped at her lower lip, his possessiveness flaring. "Miguel again? Are you sure he's just your gay friend, Darby? He seems to spend an awful lot of time hanging around while you're changing clothes."

She swatted his chest playfully, her eyes gleaming. "You're absolutely impossible."

"By the way, Gramps called while I was at lunch." He reached behind her, his fingers deft as he unhooked her bra, watching the lace fall away. Her body still took his breath away, its familiar curves now subtly, beautifully reshaped by the life they'd created. For a fleeting, primal second, the thought of sharing her breasts with their son crossed his mind—a strange, ancient jealousy that vanished as quickly as it came.

She trembled as his thumbs brushed over her darkening and enlarged nipples. Their color was almost the same as the flush of her cheeks.

"What did Gramps have to say?" Her nails raked lightly up his spine, pulling a sharp shiver from him.

"Badcock's gone," Blake said, his voice dropping an octave. "Closed up the house, put a hold on his mail. A postal clerk swears she saw him and Winston in a heated argument out front yesterday, but she couldn't catch the words."

Darby stilled for a heartbeat, the mischief in her expression replaced by a faint, lingering dread. "Should I call Winston? Ask him what happened?"

Blake's jaw tightened; the mention of her father always acted like salt in a wound. He forced a grin, his eyes darkening as he focused back on her skin. "Winston who?"

He scooped her up in one fluid motion, her legs wrapping around his waist as he carried her toward their bed.

The sounds of their shared heat slowly began to fill the quiet condo. But outside, in the cool Nashville night, the front window caught a faint, oily reflection—the predatory gleam of headlights idling at the curb. The vehicle sat long enough to mark the rhythm of their lives before slipping away into the darkness, a shadow returning to the shadows.

The weekend had been a sanctuary of acoustic melodies and circling dances in the park, a mile of golden Nashville air separating them from the world's sharp edges. Dinner had blurred into old board games and easy laughter, the kind of comfortable warmth that only family—real or chosen—could provide. The Taylors had stayed late into the night, and Sunday morning had been a ritual of bagels and campus chapel bells.

But as they returned from a bicycle ride to their favorite diner, the first signs of the storm appeared. Darby was weary, her strength flagging. They had spent the afternoon on the sofa, lost in a movie about dragons, where she had whispered her love against his shoulder before drifting into a deep, heavy sleep. Blake had sat there in the quiet, watching her breathe, feeling like he was standing on the threshold of a miracle he'd waited for his entire life.

Then came Monday.

The dull ache in Darby's back had sharpened into a terrifying, bright red reality by noon. She had tried to reach Blake, but the call dropped straight to voicemail—a digital wall between her and the man who would have moved mountains to get to her.

"I'll be fine," she had told her coworker Carolyn, her voice trembling as she clutched her purse. She didn't want to cause a scene. She just wanted her doctor.

She never saw the white shape jump the curb. She never heard the screech of tires until the world exploded into a cacophony of shattering glass and tearing metal. One moment, she was reaching for her car door; the next, the concrete rose up to meet her in a sickening, violent rush.

In the sterile, fluorescent glare of the time-worn hospital waiting room, Blake Williams was a man being torn apart from the inside out. He clung to Katelyn; his body racked with sobs that sounded like something breaking deep within the earth.

"You have my son, God. Please don't take my Darby, too," he choked out, the words raw and jagged, dragged from a chest that felt like it had been hollowed by a knife.

Adam Taylor sat nearby, his hands knotted into white-knuckled fists. He was the anchor, the one relaying updates to a frantic Reece and Eric, but he felt utterly useless watching his friend's soul unravel in real-time.

In the recovery room, Miguel Garcia, MSN, Nurse Practitioner and a member of Nursing Administration at the hospital, sat in silence as an overhead monitor beeped in rhythm with her slow and weak vital signs. His credentials had gotten him past the doors that barred the rest of the family. He held Darby's limp hand, his own face the color of ash. Miguel had been standing there when the surgeon delivered the news that would forever change the lives of Darby and Blake: the fetus had not survived.

The media ghouls began to circulate Darby's name, dredging up her mother's sins and the family legacy. Winston Payne sat in his government-sanctioned office, staring at a silent phone. He was waiting for a crumb of information from Adele Carter, the designated bridge between the two families. His sons, Darby's half-brothers, had been notified, and Omalita was leading a prayer circle at the church, but Winston felt only a cold, growing dread.

Darby was finally moved to the Intensive Care Unit, a map of monitors and tubes keeping watch over her. The surgery had saved her life, but she was a mosaic of trauma—bruised ribs, a fractured ulna, and a spirit that hadn't yet found its way back to the surface.

When the hospital finally cleared the halls for the night, the silence was absolute. Adam and Kate left with heavy hearts. Reece and Eric had to practically carry Blake back to the condo. He collapsed onto the bed that still smelled like her—like jasmine—and sobbed until his body gave out, falling into a restless, broken sleep where the only sound was the ghost of a baby's heartbeat.

Tyler Payne stared at the blueprints glowing on the oversized monitor in his Knoxville apartment, tracing each structural line until the layout of the hospital's West Wing was burned into his memory. With a final, sharp tap, the screen went dark. He slid the laptop shut, shouldered the heavy tactical bag he'd packed hours earlier, and carried it out to his truck.

Two calls had already been made—one to his boss, one to his girlfriend. He'd used the same even, practiced tone for both: *Family emergency*. Neither pressed for details. Dressed in head-to-toe black, he tossed his bag onto the passenger seat and steered his truck toward the I-40 on-ramp.

The miles dissolved beneath him in a blur of white lines and taillights, the hum of the tires as steady as his own pulse. He drove hard, chasing a ghost he couldn't name. Conscious of the time difference between the two cities, he noticed the Nashville skyline looming ahead, jagged and indifferent, as his dashboard clock neared one a.m.

The hospital rose before him, quiet and pale against the

Tennessee night, its windows glowing like the watchful, unblinking eyes of a giant. Tyler parked blocks away and moved through the shadows like he'd been born to the dark. Inside, the blueprints hadn't lied. He navigated every blind spot and threaded the needle between the security camera dead zones.

It took him nearly an hour of silent maneuvering to reach her floor. Each hallway, each stairwell turn was a calculated risk. Each step on his prosthetic limb was soundless, a testament to his engineering and his willpower. At last, he slipped through the doorway and stood in the darkest corner of her room.

Darby lay perfectly still beneath the sterile sheets, her face washed in the faint, sickly spill of light from the hallway. She looked smaller than he remembered—fragile in a way that twisted something deep in the hollow of his body. He watched the rhythmic rise and fall of her chest, and his own breath hitched until he thought his ribs might crack under the pressure.

He'd told himself this was irrational. He'd told himself he had no right to be here, not after everything. But he had to see her. He had to know she was still breathing, no matter what the cost.

Memories rose unbidden, thick and suffocating. Summer evenings spent in the space between two houses. The sound of a girl's laughter drifting through open windows like a song he never wanted to end. The moment he realized his best friend had become his entire world— and then, the day the world shattered.

The DNA test. Winston's confession. The unbearable

truth that Darby wasn't just the girl next door. She was his sister. Soon after that revelation, the forklift accident had claimed his leg and nearly extinguished his will to live. He'd spent months in a darkened room, plotting his own exit—counting pills, measuring rope, staring at a revolver he was too tired to lift. He'd convinced himself it would be quiet. Easy. Just *done.*

Then Katelyn Williams, his former girlfriend, had arrived. Blake's sister had hammered on his door until the wood groaned, refusing to let him rot. She'd barged in, bypassed his pride, and thrown a credit card onto his table.

"You're signing up for those last three classes to get your associate degree, Payne," she'd commanded, shoving his laptop toward him.

"I can't let you do this, Kate," he'd rasped. "I brought this on myself. I'm a mess."

"Nonsense," she'd shot back, her eyes flashing with that Williams iron. "You'll pay me back someday."

And somehow, she'd given him back a pulse. He had paid her back—every cent. He'd clawed his way through a two-year degree, then moved to Knoxville to grind out an engineering degree, one agonizing, prosthetic step at a time.

Now, standing in the shadows of the ICU, the phantom pain in his missing leg began to throb, pulsing in perfect, cruel time with the steady *beep-beep-beep* of Darby's heart monitor.

A nurse peeked through the door, the small window of the ICU room framing her briefly as she yawned, her mind likely on the end of her shift. She moved on, the squeak of her rubber-soled shoes fading down the hall, never seeing the shadow standing in the corner.

Tyler stepped from the darkness, the prosthetic leg clicking faintly as he moved to the side of her bed. He leaned close, the scent of antiseptic and hospital soap filling his senses, and brushed his lips against hers—a ghost of a kiss for a ghost of a life they once shared.

Darby stirred. Her lashes fluttered, struggling against the weight of the sedatives.

"Hey, Ty. What's up?" Her voice was a dry rasp, caught in the haze of a half-dream, half-memory. She wasn't in the ICU; she was back in the tall grass between their childhood homes.

"Hey, yourself, neighbor girl. You had me worried." His throat tightened, the words feeling like jagged stones.

"You'd better go," she murmured, her eyes barely slits. "My parents... they'll punish me if they find you here. You know how they are."

He took her hand—it was warm, soft, and undeniably alive and held it with a crushing tenderness, as though anchoring himself to the moment before it floated away.

"You're right, I have to go. But listen to me, Darby… your parents won't ever hurt you again. Love you, neighbor girl."

Her lips curved faintly, a sliver of the old Darby shining through the trauma. "Love you too. Hey, Ty—let's go fishing tomorrow. At the creek."

He swallowed hard, the grief of their lost years threatening to break him right there. "Darby, I'd like nothing better," he whispered as her eyes softly closed and her breathing leveled out into a true sleep.

Tyler checked the hallway, timed the patrol of the night staff, and slipped back into the quiet. He vanished into the dark as efficiently as he had arrived. He sat in his truck for a long time, the engine cold, letting the tremors in his hands finally fade. His body felt wrecked, the phantom pain in his leg a dull roar, but inside, something light had finally taken hold—a fragile peace. Maybe it was closure. Maybe it was the beginning of forgiveness.

He picked up his phone and thumbed a message to Melissa: **Heading home. Love you.** It was the first time he'd said it and he realized, with a startled, heart-stopping clarity, that he meant it. He wasn't just saying it to be a boyfriend; he was saying it because he was finally ready to be a man with a future.

The eastern sky was paling to a bruised purple as he pulled onto the interstate. The city lights of Nashville dimmed in his rearview mirror, and for the first time in years, Tyler Payne drove toward the sunrise instead of away from it.

Benjamin Williams and Hawk stepped into the hospital waiting area, their polished presence drawing glances all the way from the parking lot to the Intensive Care Unit. Ben carried himself with the quiet, crushing authority of a man used to being obeyed, while Hawk followed a half-step behind, his eyes alert and scanning every face, every exit, every detail.

"Gramps." Blake rose at once, the exhaustion lines on his face deepening as he hugged his grandfather before shaking Hawk's hand with a firm, desperate grip. "Thank you for coming."

Ben's eyes softened for the briefest of moments—a rare crack in the patriarch's facade—before turning granite-hard. "What do we know this morning? Give me the facts, not the platitudes."

Reece straightened in his chair, trying to project the Williams brand of calm. "Not much. The nurse said Darby had a peaceful night—no complications. We're just waiting for the first visitation window." His words came out steady enough, but the strain beneath them was audible, like a wire pulled just past its breaking point.

He pressed on, his voice dropping to a conspiratorial low. "Eric's working the case hard. He's been back to the accident site several times and collected security footage from every business within a six-block radius—with Blake's legal muscle to back him up. Everything points to a white rental van. We're trying to piece together the license plate through all the grainy footage."

As he finished, Reece's hand drifted toward the small bottle Hawk had already placed discreetly in his palm. He shook out the tablets and swallowed them quickly, with no water and zero hesitation. The oversight of leaving Steeplewood without his blood pressure medication had finally caught up to him; he felt it in the rhythmic throb behind his eyes and the faint, cold sheen of sweat on his brow.

For once, Reece didn't look like the unshakable Williams heir—the man who always had a plan and the means to execute it. He looked tired. Mortal. And Blake, watching him from across the sterile room, felt the cold unease of seeing strength waver in the one man he had never seen falter.

"Mr. Williams?"

A woman in hospital scrubs appeared like a blue-clad apparition in the doorway.

"Yes," three voices answered in perfect, jagged unison.

"Mr. *Blake* Williams?" she clarified, her eyes settling on the youngest of the three.

"I'm Blake Williams." He stepped forward, his heart pounding a frantic rhythm against his ribs.

"Your wife is awake and asking for you, Blake."

Blake didn't wait for further instruction. He ran past the messenger, through the still-open electronic doorway, and down the hall. He moved as if he could outrun the grief waiting for them both, finally bursting into Darby's room.

"Cowboy," Darby murmured. her eyes blinked slowly, heavy with the remnants of surgery and sleep. Her voice was a weak, fluttering thing. "Where were you?"

"Right here, my love. I'm right here." He didn't care about the IV lines or the monitors. He carefully crawled onto the bed, folding his tall frame around her and tucking himself into her open arms as if he could shield her from the very air of the hospital room.

"Mr. Williams, you cannot be in the bed with the patient," the nurse firmly informed them, stepping into the room with her clipboard raised like a shield.

"I don't believe we've been introduced." Ben appeared behind her, his voice a low, velvet warning as he took the woman's elbow and began to escort her back into the hallway. "Why don't you tell me about the hospital's endowment fund while these two have a moment?"

Inside the room, the monitors continued their rhythmic *beep*, but the world outside the door had been effectively shut out by Ben. Blake held Darby, his face buried in the crook of her neck, waiting for the strength to tell her about Eli.

Reece stood like a sentinel, blocking the doorway to ensure his daughter-in-law had a perimeter of peace while he texted the news to the family.

In Steeplewood, Josephine's response was instantaneous. She was already at Reece's office, her elegant hand moving with practiced fluidity as she forged his signature on a stack of time-sensitive documents. It was a silent, efficient partnership they had perfected over decades; while the men fought the physical wars, Josephine held the line at the fortress.

The air was thick with desperate, relieved love. "Darby, I love you with all that I am, but you have got to stop this shit," Blake whispered, his voice cracking. "My heart can't take it, honey." He pressed kiss after frantic kiss to her face, her forehead, her hair.

When she let out a small, weak giggle, Blake felt the sound vibrate through his very soul. "There's my girl," he breathed.

"It's no picnic from this side, babe," she countered, but then her expression underwent a jarring, violent shift. Her hand clamped onto his arm with surprising strength. "Blake... it was a white van. The driver was wearing a frowning theater mask and a red hoodie."

Blake stilled. "A theater mask?"

"The white ones," she whispered, a shiver racking her frame despite the warm blankets. "One smiles; one frowns. He was wearing the one that frowns."

Ben, who had been watching from the foot of the bed, caught the eyes of Eric and Hawk as they slipped into the room. A silent command passed between them. The two men nodded and vanished into the hallway to track a ghost in a red hoodie.

The door pushed open again as Miguel Garcia rushed in, looking impeccably sharp in a vintage designer suit that seemed to defy the sterile hospital atmosphere. "Welcome back, *hermana*. It's about time you showed up." He crossed to her side, kissing her cheek before giving Blake a supportive pat on the back.

"Hey," Darby asked, her eyes searching the room with a hazy, dream-like quality. "Is Tyler still here?"

Blake eased back, his brow furrowing as he kept a tight hold on her hand. "Tyler? Tyler Payne?"

"Yes. Ty. He came to see me last night. I think... I think we're supposed to go fishing today."

Ben, Hawk, and Miguel stood shoulder to shoulder in the hospital's security office, the room bathed in the cold, flickering glow of a dozen monitors. Behind them, a nervous Administrator and the stone-faced Director of Security hovered, both uneasy in the presence of the Williams patriarch.

The footage of the ICU hallway rolled in a grainy, silent loop until Hawk leaned forward, his eyes narrowing into lethal slits. A single, angled glimpse of a profile—a shadow moving with a distinct, calculated rhythm—caught his attention.

"Tyler," he murmured.

No one else would have spotted it, but Hawk knew the gait of a man who moved with a purpose. Seconds later, a different camera angle confirmed it: a black pickup with Knox County plates exiting the parking lot. Hawk didn't say a word to the officials. He captured the images with silent efficiency, ensuring the hospital staff never realized he'd just identified their midnight intruder.

Ben straightened his coat, his face a mask of unreadable stone. Without a word, he stepped out into the hallway, pulled his phone from his jacket pocket, and made a call in a voice low enough that no passerby could overhear.

Tyler Payne awoke to a forceful, heavy pounding that seemed to vibrate the very walls of his apartment. He sat up, the memory of Darby's hand in his still feeling like a warm brand on his palm.

Barefoot and wearing only jeans, he yanked the door open. "Detective Jenkins?"

Tyler blinked against the pulsating red and blue lights reflecting off the hallway walls from the unmarked cruiser at the curb.

"Hello, Payne," Jenkins said, his hands deep in his pockets. "It's been a while since we had to talk about your hobbies."

The weight of the past—the investigations, the bad blood, the secrets of Steeplewood—rushed back in. Tyler knew he was caught.

Back in his expensive hotel suite, Ben Williams was perfectly composed, his suit crisp. His phone buzzed. It was a patched-through call from Eric.

"Yes," Ben answered.

"You win as usual, Ben," Tyler's voice came through the line, sounding like a man who had finally reached the end of his rope. "If these charges go through... I'm ruined. I'll lose my security clearance, my job, everything."

"I told you to stay away from her, Payne," Ben said, his voice cold.

"Dad made it sound like she was dying. I had to see her." Tyler's voice cracked, then regained its steel. "And when she spoke to me... it healed something, Ben. Something that's been rotting in me for years."

Ben's silence was heavier than a prison sentence. Finally, he asked, "So what is it you want?"

"Redemption," Tyler said.

Ben allowed himself the faintest, darkest breath of amusement. "Not sure that's mine to grant. But thank you for the compliment."

"If these charges stick, I lose my future. Tell me what it takes to make this right."

"You already had a warning," Ben reminded him. "And you squandered it. What assurance do I have that your word is worth the paper it isn't written on?"

"In all fairness," Tyler said, his voice quiet but steady, "I never gave you my word before. You have it now. I stay away. I disappear."

Ben paced the length of the suite, his reflection in the

glass looking like an ancient judge. "Fair point," he conceded. "But if you break it this time, the consequences will be final. You want a life? A family? Then learn what responsibility costs. You do as you're told."

"Yes, sir. I understand."

"Very well. The charges will vanish. But hear me, Payne, you've run out of grace."

The line went dead. Ben lowered the phone, an uncharacteristic knot of doubt coiling in his gut. He had protected the family, but he knew the truth: if Darby ever found out he had used the law to banish the brother she had asked to go fishing with, she might never look at him the same way again.

CHAPTER 10

Eric had carved a path through Robert Badcock's digital life, the trail unfolding in cold fragments across his glowing monitors. Gasoline receipts from Lexington, Kentucky. Midnight check-ins at budget motels in Asheville, North Carolina. Greasy-spoon meals on the outskirts of Savannah, Georgia. The path was erratic, a jagged line of low-rent travel that had skipped Nashville entirely. As Eric dug deeper into the archives, a chilling pattern emerged: Badcock had made this identical loop, with only minor variations, dozens of times over the years. He wasn't just traveling; he was following a ritual.

While Eric tracked the digital ghost through the South, Hawk and Ben maintained a suffocating perimeter around Darby. She was recovering with the stubborn speed of a woman who hated being confined, and she had already begun issuing demands with a sharp, impatient edge that signaled the return of her spirit.

"Tell them I don't need permission to go home!" she snapped at a young resident, her voice echoing into the hallway.

Hawk answered not with words, but by stepping silently into the doorway. He didn't move, didn't scowl; he simply existed there, a wall of suit-clad muscle that made it very clear she wasn't going anywhere until the Williams family said so.

Hospital security had reached a fever pitch. Humiliated by Tyler Payne's midnight infiltration, the administration had doubled patrols and switched every camera to a high-priority live feed. Yet, within the Williams inner circle, the tension remained taut as a piano wire. They knew this wasn't a random hit-and-run or a warning shot. The white van jumping the curb was a calculated strike. It had been meant to end her.

The media circus had begun to thin, the vultures drifting away in search of fresher blood, but the threat remained. All it would take was one hungry reporter connecting the *accident* to the Badcock name to unravel months of quiet, delicate work in a single, explosive headline.

To keep the peace, Miguel and Garcia's restaurant began a coordinated assault of its own. They delivered massive spreads of high-end catering to both ICU shifts— enough food that the nurses couldn't finish it all. From that moment on, the staff became blind to the hospital's strict visitation rules, allowing Blake to linger at Darby's bedside for as long as he needed.

Reece and Eric had already retreated to the war room in Steeplewood to follow the money, leaving the hospital in the hands of the Williams veterans. Ben had inadvertently become the darling of the third floor, the nurses affectionately dubbing him the *Silver Fox* as he charmed them with Southern grace while subtly extracting information.

Hawk, however, took a different approach. He cemented his reputation as the unit's silent enforcer when he intercepted a reporter posing as an orderly. Without raising his voice or breaking his stride, Hawk neatly disarmed the man of a hidden mini cam, crushing the device in his palm before escorting the intruder to the exit. After that, the nursing staff didn't see him as a security guard; they treated him like a guardian angel in plainclothes.

The Williams reach showed itself in other ways, moving through the city not just as a name, but as an inescapable financial force. It began with the patriarch; Benjamin Williams authorized a **$100,000** reward from Williams Inc., effectively declaring open season on the van driver. This wasn't a static figure for long. To show their loyalty to the family, the team at TNT—the family's engineering arm— immediately added another **$25,000** to the pot.

The momentum continued to build as Blake's own law firm matched that contribution with **$25,000** of their own, signaling that the legal community stood firmly behind one of their own. Finally, the true depth of the Williams influence was revealed when a long list of Blake's high-profile clients—men and women who owed their livelihoods to his counsel—pooled their resources to add a final **$100,000**. By the time the figure was announced on the evening news, the reward stood at a staggering **quarter-million dollars**. It was enough to turn whispers into leads and transform the faceless driver into a hunted man, priced out of his own life by the people he had sought to destroy.

Inside the hospital, that mountain of money couldn't buy a single second of the life they had lost. Katelyn was with Blake when the OB/GYN doctor stepped into Darby's room. She clung to her brother's hand while Blake held Darby's with the other, forming a silent chain of support as the air in the room grew heavy. When the doctor moved closer to the bed and explained that they couldn't determine if the miscarriage began before or during the accident, but that the fetus had not survived, Darby's reaction was a jagged edge of sarcasm. She mocked the *five-dollar words* the doctor used to wrap a death sentence, her voice flat as she acknowledged her son was dead.

The doctor's expression crumpled, offering sympathies and promises of future health before Katelyn quietly followed her into the hallway to give the couple space. Left alone with her husband, Darby's grief turned inward, sharpening into a bitter self-loathing. She exhaled a shaky breath, labeling herself a failure and a *fucking screw-up* before tearing her hand away and demanding everyone go home.

Blake refused to flinch. He leaned in, his voice dropping into a low, unyielding register as he told her it was okay to rage, but he wouldn't let her turn the knife on herself. When she laughed at him, a harsh and jagged sound, he countered with a vulnerability that broke through her defenses. He told her how he'd thanked God on his knees that she was still alive, and promised that they would walk through the grief together. To anchor her back to reality, he added with a soft murmur that as soon as she was strong enough, he was going to spank her ass for trying to push him away.

Kate watched from the doorway, transfixed by the strange alchemy of pain and devotion. She watched Darby's face cycle from fury to raw grief until love finally broke through the static. Tears streamed as Darby reached for him, whispering an apology that Blake caught against his chest as he climbed onto the bed to hold her. He promised they would grieve one step at a time, his voice cracking even as he teased her again about the *busting* she had coming. Her laughter tangled with her sobs as she clutched him, and Kate, shaking her head in disbelief at the intensity of their bond, slipped silently away into the hall.

Darby was visited by a priest, a rabbi, and a Baptist minister, all in the same morning, her religious affiliation *unknown* at the time of her emergency admission. She appreciated their efforts, but felt like the central character in a cliché older than herself. John Hawk, acting as bodyguard, was sitting at her bedside, the two of them gently laughing, when Blake entered the room after work.

She had insisted he return to the firm, reminding him they had responsibilities beyond her hospital bed. Blake had relented for her sake, but the sight of his wife laughing with another man, his grandfather's trusted bodyguard or not, stirred something hot and jealous in his chest. Hawk was competent, loyal, and utterly professional, but Blake couldn't shake the instinctive burn of seeing him occupy the chair he considered his.

"You two apparently had a good day," Blake said, crossing to his wife and kissing her lips with a territorial side glance in Hawk's direction.

"That's my cue to leave, Mrs. Williams. I'll be in the waiting room." In Blake's direction, he said, "Your grandfather has a date this evening with a nurse by the name of Mindy. I'll be doing double duty until they kick me out of the building."

"No need to worry, Hawk. I'll be here." Blake tried to reassure him.

"No offence, sir, but it's my responsibility to worry." Hawk exited the room, knowing that his presence was no longer wanted.

Miguel Garcia rushed past Hawk and entered the room carrying two aromatic bags with the prestigious Garcia restaurant logo printed on both sides. "My little sister has been upgraded to a regular diet. I brought you dinner prepared by my brother, Eduardo himself. The family sends their love. I also dropped off dessert down at the nurse's station for the staff, which should get you a few extra favors this evening." He set the bags on the bedside table and leaned in to kiss Darby's cheek. Miguel had the distinction of being the only male that Blake wasn't jealous of.

"Thank you, Miguel. It smells wonderful," Darby said.

"I hope you enjoy it. There is an extravagant meal for that gorgeous Hawk as well. He is currently the apple of the nursing staff's eye. Now, I have to rush off to a meeting, but if you need me for anything, text me, and I will appear." Miguel dashed back out of the room.

"I think I'll get to go home tomorrow, cowboy." Darby squeezed her husband's hand.

"Honey, my mother wants to come down and spend a few days in the guest room once you're discharged."

"Oh, I don't think that will be necessary." Darby looked alarmed. "I'll be able to take care of myself."

"Darling, don't be stubborn. You know I'll do everything possible to take care of you, but you might need someone around while I'm at work."

"I'll be perfectly fine, Blake." She tried to reassure him. "Otherwise, that's why God invented the cell phone."

Blake couldn't help but grin. "Darby, I need to know that someone I trust is watching over you while I'm at work. I suppose we could hire a stranger to come into our home."

"No. That would be worse." She looked stressed.

"Yes, it would. Besides, my mother isn't going to charge us for her services."

"Oh, I'm sure I'll pay," she whined.

"You know I'm right, pretty girl."

"Well, at least I'll know that *you'll* be taken care of." She pouted.

"Don't be that way, wife. I already owe you a spanking. Don't make it two," he laughed as she rolled her eyes. "On a positive note, my therapist has agreed to meet with us online until you feel well enough that we can go to her office."

"Blake, I'm sure I could use counseling, but..." Darby reached for the bags of food that were positively assaulting her salivary glands.

"No buts, babe. We're doing this. There is a big hole in my heart where our son was. Can you honestly say that you feel nothing?"

A dark and frightening grimace consumed her face. He had to meter his gaze to keep focusing in her direction. Blake had unintentionally crossed a line and triggered a response in Darby that he realized, too late, had been smoldering inside her since she had awoke from the accident.

She closed the lid to her food container and dropped it into the trash can beside her bed. "I think it would be best if you left now, Blake." Her voice was firm, as was the look in her eyes.

"Not happening, Darby." His jaw clenched.

"Cowboy. Get. Out."

"No. Ma'am." He pushed the bedside table out of the way to stand against the side of her bed. "You can't send me away, honey. You're mine, and I'm yours. I'm sorry for what I said. I know you're grieving, but you're trying to push me away as punishment. We've been down this road before, and I love you too much to let you get away with it." His first tear trickled slowly down one cheek to quickly be followed by more, and then he was holding her hand and openly sobbing. "I know you're bruised from your breast to your knees, but I need you, Darby. I need to go to sleep at night and wake up with you in the morning."

"Oh, Blake." She crumbled and softly pulled him to her. He went willingly, trying not to cause her pain. "I don't think you realize how much you affect me." Her tears were starting to drop along with his.

"Please, Darby. We can't change what happened, but we can seek counseling to help us deal with the loss. Are you with me, honey?"

Reality slammed across her senses. "Yes, Blake. I'll do whatever you need, including welcoming your mother into our home." She didn't say that she had been afraid the entire time she was pregnant. But she realized that Blake might need Josephine to be with them more than she did. Darby had never truly known a mother's love, but her husband had. And there was no doubt in her mind that Josephine Williams loved her son.

"Excuse me, Blake. I'm sorry to interrupt," Hawk said from the doorway, "but Reece is trying to reach you. He says it's crucial."

"Thank you, Hawk, and please take one of the bags on the bedside table. Miguel brought you dinner."

Blake reluctantly left Darby's bedside and stepped into the dim hallway, phone already buzzing in his palm. He slid his thumb across the screen.

"What's up, Dad? It's been a long day, and I'm spending time with Darby."

"This is important, Blake," Reece exhaled loudly, his voice edged with irritation.

"With all due respect, sir, there's nothing and no one more important to me than my wife." Blake's tone was rigid.

For a moment, Reece Williams closed his eyes, mentally chastising himself. His son was clearly a man in charge of his own destiny. "I apologize, son. How is Darby today?"

"Improving despite her obvious physical limitations. We're ninety-five percent sure she'll be discharged tomorrow. And, believe it or not, she's agreed for Mom to move in and stay with us while I'm at work."

"That's amazing. I'll call JoJo as soon as we're off the phone and make arrangements for one of the security team to drive her to Nashville tomorrow."

"Thank you both. Now what's so important?" Blake's impatience bled through.

"Nelson Pedigo insisted I meet him at the Phase Two development site today," Reece said.

"Dad, I don't care about Judge Pedigo's issues right now, or the new site."

"You'll care about this one. Seems Nels had a visitor who brought information regarding Robert Badcock's recent activities. Badcock had his mail held before he disappeared from town. A certain postal worker noticed something interesting that could blow the mysterious hit-and-run wide open—if we can figure out how to leak it to the authorities."

"Go on," Blake said, glancing at his *Rolex*. Visiting hours were a dwindling currency.

"The Judge's visitor was Winston Payne—Darby's biological father. Winston and Nelson go way back."

"Why didn't Winston come directly to you?" Blake's voice sharpened with suspicion.

"I'm guessing it would have been too obvious. And you know we keep the Payne family at arm's length because of Darby's preference. The only one she lets anywhere close is Wyatt, and only God and his handler know where in the world he might be."

"So what's the problem? I already told you and Gramps I want blood—every drop you can get. Do you understand me?" Blake's voice went low and dangerous; each word was edged like a knife.

"The problem is, Winston Payne's been arrested. The state police positively identified his thumbprint on the fancy door handle leading into Robert Badcock's residence. And no one's heard from Badcock since he left the building where Winston is Postmaster."

"Damn." Blake's response was a mere whisper of breath.

"Exactly," Reece said. "Now let's complicate it even more, shall we? Winston wants Benjamin Williams as his attorney. Got any clue where your grandfather is right now?"

"According to Hawk, Gramps is fucking some nurse named Mindy tonight. My guess is you need to talk to Hawk and get Gramps back to Steeplewood as soon as possible. And Dad—"

"Yes, son?"

"Tell my mother that I refuse to referee between her and Darby. If it comes down to a choice, I will choose my wife first. Every time."

"I'll tell her those exact words, Blake." Reece smiled on the opposite end of the call, even though Blake couldn't see the pride in his father's expression.

"Thanks, Dad."

Tyler Payne paced the narrow aisle of the Knoxville

hospital chapel, the rhythmic *thud-click* of his prosthetic leg sounding against the carpeted floor. At 7:15 p.m., the chapel was mostly empty, but a few seated visitors offered him quiet, sympathetic smiles. He had driven straight from the engineering firm, still wearing his best knockoff suit; the cheap, synthetic fabric itched against his skin, a nagging reminder of the life he was still trying to build. Melissa was upstairs, finishing a grueling twelve-hour shift, desperate to change into the simple white dress she'd packed that morning.

Melissa Algood had been more than his physical therapist. She had been the one to guide him through his most recent prosthetic fitting, pushing him past exhaustion and serving as a bedrock of stability when the frustration of his "new normal" threatened to undo him. On his final day of formal therapy, she had asked him a question that stripped him bare: *"What's your biggest fear now, Tyler?"*

He had swallowed hard, the truth tasting like ash. *"That I'll never be with anyone again. That no one will ever want me like that."*

She hadn't flinched. She hadn't offered the hollow pity he'd grown to loathe. She had only nodded, as if she understood a secret language he was only just learning to speak. The dinner at her apartment the following night had changed everything. With a patience that unmade him, Melissa had shown him he was neither broken nor unwanted. He had initially thought it a one-time act of kindness—a mercy, but he had been wrong. She was clever, frugal, and radiant; and though he never dared say it aloud, there was something about her fierce spirit that reminded him of Darby Hart Williams. He still wasn't sure if that was a blessing or a curse.

He checked his engineering Casio for the fifth time just as the chapel doors swung open. Melissa appeared, breathless and beautiful, followed by a small parade of coworkers still in their scrubs. The room filled quickly, fifty people packed shoulder to shoulder in the tiny space. But when her eyes locked onto his, the crowd vanished into a blur of white noise.

He hadn't told a soul his plan to marry her tonight. The plain gold bands were a heavy secret in his pocket. He had left his anger behind, along with the compact pistol tucked beneath the driver's seat of his pickup. As the young, inexperienced chaplain began the ceremony, Tyler felt the weight of his old life slipping away. Two of Melissa's coworkers signed as witnesses, and just like that, Tyler Payne was a married man.

The reception in the Physical Therapy Department was a humble affair—white plastic tablecloths taped over rolling therapy tables and a punch bowl filled with syrupy, pastel liquid. A sheet cake sat under the harsh fluorescent lights, but to Tyler, Melissa had never looked more radiant. He was bone-tired, his stump aching inside the socket of his leg, but he refused to let the fatigue show.

Then, his pocket began to vibrate. He stepped into a quiet corner, away from the laughter and the smell of sugar.

"Hey, bro. You in a bar?" Colt's voice sounded miles away.

"A wedding reception, actually. What's up?"

"My flight from Dallas to Nashville's been delayed—

weather issues. I was hoping you could head to Steeplewood tonight."

"Kind of busy, Colt. I'd rather not include Steeplewood in my plans."

"Ty, Dad's in jail and someone has to bail him out."

The world tilted. The phone slipped from Tyler's fingers, hitting the tile with a sharp crack that cut through the music like a gunshot. He stared at the device, wishing he could will the news away, wishing he could stay in this fluorescent bubble of happiness. Across the room, Melissa was laughing, wiping frosting off her wrist with a napkin. She looked tired, human, and perfect.

He bent, retrieved the phone, and pressed it to his ear. "Say that again."

"Dad's in jail," Colt repeated. "State police found his thumbprint at Robert Badcock's place. Badcock's missing."

"Jesus," Tyler whispered. He looked at Melissa again. His wife. Then he heard his father's voice in the back of his mind: *Be a man when it counts, son.*

"Text me the details," Tyler said, his voice going flat.

"You just got married, didn't you? Man, I'm sorry. I wouldn't call if it weren't bad."

"Just do it." Tyler hung up and squared his shoulders. He walked back to the table, took Melissa's hands, and led her into the quiet of the hallway. When the elevator doors closed, he told her the truth. "It's my dad. He's been arrested. I have to go to Steeplewood tonight."

"You mean now? Ty, we just—" Her brow furrowed, her joy dimming into confusion.

"I know." He brushed her cheek with his thumb. "I don't have a choice."

"Will you come back?" she asked quietly.

"As fast as I possibly can. Count on it."

The drive to Steeplewood was a three-hour blur of rain-slicked asphalt and the rhythmic hiss of tires. The gold band on his finger felt heavier than steel, a constant reminder of the life he had just started and the one he was being dragged back into. The sign for **Welcome to Steeplewood** emerged from the mist like a grim accusation. The sheriff's department was a beacon of harsh floodlights and idling patrol cars.

Tyler parked, swung his prosthetic out of the cab, and adjusted his pant leg before heading inside. The automatic doors hissed open, releasing a stale cloud of coffee and bureaucracy.

Behind the front desk, Sheriff Vechel Locke looked up from a stack of paperwork. His expression shifted from weary to wary. "Well, I'll be damned," he said, leaning back in his chair. "Tyler Payne, back from exile."

"Evening, Sheriff," Ty said, his voice like flint. "I'm here about my father."

CHAPTER 11

Blake tapped the end of a pen against his desk, the rhythm sharp and restless, echoing the fractured tempo of his thoughts. His phone was pressed tight to his ear, the silence of his office amplified by the heavy weight of the secret he was carrying.

"Blake, you should tell her," Katelyn said on the other end, her voice a mixture of sisterly concern and common sense. "It's been two weeks. If things weren't so crazy back in Steeplewood, Omalita would've spilled everything by now. You have nothing to be afraid of."

"I know, Kate." He exhaled, staring at the silver nib of the pen as if it held the answers. "It's just… things have finally started going well. Darby's healing fast. She never complains about the pain, she's participating in the therapy sessions, she even—" He broke off, his voice dropping to a low, rough rasp. "She offered me something intimate the other night. I turned her down." He had managed to swallow the words *blow job* before they left his mouth. "She and Mom actually got along while JoJo was there. But now she's on her own during the day. I don't want to be the one to shatter the peace."

"What about your feelings, brother? I'm worried about you. You're carrying the world on your shoulders again."

A long, heavy silence stretched across the line, filled only by the distant hum of the office air conditioning.

"Blake?" Katelyn's voice softened, sensing the crack in his armor. "Are you still there?"

"I'm here, Katie. Thank you." He forced the words out past the lump in his throat. "I'm coping. I'm dealing with the loss as best I can."

"Well, Adam and I are here for you both," she said, her tone shifting toward the practical. "I love you, big brother. Call me if you need me or if you just want to talk."

"I love you too, baby sis." His voice steadied, sounding like the man the world expected him to be, but his hand never stopped that relentless, sharp tapping of the pen against the desk.

Blake arrived home that evening expecting, for the first time in weeks, to have his wife entirely to himself. The silence of the condo felt like a luxury he'd earned. Instead, he froze in the doorway, the air in his lungs hitching. A man sat beside Darby on the sofa, her hand resting comfortably in his.

"Blake." The man rose, his sharp, tailored suit catching the ambient light. The voice was familiar even before the face clicked into place. Wyatt Payne—Darby's half-brother—looked more like a high-fashion model than a specialized soldier, his hair grown out into a stylish length and his beard neatly trimmed.

"Wyatt?" Blake took the outstretched hand, his grip firm. "Did you leave the military?"

Wyatt grinned, a flash of white against his tanned skin. "Not exactly. The look's part of my new cover, and that's all I can say."

Blake's mouth curved faintly. Wyatt was the only Payne brother he genuinely liked—the one who lacked the family's typical chip on the shoulder—but even so, the timing felt like a jagged intrusion.

"I'm passing through on my way to Steeplewood," Wyatt said, glancing at Darby with a flicker of regret in his eyes, "and I couldn't resist seeing you both. But I may have said too much about Dad and Tyler."

Blake kept his expression as steady as a marble bust. "I'm sure everything will be fine."

Wyatt caught the polished smile—the defensive wall Blake used on difficult clients. He answered with a knowing one of his own. "I hope so."

"Stay for dinner?" Blake offered the invitation, a calculated move to buy time he wasn't sure he wanted.

"I'd better not. I need to hit Steeplewood tonight, and Omalita's kitchen will be overflowing as it is. If I eat here, I'll have to eat again there just to keep the peace." He patted his stomach, then looked at Blake. "Walk me to the car after I kiss my sister's cheek?"

Outside, the rain had picked up again, a soft, steady drumbeat against the pavement. Standing beside the nondescript rental car, Wyatt's easy charm evaporated. "Blake, I didn't realize Darby didn't know about Dad's arrest or Tyler's marriage. I never meant to cause a problem, but looking at her face... I'm certain that I did."

"Not your fault," Blake said quietly, the rain cooling his skin. "I'm the one who chose to keep the information from her."

Wyatt frowned, his tactical mind trying to parse the logic. "That's your call, man, but why?"

Blake hesitated, then met Wyatt's gaze. "A son we never got to meet died in an accident. We've been off-balance ever since. I didn't want to be the one to push her any further into the dark."

Wyatt's expression softened, the soldier replaced by the brother. "I'm sorry, man. That's got to hurt in ways I can't imagine."

"I hope you never do." Blake accepted the brief, rough embrace, the only comfort men like them knew how to give.

When he stepped back inside, the silence felt sharper, almost hostile.

"Is he gone?" Darby asked. Her voice was too calm, a sure sign of a gathering storm.

"On his way to Steeplewood." Blake loosened his tie, the silk slipping through his fingers as he moved toward the bedroom. "I was thinking of making dinner in my birthday suit—a little celebration for your mother-in-law having vacated the premises." He turned, expecting the usual flash of mischief in her eyes. None came.

"You and Wyatt share any more secrets out in the parking lot?" she asked.

He paused mid-motion, his shirt half-unbuttoned. "Was that supposed to make me feel guilty?"

"I don't know. Should it?"

Blake finished undressing and pulled on a pair of soft cotton shorts, brushing past her toward the kitchen, his jaw set. "Darby, I understand that you're upset."

"How about you kiss my ass? Understand that?"

"Oh, I don't have a problem with that request." Blake started toward her, a low, dangerous rumble in his voice.

"Don't even think about it." She held up a hand like a stop sign, her eyes blazing.

He stopped, a half-smile playing on his lips despite the tension. "How did you expect me to respond, honey? I decided to withhold information from you temporarily. I believe you've done the same in the past when you thought it was for my own good. The goal wasn't to upset you." He pointed a finger toward her, the lawyer in him demanding a closing argument. "Your turn."

"Why didn't you tell me?"

"Because, Darby, you punish yourself for things that are out of your control."

She folded her arms, her jaw setting in that familiar, stubborn line. "Because this started when I kicked Robert Badcock's ass?"

"No." His voice softened, losing its defensive edge. "It started when I didn't want my pregnant wife on the back of a horse. You think I haven't run that through my mind a million times? If I hadn't pushed, if I hadn't made an issue of it, maybe you wouldn't have been on that sidewalk."

Her face changed—the flash of anger cooling into a dull, resonant ache. She straightened her posture, her voice gentling as she reached for him. "Blake, nothing that happened is your fault."

"It isn't yours either," he said quietly. Then, after a beat, he shifted gears. "Wine?"

He reached into the refrigerator, pulled out a half-empty bottle his mother had left behind, popped the fancy stopper, and took a long pull straight from the glass before offering it over.

"Truth is…" she said after taking a swallow, the cold liquid cutting through the tension, "it started when I was born."

She handed the bottle back. Blake's eyes flicked over her face, assessing her with the precision of a man who spent his days reading clients. Years of experience told him she didn't need more wine—she required grounding.

"I need a minute, Darby." His voice was low now, a velvet command. "Let's sit. Drink our appetizer. I want to understand where you're coming from."

She gave a small, tired smile. "I agree with your menu plan, cowboy. And for what it's worth, I accept the role I played in what happened."

At least she didn't sound disappointed anymore. That tone from her always gutted him—it felt like a personal failure, a verdict he couldn't appeal. He slung an arm around her shoulder, the wine bottle dangling from his other hand, and led her to the sofa. Not long ago, this setup—plus a bag of microwave popcorn and the remote—was their idea of a perfect night in.

"So, Blake." She sank into the sofa cushions, the fight seemingly drained out of her. "Tell me about Winston."

He exhaled, the story coming out in measured pieces.

"Winston Payne was arrested after police found his thumbprint on the fancy storm door handle at Robert Badcock's place. Badcock was discovered unconscious by his sister, taken to the hospital, and woke up the next day. Later, he went to the post office to put his mail on hold— probably exchanged words with Winston before leaving town. He hasn't been seen in Steeplewood since."

"How did they know it was Winston's print?"

"His prints are on file—he's a federal employee, a postal worker," Blake said, explaining the logic of the system.

"Is he still in jail?"

"No." He left out the part about Tyler's midnight ride to Steeplewood on his wedding night to post bail—one more secret he wasn't ready to untangle just yet.

"So what happens now?" Darby asked, taking another pull from the bottle.

"Winston has retained Benjamin Williams as his attorney."

"What?" She jerked upright, too fast for her injuries. A flash of sharp pain sliced across her face as her body reminded her she was still in the middle of a slow healing process.

"Careful, Darby!" Blake shot to his feet, then dropped to his knees in front of her. The empty wine bottle sat forgotten on the side table. His hands began to massage her thighs—gentle, firm, grounding her. "You okay, honey?"

"I'm okay," she said with a soft, breathy laugh, the wine starting to loosen her tongue and her nerves. "I haven't moved that fast since I broke out of the hospital."

"I'm going to open another bottle. What say you?" He leaned in and kissed the tip of her nose, the scent of her skin finally beginning to chase away the stress of the day.

"I think that sounds lovely."

He dragged over the heavy ottoman he'd built back when they lived in that concrete efficiency apartment with a clothesline strung overhead—a relic of their leaner days. He lifted her feet to rest on it, a gesture that was instinctive, domestic, and tender.

"Has Ben agreed to represent Winston?" she asked, watching him work.

"Yes, as far as I know." He pulled the cork on the second bottle with a low, satisfying *pop*. "Gramps is one hell of a trial attorney, Darby, but whatever passes between them falls under attorney–client privilege. Even I won't know the full story."

He took a drink and handed her the bottle. She nodded, sipping slowly. As she did, Blake reached out and unbuttoned the front of her blouse, revealing a flash of fuchsia lace beneath. She passed the bottle back without a word, the air between them shifting from confrontational to intimate.

"Now, why didn't you tell me Tyler got married?" Her wine-fueled tone sharpened again, the memory resurfacing. "What harm could that have possibly done?"

He winced. Silence stretched between them, taut and heavy. "Darby," he said finally, "do you remember anything about Tyler coming to your hospital room?"

"Mostly a fuzzy dream." She looked down at her hands. "I think we talked about fishing. We used to do that a lot when we were kids." She didn't mention the part she remembered with startling clarity—the feel of Tyler's lips brushing hers in the dark.

"Honey," Blake said quietly, his voice heavy with the truth, "after he went back to Knoxville, Tyler was arrested for trespassing."

"What?" Darby lurched forward again, pain slicing through her expression. "How could you do that to him?"

"Baby, I didn't." Blake caught her before she could strain her healing stitches, his arms steady but careful. "Easy now. Do you see why I kept this from you? Two minutes into the conversation, and you've hurt yourself twice."

He eased her back, his throat tightening. That look in her eyes—hurt, accusing—stabbed at him every time. It made him feel like he had failed her, even when he was trying to protect her. He pressed her gently into the curve of the sofa until her body rested against his chest. His hand lingered on her shoulder, his thumb brushing slow, easy circles into her skin, trying to communicate what words couldn't: that he loved her too fiercely to let the world wound her again.

"Tyler somehow slipped past ninety-nine percent of the hospital's security," he went on, his voice low and steady. "That made it trespassing after posted hours. Don't worry—the charges were dropped." He didn't mention Ben's involvement. Some things were better left untold, buried in the name of family peace.

Blake took another long drink. He knew he shouldn't— he knew he was self-medicating the stress—but he did anyway, letting the burn of the wine settle his nerves.

"And for the record," he said, finally meeting her eyes with a raw honesty that hadn't been there before, "I was pissed that the first person my wife saw when she woke up after the accident and surgery was that fucking Tyler Payne. I wanted that moment to be mine, Darby. Not his."

Darby took the bottle from him and enjoyed a long drink of her own, the silence between them softening. Blake carefully began to ease the lounge pants off her, his movements gentle and methodical to avoid jarring her healing frame. He reattached the soft cast after removing her blouse, his touch lingering against her skin as if reassurance could be transferred through a simple touch.

"You forgot the bra and panties," she teased, her eyes glinting with a spark of the old mischief that had been missing since the curb jumped up to meet her.

"That's amateur stuff," he said, flashing her a crooked grin. "Takes skill to work around a cast and a rib belt without causing a patient to scream. I'm a professional."

It was the same grin she remembered from high school—the one that always undid her a little, the one that promised both trouble and absolute devotion all at once. It was the look that had convinced her, years ago, that a Williams might actually love a girl like her.

"So, boyfriend," she murmured, the wine beginning to haze the edges of her grief, "what does any of that have to do with Tyler getting married?"

"Beats me." He kissed her lightly, just at the corner of her mouth. "All I know is, shortly after the charges were dropped, he and Melissa got a marriage license and were married in the hospital chapel where she works. Apparently, the man doesn't waste time."

"That's… actually sweet," Darby admitted, her shoulders finally dropping an inch. The image of Tyler finding happiness seemed to act as a balm for her own guilt.

"So are you," he said softly. "Still mad at me?"

Her lips curved. "I'm working on it."

"I thought we had moved on to pleasure," Blake said, his voice dropping an octave. "But if you insist…" He paused, his expression turning serious again. "Honestly? I stripped you down so you wouldn't get angry and try to run away. It's hard to storm out when you're missing your pants." He caught her gaze and held it. "From now on, if we disagree, we strip down to at least our underwear. It forces us to stop hiding behind our clothes, our titles, our defenses. If it leads to the bedroom afterward, great. If it doesn't, that's okay too. But we don't hide."

Darby swallowed hard and stared at her clasped hands resting in her lap, the weight of his honesty pressing down on her.

"And don't you dare feel guilty, Darby," Blake went on, sensing the shift in her mood. "You've got to knock that off once and for all. I could probably write down the words running through your brain right now, and they're all lies."

"I was wondering," she murmured, her voice trembling as a fresh wave of vulnerability hit her, "if I was born stupid—or if God was just punishing me for being born."

"I was wrong," Blake said quietly, the pain in his own chest mirroring hers. "I would not have written those words." He reached for her hand, lacing his fingers through hers. "Darby, while working full-time, you graduated third in your class with a master's degree. We can safely rule out dumb. As for punishment... the God I believe in doesn't work that way. He doesn't settle scores with car accidents and loss. Please look at me, sweetheart, and tell me what I'm missing. Why do you think you're being punished?"

Darby lifted her eyes to him. She obeyed, as she always had when he asked gently instead of demanding, searching his face for the truth she couldn't find in herself.

"When I was very young, I prayed over and over for God to make my parents love me. When that didn't happen, I started praying that the man I thought was my father would stop hurting me. We know how that went." She drew a shaky breath, the weight of a thousand unanswered childhood pleas hanging in the air. "Later, I realized it must have been God who brought you into my life. I was in love with you, cowboy. I still am. I suppose HE had other commitments before that point. Let's face it—there was worse stuff going on in the world than me." She swallowed hard, her eyes glassing over. "But now... HE took our son, Blake." Her voice broke, the finality of the loss crashing down on her.

Blake felt her pain radiating from her like a physical heat. He reached out and brushed a stray tear from her cheek, his own throat tight. He steadied his voice, needing to be the anchor she could no longer find within herself.

"Darby, God gave mankind free will. HE didn't make Luis and Malina Hart evil—they chose to be. And I believe our son died because the driver of a rental van made an awful, human decision. That was not God punishing us." He squeezed her hand, his gaze unyielding. "What God did do was make you strong, beautiful, and the love of my life." He paused. "I never told you this before, but I prayed for a girl who would believe in me, who would love me for who I was, not for the Williams name. The next night, I went to a high school dance, and there you were, sitting in a dark corner of the gym. Bright. Beautiful. Darby Hart. I already had a crush on you." He chuckled, the memory a rare spark of light in the dim room.

Her lips curved into a small smile, a faint blush creeping up her cheeks. She looked down and then back up at him through her lashes, the sarcasm and fury finally replaced by a fragile hope.

"That moment changed my life," he said, his voice dropping to a low, intimate rasp. "That was God answering my prayer."

"Oh, Blake," she whispered, her voice barely a breath. "Maybe HE was answering both our prayers." She shifted, wincing as her ribs protested the movement, but she was determined. She moved closer, seeking the heat and safety only he provided.

Blake carefully guided her onto his lap, mindful of the soft cast and the remaining bandages, and held her tight. "There were bumps along the way, honey, because that's how life works. But no matter how you look at it, you are mine, Darby Williams, and I am yours. We're both still here."

He kissed her tenderly—a promise of a future that

didn't feel so dark anymore—and his heart lifted when she kissed him back, the connection between them sealing out the rest of the world.

CHAPTER 12

Winston Payne and his son, Wyatt, entered the Williams Law Office late Saturday morning, their expressions carved from stone and their presence heavy enough to alter the room's atmosphere. The building was still and expectant; no other clients had been scheduled, ensuring the stillness would remain undisturbed. Ben rose to meet them, his handshake firm but brief, and led them to his in-town private office.

Inside his own open-door office, Reece appeared absorbed in his typing, the soft, tapping of keys filling the silence. In truth, he was a silent sentry, his ears tuned to the building—backup disguised as routine. When the heavy door to Ben's office finally clicked shut, Reece rose with a fluid motion. He crossed the professional lobby and engaged the metallic slide of the bolt on the front door. The sound echoed faintly through the quiet building, a subtle but deliberate barrier against the outside world.

As he turned back, Reece caught Wyatt's glance through the narrow pane of glass in Ben's office door. The younger Payne's stance was loose, almost careless, but his eyes flicked over the lobby with practiced, lethal calculation. He was measuring the angles, the exits, and the distance between everything and himself. Winston, by contrast, carried his weight forward with the certainty of a man who believed walls simply bent around him. Reece filed the contrast away in silence. In his experience, it was men like Wyatt—the ones who looked casual while counting doors—who mattered most when things finally broke.

Inside Ben's area, the air was thick with the scent of old paper and expensive leather. Ben motioned to the two guest chairs he had strategically placed in front of his desk years ago. "Gentlemen, please make yourselves comfortable."

He was fully aware that Wyatt was tactically scanning the room for bugs or recording devices, but Ben pretended not to notice. He waited with the patience of a predator until the two Paynes were seated before he claimed the high-back executive chair behind the desk—a seat selected to remind everyone who held the authority.

"All right, Winston." Ben steepled his fingers, pinning his client with a sharp, focused gaze. "I'm both flattered and dubious that you've asked me to be your attorney. The best bet is that you have confidential information you are not willing to share otherwise, which is the only reason I agreed to this meeting. I don't dislike you, Winston, but legally, I feel compelled to remind you that your daughter is married to my grandson, and he is also an attorney."

"I get it," Winston said, his voice a low rumble. "A lot of lawyers in the Williams clan."

Ben didn't react, his face a mask of professional neutrality.

"I think Robert Badcock is responsible for what happened to Darby," Winston continued.

"Go on," Ben encouraged.

"I went to Badcock's place to tell him to leave Darby alone after he threatened to have my little girl arrested. The conversation got heated. He took the first swing and missed. I didn't miss, but I only hit him once. He was cussing and standing on his own two feet when I left. I'm thinking his alleged unconscious state probably had more to do with the bottle of gin sitting next to his chair than my fist."

Winston leaned in, his eyes dark. "When he came to the post office to have his mail held, he told me he'd get even in a way I'd never forget. Anyway, I'm reasonably sure I have information that I can't share with the law—something that tells me Robert Badcock will be back in Steeplewood soon."

Ben leaned forward slightly, a posture designed to assure a client they were being seen and heard. He noted Wyatt recognized the move with a thin, knowing smile.

"Show him the pictures," Wyatt said, mirroring Ben's forward lean.

Winston pulled his phone from his pocket, brought up an image, and slid the device across the mahogany toward Ben.

"Explain to me what I'm looking at," Ben said, knowing that every syllable in the room was being recorded—both by his own security and likely by Wyatt Payne.

"You'll recall that Badcock was having his mail held, so I recently went through it after everyone else had left for the day," Winston explained. "What you're looking at is a photo of an envelope from a bank in Gallatin, addressed to Janiece Badcock—Robert's mother, who passed away six months ago. I held the envelope; I felt the contents. I firmly believe it contains a bank-issued credit or debit card. Something tells me the card Badcock is using to cover his tracks is about to expire. He'll have to come back here to get the new one, which means the bank is currently unaware that the true cardholder is deceased."

"Does Robert Badcock always have his mail held when he goes out of town?" Ben asked.

"No. This is the first time. The route delivery guy mentioned that Badcock's sister-in-law usually checks his box when he's away. Sometimes she's even waiting in her car when the truck pulls up."

"Huh. I thought he and his brother's family were estranged," Ben mused, pushing the phone back with his knuckles. "This could have been a joint account. Did you leave your prints on the mail?"

"I wore disposable gloves," Winston said. "We keep them in stock."

Ben rose, pointing toward the exit. "Let me walk you to your car, gentlemen."

Once in the parking lot, the midday sun reflecting off the asphalt, Ben turned to Wyatt. "What do you need?"

"I'll need access to that special equipment you are rumored to have on the farm."

"You're asking a lot, Wyatt." Ben stared directly into the

younger man's eyes, searching for the limits of his loyalty.

"Ben, I'm positive that a Badcock has something to do with what happened to my sister. I can show you why if you give me access. But I'm not an attorney, and I need to return to my job. Time is running out."

Ben nodded. "Give me fifteen minutes to make some calls, then come to the farm. The gatekeeper will direct you. Only Wyatt will have access to certain areas. Winston, you'll be either eating pie at the main house or having a drink. I'll ask Reece to join you. You'll be two in-laws getting together to discuss your children."

A short while later, the heavy security gates at Williams Farm swung open. John Hawk was waiting in a farm truck to whisk Wyatt away to the multifaceted bunkhouse. Winston drove ahead on the immaculate driveway, his eyes scanning the livestock in the pastures—well-bred animals that screamed of wealth and high-dollar auctions. Despite his pride, Winston was undeniably impressed.

In the bunkhouse AV room, Ben was waiting alongside Eric Youngman. Eric looked visibly annoyed at the prospect of sharing his high-tech domain, standing back from the massive control console and the glowing row of monitors.

Wyatt offered a sharp nod and approached the console. He visually scanned the array of equipment before his fingers began to fly across the keys with a speed and precision that made the monitors flash and reorganize around the room.

Show off, Eric thought silently, watching the soldier dismantle his digital walls with terrifying ease.

Within seconds, the central monitor displayed a current bank statement belonging to the not-so-current Janiece Badcock. Wyatt pointed to the screen with the clinical detachment of a professor teaching a graduate-level seminar.

"What we see on the screen is the current statement for the Gallatin bank account in question," Wyatt explained, his eyes never leaving the data. "The first line is a hefty payment made to Lyonhurst Security in Nashville. Lyonhurst doesn't just provide bodyguards to the rich and famous; it also conducts specialized private investigations when the circumstances warrant. The second transaction was made near a private rental location in Georgia, exactly twelve hours before Darby was struck by a white rental van while walking outside the TNT offices."

He paused, letting the timeline sink in. "Additionally, in-depth details reveal that Janiece Badcock was the sole owner and signatory. No *pay-on-death* arrangement was ever documented. This account was set up in person by Mrs. Badcock a year before her son Robert became her primary caregiver. It appears Janiece went to a great deal of trouble to hide money—likely from her own son—for some unknown reason."

"Now," Wyatt continued, his fingers flying across the keys again, "we already know what Robert Badcock's personal credit card statement looks like, but let's look at his personal checking account at the bank here in Steeplewood."

An image appeared on a separate monitor, glowing bright in the dim room. "I'd like to point out the two most notable transactions that recently occurred at a post office in Hendersonville. The first involves using his debit card for facility services. The second is a personal check made out to the U.S. Department of State."

"I'll be damned," Ben said, a grin tugging at the corner of his mouth despite his best efforts to remain neutral.

"Gentlemen," Wyatt said, nodding toward Ben. "I can think of only one reason why this information exists. Since Janiece Badcock is no longer among the living, the obvious party responsible for the fraud would be Robert. And we have the digital breadcrumbs on his own credit card showing he was in the state of Georgia at the time of the van rental."

Eric, recognizing a smoking gun when he saw one, reached into his pocket for his cellphone and began taking rapid-fire pictures of the screens. Sensing the job was done, Wyatt worked with surgical speed to exit the sites and scrub any digital evidence of their intrusion.

On the shaded patio behind the main house, Winston accepted a cold beer from Reece. They sat in a pair of high-end outdoor chairs, admiring the manicured view of the Williams estate.

"Nice place you got here," Winston admitted, looking out over the rolling pastures. "You can't tell from the road exactly what's back here this far."

"I believe that was the plan," Reece replied, taking only micro-sips from his bottle. "I'm pretty sure Pops built this house specifically for my mother, and he's always been a man who values his privacy."

"Real shame about our grandson," Winston said, his

voice dropping into a somber register.

"Truer words were never spoken. My heart breaks for our kids," Reece said, staring out at the horizon. "But Blake assures me that they are healing, both mentally and physically. My wife spent a couple of weeks with them after Darby was discharged. JoJo's glad to be home, but she's ready to go back the second they need her."

"At least you get to spend time with them," Winston sighed, a trace of bitterness in his tone. "I imagine you hear from them whenever you want to. I don't think Darby has ever truly accepted me as her father. She responds faster to my wife, Omalita, than she does to me."

"Do you blame her, Winston?"

"No," Winston said after a long, heavy pause. "I don't. I shudder to think about what might have happened between her and Tyler. That boy was clearly in love. At one point, I figured Darby would be my daughter-in-law, but as it turns out, she was my daughter all along. I thank God that she and Blake found each other when they did; otherwise, I'd be living with a different type of disaster entirely."

Reece reached over and handed his guest another beer, a silent gesture of solidarity between two men who had spent their lives trying to protect complicated legacies. "Well, if it helps to know, I never realized a person could humanly love someone as much as my son loves your daughter."

"Good to know, Reece. Your son is a fine man."

The two men clinked their bottles together, the glass ringing out in the quiet afternoon air—a temporary peace between two families bound by a tragedy and a shared enemy.

Minutes before midnight, Reece brought his recliner to the upright position and turned off the television, the blue glow of the screen fading just as his cell phone began to vibrate on the side table.

"Hello." He answered.

"Omalita just got a phone call saying that Robert Badcock is back in town." Winston Payne didn't bother to identify himself; the urgency in his gravelly voice was unmistakable.

"I need a little more information, Winston," Reece said, his mind instantly shifting from late-night relaxation to tactical assessment.

"Clara was double-checking the door locks inside the Thrift Shop a few minutes ago when she recognized his car at the stoplight outside her store. She and her husband live over the shop now, and she was downstairs in the dark. She's positive that Badcock didn't see her."

"So, she automatically called Omalita at this late hour to tell her the news?" Reece questioned, his internal lawyer skepticism kicking in.

"They're both members of the church's Ladies Auxiliary. Seems like a lot of people in this town think Robert might know something about what happened to Darby. Most people don't like the man, and some of the ladies are actually afraid of him," Winston pointed out.

"Why didn't you call my father? He is your attorney."

"I tried. It went straight to voicemail. And before you

say it, yes, I know it's late."

"Tell Omalita not to discuss the situation with anyone else. It could hurt your case," Reece warned, rubbing his forehead as a headache began to pulse behind his eyes. He almost wished he'd let the call go to voicemail himself.

"She says she hasn't, but she also says that Clara doesn't speak up unless she thinks something is significant—especially not in the middle of the night."

"All right, Winston. I'll let Dad and Blake know. You and Omalita watch your backs. We know what Badcock may be capable of."

Reece ended the call and stared at the dark TV screen for a moment. The *wait-and-see* portion of the investigation had just ended. If Badcock was back, he was either here to finish what he started or to grab that new passport and disappear forever.

CHAPTER 13

Robert Badcock, dressed in a cleaner-than-usual red hoodie, had been loitering outside the post office since dawn, pacing and muttering under his breath as he waited for the clerk to turn the key in the lock. When the doors finally opened, he was the first customer across the threshold. He demanded his held mail and snatched up the bundle with twitching fingers, his eyes darting as if he expected a lifeline to leap out from the stack of bills and circulars.

Less than an hour later, the red hoodie came storming back through those same doors, the earlier pretense of composure completely shredded. Badcock shoved through the line with the force of a man who believed the world owed him an explanation. His face was mottled with a sickly purple rage, his voice ragged.

"I want the rest of my mail!" He pounded a fist on the counter, the sound echoing like a gunshot in the small lobby.

"Uh, sir," the seasoned window clerk said, remaining remarkably calm despite the spittle flying toward him.

"You picked up your mail this morning, but you'll need to wait patiently back in line. I'll double-check as soon as I wait on the folks who are ahead of you."

The tension in the room was palpable. Two of the female customers looked at Badcock's shaking hands, grew nervous, and quietly slipped out the door. The remaining two men in line held their positions, their stares heavy and expectant, fixed squarely on the back of the hoodie.

"You tell Winston Payne I want to see him," Badcock snarled, lowering his volume to a dangerous, vibrating whisper.

"Boss," the clerk called out, stepping back from the counter without turning his head. "Someone here to see you."

Winston Payne strolled casually to the front counter, both hands buried deep in his pockets, and looked Badcock directly in the eyes. He didn't blink. He didn't flinch. "Hello, Robert. Something I can do for you?"

"You can give me the rest of my mail. Something seems to be missing."

"Let me double-check in the back, but please keep your voice down," Winston said, his tone smooth as polished stone.

Winston moved deliberately through the back sorting area, opening and closing mail cubicles with practiced precision. The act was a perfect cover. Hours earlier, in the dead of night, Winston had cut the building's power, giving Eric Youngman the window he needed to slip inside and plant the mini-cams. Those cameras were currently streaming live high-definition video to the farm's bunkhouse AV room—and, unknown to Eric, Wyatt Payne was monitoring the same feed from a secure, remote location.

"Sorry, Robert. It appears that we gave you everything this morning." Winston returned to the counter, wearing a mask of fake concern. "What is it in particular that you think you're missing? If you tell me, we can keep an eye out for it. That way, if it comes in, I can personally run it out to the house for you."

"Never mind!" Robert Badcock's fist slammed down hard on the counter one last time as he turned and stormed out of the building, the bells on the door jingling frantically in his wake.

"Damn, patient of you, Winston," one of the remaining male customers said, letting out a breath. "That Robert has always been a piece of work."

"All in a day's work, boys," Winston replied with a modest nod, though he was mentally patting himself on the back. He had just set the hook, and now all they had to do was wait for Badcock to lead them to the rental van.

Benjamin Williams was sitting in the micro-kitchen on the second floor of *Clara's Thrift Shop*. Her newly retired husband was temporarily minding the shop below.

"You're afraid of Robert, and something tells me that you have a specific reason why. You're a good person, Clara. Any knowledge you share with me may help save lives," Ben said.

"Ben, the last thing I want to do is get involved in anything to do with Robert Badcock. My husband and I have turned the farm over to our son and his family. Our daughter lives next to them on the old place where my grandparents used to live. Life is good, and we enjoy living in town now. We've worked hard to enjoy our retirement, and the last thing we need is a feud with that short-fused Robert." Clara was not smiling.

"I understand that by asking you these questions, I am placing you in a precarious position," Ben said.

"Ben, the whole town is sorry about Darby losing her baby. That girl has endured enough for two lifetimes, but Robert is unpredictable, and you know it."

"Yes, Clara, I do. That's why we need your help." Ben briefly checked his watch, only to make her think that she was wasting time.

"All right, truce," Clara said. "Fact is," she paused to gather her thoughts, "Janiece Badcock was afraid of her youngest son."

"She told you this herself?" Ben asked.

"She did. As you know, she was a lifetime member of the Ladies Auxiliary at the church."

"Uh, hum," Ben nodded in affirmation.

"Anyway, her children took her license and car keys away when Janiece was 80 because she took down her big fancy mailbox while backing out of the driveway. Since Robert had been living with her in the same house ever since his daddy died, Rob got responsibility for driving Janiece anywhere she needed to go."

"Go on," Ben encouraged, taking a sip of the now lukewarm coffee she insisted that he have. Clara was a charming southern woman. She had to offer him some form of food or beverage, and he was obliged to accept her generosity under the circumstances.

"Well, Janiece Badcock started showing up at the Auxiliary meetings wearing a lot of long sleeves, even in the summertime. The woman was clearly uncomfortable. So, one day her sleeves rode up on her forearms, and I saw several deep bruises. I asked her about it. She seemed anxious and tried to pull the fabric back down to cover it up. Then she said that Robert had been helping her with something a few days earlier and had gotten carried away. She couldn't look me in the eye when she said it, so I asked her outright if she was afraid of Robert, and she said 'yes'."

"Why didn't you notify the authorities, Clara?" Ben asked.

"Because she asked me not to." Clara paused and looked sad. "Later, after she supposedly died in her sleep, I wondered if that was true or not. She had been down at the church that day for the monthly meeting of the Auxiliary. Seemed to be in good spirits and appeared to be in good health for her age. The coroner's report said that she died of natural causes. Went to sleep and didn't wake up. I guess we should all be that lucky when our time comes, but I've always wondered. I don't know if anyone stood to benefit more from her death than her son, Robert."

Ben leaned forward, his expression grave as he addressed Reece. "What do you think?" he asked, the weight of the meeting with Clara and the troubling shadow of Janiece Badcock's death hanging between them like a physical presence.

Reece considered the situation with the cold calculation of a man who had spent his life managing risk. "There isn't enough evidence to exhume Janiece Badcock's body," he said, his tone low and measured. "But I do believe we have plausible information suggesting that someone in that house would commit murder to maintain their lifestyle." He paused, his gaze narrowing. "Where do you stand on the subject of the Badcocks? I want the history, Pops."

Ben leaned back in his leather chair and steepled his fingers, his eyes distant as he reached back into the archives of Steeplewood's darker history. "We're polite in public, but there's a common saying among local businesspeople: *never turn your back on a Badcock.* People who stand in their path have a way of getting hurt or disappearing altogether."

Reece leaned in, his interest piqued. "Are you saying they actually kill people who get in their way? That it's a family tradition?"

"There have been rumors for years," Ben said, slowly shaking his head. "Just like the rumors that Morgan Senior was involved in all types of illegal activities back in the late sixties and early seventies. Back then, every wide spot in the road around here had a branch bank. Morgan Badcock Senior had multiple accounts at each one. He would spend his days driving a circuit, making massive cash deposits. Clearly money laundering, but the source was always a mystery. The ambiguity of the situation was apparent; multiple scenarios were possible, and none could be ruled out without further proof." Ben's forehead wrinkled as he sighed. "I have a strong feeling that we are overlooking an important detail, Reece. Something hiding in plain sight."

In the farm AV Room, Eric Youngman worked with clinical efficiency. He printed Janiece Badcock's obituary from the local funeral home's website, the ink barely dry before he slid it into a legal-sized envelope addressed simply to **CUSTOMER SERVICE**. Wearing thin latex gloves, he folded the death announcement, placed it inside the self-sealing envelope, and handed it to John Hawkins.

Hawk, wearing his heavy farm-issued work gloves, accepted the packet.

"Make damn sure Hunter North knows what he's doing when he puts that in the night drop box at the bank," Eric warned. "If the bank gets this notification tonight, that account freezes by morning."

"He'll be fine." Hawk nodded, his expression grim. "Besides, he'll be doing the drop on his way to Georgia to check those rental leads. We underuse his talents as it is. I know that Boyd and Ben both trust him with their lives."

"Good luck in Nashville, Hawk." Eric returned to his monitors, his fingers flying across the keys. "I don't envy you. One wrong move and Blake might snap your neck if he thinks you're scaring Darby." He paused, his typing slowing. "You think he'll ever move back to the farm permanently?"

"Honestly, I don't know why he would, Eric." Hawk scratched his head, thinking of the high-rise life in the city. "Blake is a good man, and he married a damn fine woman, even if she is a firecracker," he chuckled. "Reece will do a good job when and if something happens to Ben, but I'm not sure Blake has anything to gain by returning to Steeplewood. There are too many bad memories buried in this soil for both him and Darby."

By the next business cycle, the bank's legal department in Gallatin moved with the cold precision of a federal institution. Upon receiving the anonymous notification of the death, they filed a fraud report and a Suspicious Activity Report (SAR) with FinCEN. This was a federally insured bank, and with an account balance too high to ignore for a deceased cardholder, they weren't taking chances.

The digital doors slammed shut. Robert Badcock—or whoever had been illegally bleeding the account—was now officially cut off. The money that might buy freedom was now a frozen block of evidence.

Reece's voice carried that steady, paternal fatigue—the sound of a man who had spent his life calculating risks and was tired of the math. "Hawk will be there first thing in the morning."

"Are you sure that's necessary, Dad?" Blake asked, his phone tucked to his ear as he leaned against the granite kitchen counter. The condo was quiet, a stark contrast to the storm brewing in Steeplewood. "I've got Darby under control. She's resting, and the security system here is top-of-the-line."

"Yes, I'm sure." Reece's tone left no room for debate. "We need Eric here to handle the digital side. Your mother is volunteering at the library to keep an eye on Omalita.

We've got one guard posing as your grandfather's driver and another rotating between my office, the post office, and the library. Resources are stretched thin, Blake. We're covering the farm and the development site, too. We can't afford a single weak link right now."

Blake rubbed at his jaw, the stubble rasping against his palm. "Then it sounds like you need Hawk in Steeplewood more than I do. I can ask Darby to stay inside and away from the windows while I'm at work. I'll lock it down."

Reece snorted, a dry, cynical sound. "Because that's worked so well in the past."

"Thanks a hell of a lot, Dad. Low blow." Blake caught the sharper response before it slipped out, but the tension sat heavy between them.

"Blake," Reece said evenly, his voice dropping into a tactical register, "if anyone can keep Darby in one piece while you're gone, it's John Hawk. You need to go to work. Keep things looking normal—switch up your route, vary your entrances and exits, use taxis or ride-shares. You know the drill. Pops and I both believe Darby is still the primary target. She humiliated Badcock, and Winston doubled down on the beating. She is Winston's daughter and Ben's granddaughter-in-law. If Robert Badcock manages to take out Darby Williams, he scores the revenge trifecta."

Blake exhaled through his teeth, the reality of the threat settling in his gut like lead. "Alright, Dad. I'll tell her."

There was a pause, the kind of silence that usually preceded a question a father didn't really want to ask. Then Reece spoke: "You have a problem with Hawk I should know about?"

"Yeah." Blake's tone hardened, the possessive edge he usually kept in check surfacing. "I think his feelings for my wife run deeper than they should—especially for an employee, even one that good."

A long beat of silence stretched over the line, the hum of the city outside Blake's window filling the void. Then Reece's voice came low, deliberate, and chillingly pragmatic. "Son," he said, "I'm counting on it."

"Blake, Hawk should be shadowing you, not me." Darby's hands rested on her denim-clad hips, her posture defiant despite the lingering stiffness in her frame.

"Darby, he'll be here any minute. I would consider it a kind gift if you would try not to be difficult about this." Blake had not slept well after his father's phone call, and the exhaustion was etched into the shadows beneath his eyes and the tight set of his jaw.

"Cowboy, I promise to stay inside. Doors locked. Curtains drawn. Please, take Hawk with you today. You're the one out in the open."

"Honey, since you came into my life, you have been beaten, shot, and run down by a moving vehicle," he said, his voice dropping to a low, painful rasp. "In all that time, did anything ever happen to me?"

"No, but—"

"No *buts*, honey." He cut her off, his hands coming up to rest on her shoulders. "I have an intense and busy week ahead with an enormous amount of responsibility. I can't properly do my job if I feel you're unsafe. John Hawk is our best option. I'm pretty sure that man would put his life on the line for you."

"Blake…" Her voice broke, and her chin fell against her chest. Her fists clenched and unclenched as the buzzing notification from Blake's phone vibrated through the quiet kitchen.

"He's here." Blake looked down at his phone and then back up at his wife, his expression softening with a desperate kind of love. "Come give me a kiss, pretty girl."

Darby rushed into his arms, clinging to him as if he were the only solid thing in a shifting world. His fingers lifted her chin to meet his lips, and the kiss that followed warmed her entire body, momentarily chasing away the chill of the morning. "Be good today, honey." His free hand popped her affectionately on the behind. "I'll be home before you know it."

"You better be," she said, the unshed tears making her voice thick. "I love you, Blake."

"I love you, Darby, always and forever." He reluctantly released her and punched in the security code that allowed Hawk to enter the building.

She kept her back to the room, focusing on hand-washing Blake's coffee cup at the kitchen sink. He had refused breakfast, preferring instead to spend those extra minutes holding her in the quiet of the morning. Near the front door, Blake spoke with Hawk in low, serious tones, his recycled leather briefcase already in hand.

"Alright, babe. I'm out of here." Blake was swiping through the security screens on the mini-monitor near the door, checking the exterior hallway and the street-level feeds. She ran to him one last time, and they shared a quick, fierce kiss as Hawk tactfully looked away.

"Call me, please." She backed away, her heart hammering against her ribs. Blake offered a final nod, stepped into the hallway, and pulled the door securely closed behind him. *Click.* Hawk reached over and tested the handle by hand, ensuring the bolt had fully engaged.

Darby's face dropped into her hands, her shoulders beginning to shake with silent, jagged sobs. Hawk fought every instinctual urge to cross the room and pull her into his arms. He knew the boundary, and he knew how much Blake trusted him with this assignment. He decided on a safer, more domestic tactic.

"Could I trouble you for a cup of coffee, Mrs. Williams?" he asked softly.

"Sure, Hawk." She wiped her eyes on her sleeve, taking a shaky breath to steady herself. "How about some eggs and toast to go with that?"

"That sounds good, Ma'am." He didn't mention that he'd already put away a full breakfast at the hotel over an hour ago. Keeping her busy was part of the job.

She turned toward the kitchen, her spirit flickering back to life. "And, Hawk?"

"Yes, Ma'am."

"Call me Darby, or I'm going to slap you across the face with a hot spatula."

"Yes, Ma'am. I mean—yes, Darby." He chuckled, relieved when a wide smile finally graced her tear-stained face. But John Hawk was no fool; he had seen her in action, and he took the threat of the spatula very seriously.

Blake's day was both hectic and busy. He met with a new client in the morning and returned multiple calls. He'd also had an open-door lunch in his office with Rachel O'Rourke, his fifty-something-year-old seasoned legal assistant. It was Blake's private belief that Rachel could probably run the entire firm on any given day under any circumstance. He had selected her from a short list of hopefuls when he joined the firm full-time, primarily due to her age and the fact that she had been kind to him when he was a lowly clerk intern. Not only was she loyal and overqualified, but she was married and uninterested in making a pass at him. The bonus was that she and Darby liked one another.

The afternoon brought a call from his father relating to other business. The County Commissioners in Steeplewood voted 11-9 the night before to approve rezoning additional property on Williams Farm from agricultural to a mix of residential and commercial uses, based on preliminary plans submitted by Williams Development Inc.

"That's great news, Dad. That means we'll be able to move forward once phase two is nearing completion," Blake said.

"Blake, now is the economic time to push forward with the infrastructure for phases three and four while we are doing phase two. The longer we wait, the more expensive it gets."

"I understand that, sir, but that means we pull Turner, Nealy & Taylor into the picture immediately."

"You have a problem with that, son?"

"I refuse to do business with Greg Turner."

"I saw what happened between you and Turner, but are you willing to discuss this further?" Reece asked.

"No," Blake replied.

"Are you asking me to trust you as my son or as my partner?" Reece asked.

"The choice is yours."

"Blake, with one exception, Turner's work has been exemplary."

"Sir, my position on the subject will not change, and I will not discuss it again." Blake's voice was firm, even though he was casually sorting through his interoffice email.

"All right, Blake. I'll pass this along to your grandfather." Reece sighed and changed the subject. "How are Darby and Hawk getting along?"

"Fine, I believe. I spoke with her at lunch. She says she owes Hawk five hundred. I hope that's not dollars, but knowing my Darby, it could be anything. Whatever it is, we'll make it good." Blake glanced up to see local talent agent Chelsea Lambert heading straight for his office door. "Got to go, Dad. A big snake is about to slither into my office."

Blake disconnected the call. The only thing shorter than Chelsea's skirt today was Blake's patience to deal with her rude interruption.

"Blake! You handsome devil. Give a girl a kiss." She started around the side of his desk and ran into the heel of Blake's leather shoe.

"You do not have an appointment, Chelsea, and you

and I will never kiss."

"Why do you have to be so mean to me, Blake Williams?" Chelsea turned around only to plop down in one of the chairs in front of his desk. In doing so, she made sure to leave her legs wide enough for him to see that she wasn't wearing any underwear.

"I'm sorry, Mr. Williams," Rachel rushed into the room. "I was away from my desk."

"Not your fault, Rachel. Chelsea had to pass two other checkpoints before arriving here. Now, if you would be so kind as to ask security to escort Miss Lambert to the safety of the parking lot."

"Yes, sir." Rachel stifled a laugh as she backed her way out of the room, being sure to leave the door open. Chelsea Lambert was on her mental list of least favorite individuals to deal with at work.

"Blake, I have this hot new artist, Jackson Green, that you simply have to sign as a client." Chelsea did her best to sound sexy and breathless. She honestly believed she was the solidifying force in all of her clients' lives.

"Chelsea, my roster is overflowing as it is. This building is filled with capable attorneys. Pick one and make an appointment."

"Blake, nobody in the business negotiates a better deal than you do. Besides, I thought of you first because of the Steeplewood connection." She was serious now and crossed her legs, removing the offer of herself.

"Chelsea, I am aware of Green's lineage, but I seriously doubt that, beyond his place of birth, he can claim any knowledge of Steeplewood. Not that it would get him special consideration if he had. You're looking for a hard launch for this person, and it's not going to happen with me. Besides, it would not be fair to my other clients, some of whom are also yours."

"How's your wife, Blake?" she abruptly changed the subject. "I was sorry to hear about what happened."

"My private life is none of your concern, but for the record, she is recovering well. Please leave my office. I see security approaching. Try not to make a scene, Chelsea."

"Blake, most of the information was on the news. I'm very sorry about the loss of your baby."

Blake remained silent. His stare in the woman's direction was cold and unsettling.

A tall, muscular, and well-paid security guard stood in the doorway. "Please come with me, Miss Lambert. I'll escort you to your vehicle."

Both Darby's and Hawk's cell phones chimed. Darby dropped her cards on the table as the front condo door opened and Blake walked in, allowing the door to close and lock behind him. Darby didn't walk; she sprinted across the room and melted into him as he dropped his briefcase onto the floor.

"You're home." She sighed as her face tilted upward, and he kissed her like he'd been lost at sea.

"Did you have a good day, my love? Whatever you're cooking smells great. You didn't overextend yourself, did you?"

"No, cowboy. Hawk and I cooked and played penny poker." Her smile was wide and reassuring. "You look tired."

"I was too tired to stop by the gym today, that's for sure. Hawk, you can go unless you want to stay for dinner."

Hawk was cautious not to appear over-eager to leave. "You know where to find me this evening if necessary; otherwise, I'll be on my way and see you first thing in the morning."

"I take it there's nothing to report?" Blake asked while he was busy staring into Darby's eyes.

"No, sir. Life was quiet here except that I probably gained five pounds. Mrs. Williams is an exceptional chef."

"I'm only a country cook, Hawk." Darby never took her eyes off of Blake.

"And a fine one at that, Ma'am. Again, you two know where I'll be this evening. Blake, if you plan to drive your car tomorrow, I need to check it out first, so I'll be here thirty minutes earlier in the morning. Otherwise, I'll see myself out."

Hawk passed the couple who looked like they might devour one another at any moment, and he was envious as hell. No one had ever looked at him like that, and he guessed they never would.

"See you tomorrow, Hawk," Blake said as he leaned in and claimed his wife again.

CHAPTER 14

Early over dinner, the conversation stayed light—banal chatter about Blake's newest client, the weather, a story Hawk had told, but Blake knew her too well to be fooled. Something was pressing on Darby's mind, and she was dragging her feet. Her laughter was off by half a beat; her eyes, bright as glass, were elsewhere.

He let it go for a while, watching her move through the small domestic rituals—the careful cut of her steak, the neat fold of her napkin, the way she brushed a stray hair behind her ear without realizing it. He knew every gesture of hers like a melody he'd memorized. When he finally leaned back in his chair, it was with the slow patience of a man who'd been waiting for a storm to break.

"Alright, pretty girl. You've got something to say. Out with it."

Darby hesitated, twisting the napkin between her fingers until the linen looked wrung out. "Am I that obvious?"

"No, babe. I just know you. Go ahead."

Her voice came softer now, but steady. "I've been thinking about this for a few days." She hesitated. "What if I wasn't the actual target when that van hit me?" She lifted her gaze then, eyes darkening, reflecting something sharp and dangerous beneath the calm. "What if it was all a setup?"

Blake stilled his fork halfway to his mouth. The sound of the clock on the wall filled the pause. "To what end?"

"Blake, what would have happened to Robert Badcock if I had died—and you believed he was responsible?" The silence between them thickened. Even the air seemed to slow down.

"Darby--" he started carefully.

"Blake," she interrupted. "Please answer the question."

His jaw flexed. He placed the fork down on his plate before speaking. "He might suffer the consequences, but not without proof."

Her eyes didn't waver. "What if someone wanted that? What if someone wanted the Williams family to do their dirty work? Who benefits if Robert Badcock suffers the consequences?"

Blake's voice dropped, slow and measured. "You talk to Hawk about this today?"

"No," she said, shaking her head. "I wouldn't have this conversation with anyone but you."

He gave a short nod, watching her closely. "Clever girl. There's more, isn't there?"

"Yes." She drew a breath, as though reaching backward through time. "You may remember my sister Jade was a cheerleader. Every year, she'd host the squad at the Hart farm for a weekend sleepover. That meant my brother Wade went next door to the Payne boys' house. They'd camp out with binoculars, spying on the girls."

Blake smirked faintly. "Got it. Topless cheerleaders and rural espionage."

She rolled her eyes but pressed on. "Well, sometimes the girls let me hang out with them, but mostly they forgot I was even there. One time, one of them lit a joint, trying to look cool. She said she got it from her boyfriend, who worked *down in the caves* at the Badcock farm. I thought that was strange. But later, when we were in high school, I heard rumors that the Badcocks had a grow operation in the caves under their farm."

Blake's brows knit together. "That's an interesting story, Darby. But what's your conclusion?"

"That the Badcocks are dangerous people. Probably explains why the town has tolerated Robert Badcock's behavior for so long. But what if whoever's behind this didn't actually want me dead? What if they wanted the Williams family to get rid of the alcoholic Robbie for some reason?"

He leaned back, studying her. "Why not just get rid of Robert themselves?"

"I believe someone tried, and it didn't go as planned. Maybe Omalita spoiled the setup when she called Robert's sister, Terry. Even Winston got involved when he should've minded his own business."

"You're saying if Winston and Omalita had stayed out of it, Robert would've died in his recliner from a combination of gin and sleeping pills, and no one would have questioned it—but because that failed, someone escalated to a bigger, more complex plan."

"Exactly."

Blake exhaled slowly, the movement deliberate, controlled. "Huh. Interesting." His eyes were fixed on her face. "While we're on the topic, Darby, you've always known I would do whatever's necessary to protect you. To protect what's ours. Right?"

Her breath caught in her throat. "I suppose I did—or do. But reality can be enlightening."

He leaned forward, voice soft but carrying a dangerous gravity. "When I tell you that you are mine and I am yours, those aren't just words meant to romance and seduce you."

The air seemed to shift between them—intimacy turning to tension. Darby stared at him, seeing something in his eyes she couldn't quite name: possession, devotion, both. A flicker of unease rippled through her.

"Are you afraid of me now, woman?" he asked quietly, though his tone carried a challenge. His eyes didn't move from hers.

"No, but I don't think you realize how scary you can be."

He grew still, eyebrows drawing together. "You make it sound like I go around deliberately trying to frighten people." "That's not what I mean at all." A chill drifted through her. "I am afraid of the chances that you might take," she whispered, though the words came out more fragile than she intended. She comprehended that he never intended to be a threat to her, but he would die to protect her. "And consider this, Blake. If I had died, people would say, *Oh, how sad.* You take out Robert Badcock. You remarry. Have a family—a Williams heir. Life goes on. Whoever is behind this didn't try to kill an actual Williams. They went for the expendable one."

The scrape of his chair breaking the silence was almost violent, causing her body to jerk in reaction. Pushed back, he planted both hands on his thighs and looked at her like a man steadying himself on a precipice. His chin trembled once, twice, before he forced it still.

"Darby," he said finally, her name raw around the edges. "You are not expendable. My world begins and ends with you—and you alone. And I would never, ever intentionally hurt you. Please. Please say that you understand that, my love."

She wanted to look away from the intensity in his eyes, but she couldn't. His devotion was both anchor and chain. She wanted to run away and, at the same time, to fling herself into his arms. Instead, she stayed very still. "Yes," she said quietly. "I understand, but it's not me I'm worried about. It's you, Blake. I don't want you to take any unnecessary risks. I don't want to lose you. I can't. I'm not that strong. Not anymore."

Blake slowly stood, something calmer behind his gaze, and extended a hand toward her. "Come to me, please."

Darby hesitated, then slipped her fingers into his. His grip was warm, steady, and absolute.

"Alexa," he said to the AI device across the room, eyes still locked on hers. "Play *All of Me* by John Legend."

"Playing *All of Me* by John Legend," the device replied in its pleasant, synthetic voice as the song surrounded them.

"Dance with me?" he invited.

"Of course," she replied, her voice barely audible. Confusion flickered in her eyes, but she didn't resist as he drew her close. He held her perfectly, as if they were on some polished ballroom floor instead of their kitchen. His hand pressed against the small of her back. His breath brushed her hair.

"I'm not going anywhere, honey. And Darby?" he murmured.

"Yes."

"You are mine, and I am yours. Now and forever."

"Yes, Blake," she whispered. "You are mine, and I am yours. Now and forever."

She melted against him, feeling the weight of his sigh against her temple. And in that long, swaying moment, she realized the truth: love wasn't always safety. Sometimes, it was the most beautiful kind of trap.

"I need to make love with you." His voice was a whisper as he kissed her with a slow, relentless deliberation.

Later, while Darby was in the shower, Blake quickly made a phone call to Reece.

"Dad, I have to make this conversation quick. Darby has an idea that is worth looking into." He quickly summarized her theory.

"I'll start that ball rolling right now. Goodnight, son."

"Thanks, Dad. Goodnight."

Long after the music ended and Blake had fallen asleep, Darby stood barefoot in the living area outside their bedroom. The air was still, the hum of the refrigerator the only sound in the condo. She pressed a palm to the wall, steadying herself, unsure whether the faint tremor in her body came from fear or from the echo of their dance.

The song still looped in her mind; its sweetness curdled now into something that made her throat tight. The way he had looked at her—devotion wrapped around control—lingered in her chest like a bruise she couldn't touch.

In the half-dark kitchen, she held a glass of water. Her reflection in the window stared back, ghost-pale. *You are mine, and I am yours.* The words pulsed through her, steady as a heartbeat, binding as rope.

Darby loved him—she did. There was no pretending otherwise. Blake could be tender, funny, fiercely loyal. He had built her a life of safety after years of chaos. But tonight had shown her something she'd only ever caught in glimpses before: the depth of that loyalty and how close it lay to possession.

She turned the faucet off and listened to the silence. Her mind retraced every line of their conversation at dinner, every veiled implication. If she was right—if someone had staged her accident to provoke Blake—it meant they understood him better than she wanted to admit. They knew exactly how far he'd go.

The water glass trembled slightly in her hand.

She thought of Robert Badcock—his drunken eyes, his ruined life—and of the rumor about the caves beneath his family's land. But mostly, she thought of Blake. Of how easily love could turn into a mission.

Back in the bedroom, she slipped quietly under the covers. Blake stirred in his sleep, instinctively reaching for her, his arm looping around her waist. The weight of it was familiar and comforting, a heavy anchor in a storm. Darby lay awake in the dark, eyes open, waiting for sleep that wouldn't come. When it finally did, it was full of dreams where the line between lover and protector blurred, and every embrace ended in the same whispered vow:

You are mine. You are mine. You are mine.

Adam Taylor stared at his TNT partners, his eyes moving between them with a weight that matched the silence in the room. "You both realize that Williams' phases three and four are on the line, right?"

"I know that the rezoning was approved, and that Turner's bald spot on the back of his head that Blake gave him is finally filling in." Richard Nealy said it casually, as if he were discussing the weather rather than a violent physical altercation.

"Very funny. Thanks." Greg Turner rubbed the back of his head lightly with his fingers. He had opted for a shorter, though unappealing, haircut to mask the damage and was clearly still struggling with his patience as it grew out.

"It means a significant amount of money to the firm," Adam pointed out. "But Blake wasn't joking when he said we'd get no special consideration because I'm married to his sister."

A heavy silence fell between the three men, the kind of stillness that usually precedes a confrontation.

"Do you think Darby will come back to work here?"

Greg asked, his voice sounding oddly hollow.

"That's a question wrapped in a problem, Greg," Richard Nealy said. "Do you even realize that the last two women you dated were Darby Williams look-alikes?"

"Yeah, dude. It was as if you called a Nashville casting agency and sent them a picture of my sister-in-law as a guide," Adam added, his exaggeration carrying a sharp edge of warning.

"Come on, guys." Greg threw his ink pen down on the conference room table with a sharp *clack*. "I have never touched her." He gritted his teeth, his frustration boiling over.

"You don't have to, man. It's written all over your face every time you look at her." Richard's hand slapped down hard on the table as he leaned toward Greg. "We've cautioned you about this in the past. When you came back from Steeplewood with rejected plans, a bruised jaw, and a bloody scalp, we told you to seek counseling."

"It took weeks to get into a good practice. You two want to see my receipts? Do you have any clue how much therapy costs?" Greg pushed back from the table and marched over to the coffee cart, needing the distance.

"Do you have any clue how much your obsession with Darby Williams could cost our business?" Richard's glare was persistent.

"We have no reason to deny her employment, and we all know that things run smoother whenever Darby is around," Adam said, maintaining his role as the calm center of the storm. "But the Williams and the Taylor families have a great deal in common. Trust me when I say that Blake was kind and gentle compared to what he will be if there is a next time. You got off easy, Greg. I can guarantee that there will be no additional warnings."

The silence of reality hung in the room for much too long, thick and suffocating.

"We've hired a new Office Manager who'll be here in a few weeks," Adam continued. "I think we agree that it would be advantageous for Darby to be part of his training. Plus, another vital employee is taking medical leave around the same time. If Darby agrees to come back, even temporarily, and Greg agrees to stay completely away from her, I say we go for it. All in favor?"

Both men nodded in agreement just as Richard Nealy's *Rocky Top* ringtone filled the room.

"It's Reece Williams," he shared, holding up the phone before answering. "Hello. This is Richard Nealy."

Reece paid for the pizza delivery and gave the driver a generous tip. It was worth every cent just to avoid the chore of cooking and cleaning up tonight. The house felt quiet, but the air was thick with the weight of the coming weeks.

"I approved the *Electrical Imaging Resistivity Survey* today with Richard Nealy of TNT for the Phases Three and Four development," Reece said, opening the pizza box. "He thinks they can get started in as early as two weeks. Four at the most."

"And that is...?" Josephine asked, offering him a surprisingly cheap paper plate.

"It's a test for caverns—sinkholes or caves beneath the

property. We're going to be pouring a massive amount of concrete and pavement, not to mention the weight of the buildings themselves. We can't afford any surprises."

"Uh-huh," her reply was distracted, her mind clearly elsewhere.

"So, how did things go at the library today?" Reece asked, trying to pull her back to the present.

"Surprisingly busy again," Josephine replied. "I haven't spent much time in there since our kids graduated high school, and Lord knows that was a while ago. But I don't think I'm needed there anymore. Did you talk to Blake today?"

"I did. He sounded tired but said Darby seems to be doing well. She's on her own now that Hawk is back at the farm, but she doesn't leave the condo unless Blake is with her."

"Well, I'm ready to stop volunteering," Josephine remarked. "Robert Badcock hasn't been anywhere near the library. According to Eric, 'good ole Robbie' hasn't even left the Steeplewood city limits since Hunter North covertly installed GPS trackers on both of his vehicles."

"Hunter may be young, but he is damn good at what he does," Reece noted. "He also made that trip to the Georgia rental place and came back with the mask Darby identified. Hunter saw it hanging on the office wall. The clerk said it was left behind in one of the vehicles. For a crisp fifty-dollar bill, Hunter brought it home." Reece paused, his brow furrowing. "The strange part? No fingerprints except the clerk's. Hunter checked the van, too—the front bumper was recently replaced with an aftermarket part.

What doesn't add up is why someone would wipe down the mask so carefully and then just... leave it behind."

"Robert Badcock isn't exactly known for making good choices," Josephine remarked, wrapping the still-hot, stringy cheese around a slice of pizza.

"Eric says company records show that the van wasn't even rented out during the hit-and-run," Reece added. "Yet the vehicle and the plate are a perfect match for the surveillance footage Eric pieced together."

"Of course," Josephine smirked. "That would be too easy. What's the status on Robert now?"

"Pops and I think he's waiting on a passport to arrive before he bolts. Eric says we have to be extra cautious because we aren't the only ones watching him. He's working overtime to cover our tracks. And that business with his mother's bank account isn't over. I just wish the feds would move faster."

They ate in silence for a few minutes, the gravity of the situation settling over their dinner.

"There's too much stress on our son, Reece."

"I agree, JoJo." Reece paused. "He was looking forward to being a father. Instead, he got handed a lifetime's worth of heartache and worry."

"If that girl had simply walked away in the grocery store parking lot..." Her voice trailed off, bitter.

"This is not Darby's fault," Reece said, his tone turning defensive.

"Isn't it?" Josephine's tone was cynical as she handled a slice of pizza like a weapon.

"If Badcock had only insulted her, she would have

ignored the son of a bitch. But when he went after Blake, she retaliated. Darby is always going to have an edge, JoJo. She wasn't raised as a southern debutante like you—and even *you* have a black belt."

"Why her, Reece? Why did our son choose that girl and proclaim her the love of his life?"

Reece leaned back, letting the question hang. "I'm not sure even Blake could give you a direct answer," he said finally. "What I do know is, from the moment he opened his heart to her, he never looked away. She tried to walk— God knows she had her reasons—but Blake wouldn't let her go. He chased her with everything he had. It isn't logic, JoJo. It's love, pure and unshakable. But if anything were to happen to her, I'm afraid we'd lose him, too."

Josephine crossed her arms, hugging herself. "I fear what kind of a mother she'll be. Blake will be a decent parent, but I worry about her past. She was an abused child. Sometimes that cycle just repeats."

"So, you're afraid she'll be abusive because of how she was treated?"

"Yes, I am."

"I understand the concern," Reece said. "But do you really think our son would tolerate that? And Blake is firm with her. I've seen him swat her on the behind more than once—something I wouldn't dare try with you."

"What if he's not around and she snaps?" Josephine rubbed her forehead. "We know how stressful raising a child can be. And we've seen what she's capable of with Robert Badcock."

"On the other hand," Reece pointed a finger toward his

wife, "if she's that defensive of Blake, imagine how protective she'll be toward their children."

"I hope you're right, Reece," Josephine whispered. "I hope you're right."

CHAPTER 15

In their ordinary beige apartment in Knoxville, TN, Tyler Payne froze mid-laugh, his grin stretching wider and wider as if his body couldn't contain the surge swelling in his chest. "You're sure, Mel? Absolutely, positively sure?"

Melissa's fingers trembled slightly as she held up the little plastic test she'd bought at the dollar store earlier that day, the word **positive** faint but unmistakable. "Absolutely, positively, Ty." Her voice caught on the second word. "I'm pregnant."

For a second, all the sounds around them—the hum of the refrigerator, the low buzz of traffic through the thin windows—folded into a hush. Then Tyler let out a rough, disbelieving laugh. "That's—that's incredible."

He crossed the few steps between them in an instant, scooping her up. The kitchen smelled faintly of coffee and last night's takeout, but in that moment, it felt holy. "You're going to be a fantastic mom. When will we know if it's a boy or a girl?"

"Sooner than you'd think," she teased. "Does

it matter?"

"Not a damn bit."

He spun her once, just once, because the space was too small for joy this big. Her laughter ricocheted off the cabinets and the faded tile floor. For the first time in years, he felt weightless—like something heavy inside him had finally unclenched.

"What do we do now?" he asked, breathless. "Where do we even start?"

"We'll figure it out as we go," she said, her smile softening. "Let's call my family."

"Of course." He set her down carefully, as if she were made of glass, though a shadow flickered across his eyes. "But we'll wait on mine."

She tilted her head, studying him. "Right. Otherwise, Winston will drive you crazy. And as sweet as Omalita is, she'll have a baby-quilt brigade organized before we hang up."

Tyler chuckled, but it came out thinner than he meant it to. "As much as I miss hanging out with my brothers, I envy them for their distance." He pulled her close again, his hands spreading across her back, feeling the steady beat of her heart through the cotton of her monotone medical uniform.

Melissa had pulled him out of the dark—out of nights he didn't like to remember when the bottle had been easier to reach than hope. She embodied light and forgiveness, along with the quiet belief that life could be good again.

He pressed his cheek against her hair, breathing her in—shampoo, warmth, home—and yet another scent rose unbidden in his mind. Something sharper. Jasmine and rain. A memory that didn't belong here.

Darby.

The thought came like a pinprick, small but sharp enough to sting. Her laugh. The way her eyes flashed when she was angry. The lingering ache of realizing she would never be his. Tyler swallowed hard, tightening his hold on Melissa.

She leaned back slightly, studying his face. "Hey. You okay?"

He smiled, a practiced one. "Yeah. Just—can't believe this is real."

She slid her fingers across his jaw, her expression open and tender. "It's real, Ty. It's us."

He nodded, kissing her temple, hiding the shadow that had crept into his eyes. For her sake, he would bury the past deep—so deep it would never touch what they were building. But he knew better than anyone: the past had a way of digging itself back up.

CHAPTER 16

Darby had prepared two of Blake's favorite dishes for dinner, the savory, rich aroma permeating their entire dwelling. She was also impeccably groomed and wearing only a bra and panties—his favorite set.

Blake was back at the gym at least three times a week, and his sleep patterns had greatly improved. She, on the other hand, was secretly working out at the condo in the morning after he left for work because she was bored. She'd already washed all the walls, windows, and curtains using the ladder she kept hidden under the guest room bed. Darby felt increasingly like a prisoner in her own home. It was time for a serious conversation with her husband, but first, she had to set the stage.

"Darb…" Blake's voice caught in his throat at the sight of her standing in the living area, hands on her hips, her head provocatively tilted to one side. It was the pose of a model she had studied online, and it worked instantly. He even noted his favorite movie playing on mute in the background. The items in his hands fell away, forgotten on the floor, as he advanced on her position like he was marching into battle.

Blake's right arm circled the small of her back, his broad hand pulling her flush against him. His mouth aggressively claimed hers before he dropped to his knees. Staring up at her, his fingers began to slowly and gently lower her white, lacy panties.

At the sound of her sharp gasp, a dark and sultry chuckle escaped from deep inside his chest. "You think you're the only one with power, pretty girl?" Rising from the floor, he took her with him, hoisting her over his shoulder with her panties still dangling from one ankle. One hand reached up to massage a butt cheek for the short journey to their bedroom.

She had been busy preparing for the seduction: the crisp, unrumpled sheets and the window blinds tilted at just the right angle to let in the city's amber glow. He laid her on the bed and stepped back to undress.

"I'll do that," she said, rising to her knees.

"No, Darby. Not this time." He paused, gently pushing her back down.

"But, Blake, I want to give you pleasure. The doctor has cleared me."

"Trust me when I say that seeing you lying there waiting for me brings me pleasure." His eyes practically smoldered with desire. He quickly tossed his remaining clothes and climbed on top of her. The faint scent of jasmine in her hair reminded him of sitting next to her on a porch swing for the first time on a long-ago Sunday afternoon. She had only been sixteen then, light-years ahead of him in every way but one. Pleasure was the one thing he'd been able to teach her. He was the only man who had ever known her body, and the sight of her still took his breath away.

"You spoil me too much, cowboy."

He growled against the sensitive skin of her throat. "I'm the lucky one. Now tell me what you need, cowgirl."

"You. I need you inside me. But the doctor said we should be gentle and use protection."

"Oh, you'll definitely feel me, my love, but first…" He moved down her body and, using his hands in a prayer position, spread her thighs. "First, I'd like my appetizer." He heard the hitch in her breath as he lowered his mouth. This never got old. Pleasing her first was his priority, a silent vow he kept every time they touched.

Maybe, Darby thought as her hips began a slow, rhythmic rotation, if she played this right, he'd be smiling too much to say *no* when she mentioned returning to work at TNT.

"Oh, my god, Blake," she whispered, her fingers tangling in his hair.

"Do it, girl," he urged, his tongue returning to the magic that only he was allowed to bring.

He restarted the movie as the two of them sat on the sofa, enjoying the meal she had prepared.

"Darby, the food is amazing tonight. I mean, your meals are always good, but this is exceptional." Blake took yet another bite. "I'm glad you made so much, cause I'm going back again."

"Thanks, cowboy. I got the scaled-down recipes from

Eduardo, but the difference is in the tomatoes. I only use the ones I've canned from the garden on the farm."

"You should tell Garcia's restaurant to only use that brand of tomato. Take them a sample of your dish and compare it to theirs."

"No can do, Blake."

"Why not?" he asked, perplexed.

"The garden at Williams Farm is grown from heirloom seeds that your Grammy closely guarded for years. She was as particular regarding the genetics of her inventory as Ben is about verifying and recording the DNA of the livestock."

"And you understand all of this?"

"Yes, I do. A couple of sadistic, crazy people may have raised me, but Luis Hart was a respected instructor of animal husbandry and agriculture. My mother, Malina, was not only a teacher of consumer sciences, but she also came from a long line of Appalachian pioneers. This stuff was drilled into me and my siblings from birth."

"Changing the subject, Darby, but how do you feel about meeting up with Kate and Adam at the farm tomorrow? It's Saturday, and we don't have to be in a hurry."

"I'm listening."

"I know you're getting bored here at the condo. It would give you a chance to check out Grammy's seed inventory if you want. There's plenty to do for fun, and you know the food will be good."

"I'd love to, Blake," she said, a small spark of excitement lighting up her eyes. She decided she'd talk to him about the TNT job when they got back; for now, the idea of the farm and the soil felt like the only thing that could ground her.

Boyd sat in one of the leather guest chairs in Benjamin Williams' home office. Reece sat adjacent to him, and they both eyed Ben's reaction to the conversation they were having.

"How long have you known this man, Boyd?" Ben asked.

"Twenty-five years. Give or take."

"The real question is, can he be trusted?" Reece asked, standing to walk over to the liquor cabinet. He set three shot glasses on the corner of the Brobdingnagian desk. "Gentlemen?" The other two men both nodded in affirmation as he poured from the finest of Kentucky bourbons.

"One on one with my life on the line? Yes," Boyd answered. "But what concerns me is that he had to be hand-picked by the agency due to our prior history. I don't imagine he's any happier about it than I am."

"Boyd, both of my kids are scheduled to be here in the morning. I'm not comfortable with the DEA sending in a frontman tomorrow. Is there any way he'd consent to meet at my office in town?"

"Nope. His cover is that he's here to buy livestock." Boyd drank down half the contents of the shot glass.

"And you're sure this has to do with Badcock?" Ben spoke.

"Yes, Sir, if I decoded the conversation correctly. I

haven't had to do that in a while, but on the other hand, that's the only reason that makes sense."

"What happens if we say *no*?" Ben threw back the entire shot of bourbon in one quick move.

"Then they'll find another way in, and we'll be left totally in the dark." Boyd's tone was as flat as the look in his boss's eyes.

"Any way that we can discreetly warn the kids off? Get them to come another weekend?" Ben was looking at Reece.

"Katelyn's coming here for some damn baby shower. Blake's bringing Darby because the girl could probably use some sunshine on her face, and the farm should be the safest place for her. Besides, Blake would instantly realize that something big was going down."

"I hate to say it, Reece, but it would be good for Blake to be a part of this, but we can't tell him until he gets here." Boyd finished his drink.

"What do you think, Pops?" Reece asked Ben.

"I think Boyd's right, son. Blake needs to be ready for the unexpected if he is going to be in charge here someday."

Reece hesitated, swirling the liquid in the glass he was holding. "Alright. I guess it's a go." He set the glass back onto the desk, having never taken even a sip.

"I'll get everything set up." Boyd rose to leave the room.

"I want full coverage with snipers in place," Ben's expression was firm. "We are not entirely sure who the real enemy is. We need to take paranoia to the next level. We're missing a concrete piece of the puzzle. I can feel it in my bones. And gentlemen, my bones never lie."

"Yes, sir." Boyd nodded. He'd assign a man to the fire tower and Hunter North for the close-range security.

"Reece, I want you visible in town," Ben demanded. "Park your personal vehicle outside the law office and have JoJo pick you up in ten minutes. The two of you go to breakfast in town and take your time. Make conversation with locals so they remember you were there. Then take both vehicles and go home. Unless Boyd or I tell you otherwise, we'll see you and your missus for dinner tomorrow night."

"Why?" Reece's voice was shaky with disbelief.

"Because you're a bundle of nerves lately, and that'll get people hurt. The boys and I will take care of the kids when they get here." Ben kept his tone neutral.

"If anything happens to my children…" Reece was weary.

"Go home, son. You're too close to this for some reason, and you know better."

"I recently lost my first grandson, Pops. I'm glad you don't know what that feels like."

"I understand loss, Reece. I lost my grandparents, my parents, my only brother, a damn fine woman, all before you were ever born, and most recently, another good woman who was your mother. Don't try to compare our life journeys. Go home, and tonight, before you close your eyes, you ask God to protect your children and your heirs because in the end, that's all any of us can hope to leave behind."

"Are you sure you want me digging into Geniva's heirloom seed inventory?" Darby asked again, her voice soft but edged with caution as the car hummed along the county road.

"Darby, you spent our first two summers together in that garden," Blake reminded her. "You canned so much we barely bought groceries. Grammy even gave us that freezer chest for our little apartment, remember? She was reminding us to live off the land before we even realized it." His mind had been a storm of memories ever since last night's meal; flavors rooted in soil and family history.

"I've set up time with the grounds crew today," he went on. "Ask them whatever you want. We both know what's tucked under that farm—a hand-dug root cellar built like a fortress, simple solar backup, the whole thing hidden in plain sight."

Darby's eyes lit with reluctant wonder. "Blake, the ventilation design alone is genius. Primitive, yes, but effective. Universities would kill for access, let alone a peek at the seed stock. We're talking hundreds of years of genetic history."

"And corporations would pay millions," Blake cut in. His tone hardened. "That's why no one hears a word of this. Not Katie, not her husband. I love my sister, but..." He shook his head, jaw tight.

Darby let the silence hang a moment before nodding. "Blake, did any of Badcock's people ever work in Granny's gardens?"

Blake turned the car up the long gravel drive to the massive main house, his mind racing as he followed her train of thought. "Good question. I'll find out." He gave her a look that carried weight and tenderness in equal measure. "Clever girl." His hand gently squeezed hers.

Blake's earlier good mood evaporated the moment he found himself boxed in by Ben and Boyd. The room felt thicker, like the air was holding its breath. Outside, tires crunched on gravel—a Davidson County rental car, the kind government men favored when they wanted to be anonymous and never were.

"Are you sure you want to do this?" Blake asked, voice low, eyes locked on his grandfather.

"We don't have a choice," Ben said, steadier than he felt. Blake could see the lie in the set of his grandfather's mouth.

"I don't like surprises, Gramps." Blake's words came out clipped. "I would never have brought Darby here if I'd known. I feel backed into a corner, and I don't appreciate it."

"It happened fast," Boyd offered, but his words landed weak.

A car door shut outside, a sound of finality. Blake stood, jaw tight, the weight of what was coming pressing against his ribs. "Then let's get this over with." He pivoted and strode toward the barn, each step counting down, gravel crunching like a clock ticking out seconds.

The barn near the bunkhouse smelled of hay and motor oil, sharp and alive in the warm air. Shafts of sunlight speared through gaps in the boards, catching dust in lazy, golden motion. In the loft, Hunter North crouched with a rifle trained, a sidearm snug at his hip. Eric watched from the shadows, hidden lenses among the timbers, recording every flicker. Beyond the doors, Hawk and another male employee leaned like idle farmhands, trading casual talk that never touched their eyes. Everyone had a role; every angle was covered. On Williams' land, even the men who shoveled stalls had special skills.

"Thank you for meeting with me, gentlemen." Agent Royce Sullivan stepped into the center of the barn and let the silence answer for him.

Blake's hand hovered near the holster inside his jacket. "Look, Sullivan—or whatever your real name is. You asked for this meeting. Make it quick so you can get off Williams' land. Sound good?"

Sullivan glanced at Boyd, caught the brief nod, then met Blake's stare without flinching. "Robert Badcock did not rent the van that ran down Darby Williams, nor did he drive it. We have real-time footage of him at the Savannah docks less than an hour before Darby Williams arrived at an emergency room in Nashville."

Ben's voice was quiet, sharp. "Why are you here?"

"Robert Badcock is a low-level drug courier," Sullivan said. "We've tracked him for the last couple of years. People generally avoid him because he's obnoxious. But he's not the one calling the shots."

"My grandfather asked you to get to the point." Blake glanced at his *Timex* sports watch, knowing that Darby's tour of the gardens could end at any time.

"We believe his older brother, Morgan Badcock Jr., runs the local traffic. He inherited the business from their father and has since expanded it. But an alcoholic brother draws attention. Robert is a liability, especially now that their mother, Janiece, is deceased." Sullivan paused. "We also have evidence of multiple suspicious deaths over the years that may link back to the Badcocks."

"You're suggesting murder," Ben's voice was taut.

Sullivan didn't blink. "Possibly. And we strongly believe Morgan Jr. staged evidence to make it look like Robert was the mastermind behind Darby Williams' hit-and-run incident."

Blake's jaw tightened. Darby's theory was correct, he thought. Aloud, he asked, "So why not take Morgan Junior down and end this?"

"Because he has an accomplice and we don't yet know who." Sullivan folded his hands. "For a time, we suspected Reece or Ben Williams."

"All our businesses are legitimate," Ben snapped.

"We know that now," Sullivan said. "But you are a very wealthy family with a number of highly trained security personnel."

"There's no crime in being well invested and protected," Ben regained his neutral composure.

"Agreed," Sullivan said. "But we know you're tracking Robert Badcock, and I was sent to ask you to back down."

"No." Blake didn't hesitate. "And," he calmly added, "fuck you."

"Blake." Ben's voice warned when he should have remained silent.

Blake stepped forward, his voice a low growl. "You haven't offered anything in return while you continue to use my wife as bait. We might be persuaded to work together; otherwise, you know the way out, Agent Sullivan."

What Blake didn't voice out loud was that if Badcock or anyone else came near a member of the family, it wouldn't matter who the accomplice was. Sullivan's jaw worked once, but his tone never wavered. The air hung heavy between them, two men staring each other down— neither breaking, neither yielding.

Somewhere above, Hunter's finger rested steady on the trigger, waiting for a reason.

Darby was outside in the garden area behind the main house. She could tell that something was amiss in Blake's manner as he approached. He pulled her against him and kissed the top of her head, but she could feel the rapid, heavy beat of his heart.

"You okay, cowboy?" she whispered upward toward his ear.

"I will be. Your tour of the gardens over?"

"Yes, and it's even more magnificent than I remember. The crew left, but do you want to take a look?"

"Not this time, honey." He draped an arm around her shoulders and began walking them in the direction of their car. "We're going home to Nashville."

"Okay, Blake. Whatever you say." She felt a chill run up her spine. "I already loaded some of our canned goods into the trunk from the stock we've got stored at the guest house."

"That's good, baby, but you probably shouldn't be

lifting." Blake's eyes continually scanned their surroundings, looking for the glint of a lens or the movement of a shadow.

"I was very careful. Blake," she paused, glancing up at the intensity etched across his face, "we're being watched, aren't we?"

"Yep." He pulled her in tighter against him as they neared the aging BMW. "And for the record, you are one smart lady. Your theory regarding Robert Badcock is correct. Now, let's go home." He opened her car door while watching Boyd and Agent Sullivan from the corner of his eye as they stood by the rental car in deep conversation.

She eased into the passenger seat. "I have a feeling that information regarding the Badcocks' knowledge of Genevia's system is going to be very important to this case."

Blake returned Kate's call after he and Darby were safely back inside their condo.

"What happened, big brother?" Kate asked upon answering. "Does this have anything to do with the livestock buyer who was there today?"

"You could say that." Blake's chuckle lacked humor. "Look, quietly ask Gramps or Dad. They should have shared the information with you and Adam anyway. Otherwise, you and I can talk when you get back to the city."

"Maybe Adam and I should leave, too." Her voice sounded shaky and uncertain.

"I can't make that decision for you, Katie. Be careful whatever you do."

"I love you, big bro."

"I love you, baby sis."

Fifteen minutes later, he received a text from his sister stating that she and Adam were on their way back to Nashville. While Darby was busy putting away the supplies they had unloaded from the car, Blake made a quick call to Reece.

"Honey," Blake said, hanging up and turning to Darby, "Dad said that Grammy had the first solar panels installed on the root cellar system in the mid-1980s. There was a man named Jack Butler who was working on Williams Farm and was involved in the installation. Not too long after, he left Williams and went to work for Badcock, who suddenly began installing solar panels as well. However, Williams Farm has been using wind and solar technology as backup for years."

"What happened to Butler?" she asked.

"According to Dad, there are two possibilities. The official word was that he took a job in another state and moved on. But there was a rumor that he and Morgan Badcock Sr. had a disagreement, and Butler left town in the middle of the night, never to be seen again. Where are we going with this information, Darby?"

"I'm fairly sure that Grammy's root cellar system could be expanded on a much larger scale to work underground—like in a cave. But that's a subject for another time."

Darby knelt, lifted his feet onto their giant ottoman, and

pulled off his boots one at a time. He had never once in their entire history together asked her to do this, and he couldn't explain why he felt both pampered and guilty when she occasionally did.

"Hungry?" she asked.

"For a kiss from my girl." He reached for her, the softness in his voice undercutting the heavy weight of the day.

Darby went willingly, climbing over his lap and pressing her thighs on either side of his hips on their sofa. She brushed her mouth across his. "You were right, you know? Ben shouldn't have bushwhacked you like he did."

"Bushwhacked?" Blake grinned at her. "Have you been reading Western novels behind my back?" His fingers gently massaged her waistline as her fingers did the same to his tense shoulders.

"Tell me there is a better word for what happened to you today." Darby tapped the end of his chin with her index finger.

"Honestly, I can't, babe." Blake laughed and shook his head. "I'm sorry your first adventure out of the city ended poorly. I wanted it to be fun and to spend some time with another couple we could trust, without having to be on guard every second."

"Blake, my place is with you wherever that leads us. You are my husband, my lover, and my best friend. I'll follow wherever you lead."

"You mean that, don't you?" His eyes softened.

"I always have, cowboy. Nothing has changed. And someday soon, good Lord willing, I'll give you that family you want."

"Darby, are you positive you're willing to try again? Because I'm all in with whatever your decision is. You are my priority. I hope you understand that, woman." He sounded desperate as his eyes misted.

"Blake," she leaned in close but not touching, "I was frightened with our first pregnancy, but now I'm not. Besides, you are my world."

His insides tightened, and tears streamed down his face. She wrapped her arms around him, kissing his temples, his wet eyelids, and finally his lips.

"I shouldn't have pushed the issue before you were ready. You asked for more time, but I believe you gave in to make everyone happy. I hope you can forgive me, and I'll try harder to be a better man." He dried his eyes on the hem of his shirt.

"Cowboy, you've had a stressful and disappointing day. Besides, you are a good man." She paused. "I could have held out longer, and you would have pouted, but in the end, you would have let me have my way. I decided to get on board, whatever the reason." She ran her fingers through his hair. A child-like smile graced his handsome face, expressed equally by his eyes. "Now," she continued, "I get the feeling that something more happened today other than what we discussed on the way home. Care to talk about it?"

He hesitated and gathered his thoughts. "I had what could only be described as an epiphany." His hands relaxed on her hips.

"I'm listening." Darby's voice was strong and

reassuring.

"I looked at my grandfather and suddenly saw myself in a few years. Darby, I don't want to be like him. I know everyone expects me to take over in Steeplewood eventually, but I'm not sure that is meant to be my, or I should say our, path." His eyes appeared to glaze over, as if he were staring into the future. "I think Gramps is at the root of Dad's health issues and my parents' dysfunctional marriage. And, God bless Grammy, I believe she used alcohol to cope with him, which got worse when he went into politics. That woman was a saint. You know she taught me how to play the piano and read music from the age of four. She had me reading at a second-grade level and doing elementary math by the time I started kindergarten. I used to get into trouble at school for daydreaming because I was bored." He chuckled.

"Blake, you have many talents. You remodeled our condo yourself. You even built some of the furniture. Who taught you that?"

"A man by the name of Paul Johnson, who lived on the farm. He started out teaching me how to build and repair different types of fence, and it evolved."

"Who taught you how to shoot and to hunt?"

"My dad. He also taught me family law and how to run a business. Not to mention that he's a financial genius. Now, livestock genetics and breeding were Gramps's specialty. The veterinary skills just seemed necessary in emergency situations."

"Martial arts?"

"That was all mom's idea."

"And where did you learn that military team precision thing the crew is so good at on the farm?"

"That was a lot of different people over the years, but most recently, I'd have to say that Boyd has been the most influential. The farmhands let me participate in emergency and disaster drills from the time I was 10 years old."

"You've had the benefit of an amazing education, Blake, and you are still young. The future is yours to decide."

"It's all still a part of who I am, but at this point, Darby, I like what I'm doing here in Nashville, and I'm good at it. I like living here in the city with you. Once the contract is up, we might travel or move to a different city. We could even live in another country for a year or so. Or we could stay right here. But it's not my decision, honey. It's our decision. Does any of that sound appealing to you?"

"It all sounds appealing, Blake. I go where you go." She leaned in and hugged him to her.

"What if we have a child by then?" He looked skeptical as she raised her head.

"Well, I'm not going to leave the kid behind." She chuckled. "Blake, you don't have to do anything you're not comfortable with, and that includes returning to Steeplewood. It's your life. All I want is for you to be happy, cowboy." Her hands massaged his shoulders again. She felt some of the tension subside beneath her fingertips.

"Thank you, Darby. But it's our life, and we deserve to be happy, because none of it means anything if I don't have you." His voice was raspy and sounded a little desperate.

"Relax, Blake. You've got me now and always. Besides,

I'm pretty sure I could kick your ass if I had to."

Blake burst out laughing so hard that she bounced up and down on his lap. "There's my girl, and I don't doubt that statement for a minute." He felt a heavy emotional weight roll away. For the first time since before the accident, he wasn't afraid to feel happy. He wrapped a hand around the nape of her neck and pulled her into a kiss, which was interrupted by the ringing of his cell phone.

"Damn it, just when a man is about to get lucky." He grinned and stared at the screen. "It's Miguel Garcia." He answered the call, "Yeah, Miguel, what's up?" He paused. "Wait a second, and I'll ask the saucy minx sitting on my lap. Hey, babe, you want to have breakfast at Garcia's in the morning before they open to the public?"

"Yes, please." She straightened and flexed her back at the touch of his free hand.

"We'll be there, brother. See you in the morning." The truth was that Blake was closer to Miguel and Eduardo Garcia than he was to any of his actual in-laws.

CHAPTER 17

Tyler stared at his now obviously pregnant wife, his eyes lingering on the curve of her stomach before meeting her steady gaze. "Melissa, are you certain this is a good plan?"

"Tyler, you need to close a chapter in your life and move on for the sake of our family. If that means an open discussion between you and your sister and her husband, then so be it. You don't have to prove anything to anyone, Ty, but you appear to need closure, and I can appreciate that scenario."

"You ever think maybe it's best to let sleeping dogs lie?" Tyler asked, his jaw tightening until the muscles jumped.

"Tyler, don't tell me that you're not holding unresolved angst where Darby Hart Williams is concerned." Melissa Payne paused for a beat or two, letting the name hang in the air like a challenge.

"Let it go, Mel." He gritted his teeth.

"I refuse to live in another woman's shadow, Ty."

"Look, Darby is Winston Payne's mistake. Not mine. If I'm harboring unresolved issues, they're probably with my old man, not his bastard child. I was young and ignorant of the situation, but later I met you. You are my wife, and we are going to have a child together. Please leave Darby and my past out of our future."

"Then leave her out of our bed, Tyler."

He flinched, the sharp remark cutting deep as he watched her turn and walk out of the room. Deep down inside, in the places he didn't like to go, Tyler knew that Melissa was right. According to his wife, it had only been a few days ago when he had whispered Darby's name in his sleep. It had happened on a night when a Knoxville news station reported that the identity of the hit-and-run driver was still unknown, noting that a substantial reward remained active nationwide for information.

That evening, Tyler had retreated into the intimate memory of stealing into Darby's hospital room in the middle of the night. He had kissed her with a love that he would forever be forced to deny. His life had somehow turned into a Greek tragedy; Darby had chosen another man over him before they even realized they were brother and sister. Ty had thought he was finally beyond the anger and the obsession, but he realized now that he owed Darby an apology. He had to ask for her forgiveness to move forward. Hell, he probably even needed to apologize to Blake. They were, after all, genetically connected; their children would share DNA.

"Blake, Tyler Payne is on line one for you. He says that he's your brother-in-law?" Blake's assistant, Rachel, said over the intercom.

"Thank you, Rachel. Put him through." Blake gathered his thoughts, selecting the appropriate screen to answer the call. "This is Blake Williams."

Tyler had listened carefully to the law office disclaimer before being transferred, fully aware that the conversation was being recorded.

"Hello, Blake. This is Tyler Payne. I apologize for interrupting your day, but I would like to schedule an appointment to meet with you and your lovely wife regarding a personal matter."

Blake was momentarily taken aback—a rare occurrence for a man of his standing.

"Hello?" Tyler said again.

"I'm here, Payne. Under the circumstances, I believe that your request requires a bit more context."

"Fine. I'm requesting a face-to-face meeting with you and Darby, where I will offer a personal apology to you and my sister for past indiscretions."

"Huh," Blake said, genuinely perplexed. "Forgive me, Tyler, if I find your request surprising. Whatever your intentions, I will need to present your wish to my wife, as the decision is entirely hers."

"I appreciate your position, Mr. Williams. You have my work number in your call log. Discuss it with Mrs. Williams and get back to me at your earliest convenience." Tyler disconnected the call before Blake could respond.

"Are you sure that's all he said?" Darby asked later that evening.

"Yes, my love. I'm sure, and it's your decision as to how

to proceed." Blake took another bite of the amazing pasta dish she had prepared especially for him.

"What do you think, cowboy?"

"Well, he is a married man now with a child on the way. Maybe he has finally put the past behind him and wants to make amends. You can give him the benefit of the doubt, or you can say *no* and let it be," Blake replied, trying to be supportive while secretly hoping she would walk away from the situation entirely.

"I need to think about this, Blake." Darby put her fork down, leaving a half-eaten plate of food in front of her.

Blake mentally kicked himself. He knew better than to discuss emotional issues with his wife during a meal. The act of putting down her fork was symbolic of the heavy processing happening in her mind. At least she hadn't stomped her foot in his direction; when she did that, it meant the conversation was over, and her word was final.

Blake went to the gym after dinner. Darby hated going behind his back, but it felt like now or never. She made the call before she could change her mind.

"Darby? What's wrong? Are you safe?" Wyatt Payne answered immediately.

"Wyatt, calm down. I'm fine, and I'm alone in my condo."

"Good. Okay, what's up?" His voice returned to its usual steady baseline.

"I need your help, again, brother."

"Name it, Babygirl."

Darby laid out all the information she had to support her theory about the hit-and-run, along with everything she had learned since.

Wyatt listened intently. "I think it's certainly plausible. I remember hearing those same rumors about what was actually being grown on Badcock Farms." He paused, his tone shifting. "Which means the only way to kill the snake is to cut off its head."

"Are you saying someone would have to kill Morgan Badcock Jr.?" She was shocked.

"No. I'm saying the grow operation would have to be shut down, and the consequences will take care of themselves. There will no doubt be an intense ripple effect. Are you sure that the Williams family isn't involved in this?"

"I don't believe so, and neither did Agent Sullivan. But the only Williams that I care about is Blake, and he is definitely not involved."

"Darby," she heard Wyatt's loud exhale. "You and Blake need to stay as far away from this as possible. Are you going to tell him that you spoke with me?"

"Not planning on it," she replied.

"Good. But it sounds like the feds are dragging their feet, looking to cast a wider net."

"And they obviously don't give a damn if someone like me dies in the process."

"Babygirl, you are going to have to trust me and keep this to yourself. Can you do that?"

"Yes. It will not be the first time you saved my ass. I would not have called you if I didn't trust you, Wyatt."

"Alright, sister. Stay calm and stay low. Keep Blake close and distracted. He's no fool, but this is just between you and me. We never share this with anyone, especially family."

"Agreed." She shook her head, even though Wyatt could not see her.

CHAPTER 18

Jylene Green sat in the rented SUV idling in front of the sagging clapboard house on the edge of town. Rain streaked the windshield, the wipers dragging with a grating squeal. She hated that house. The best she could say about it was that it had once kept her—and later, her son—out of the weather. Barely.

She'd been in Nashville checking on her rebellious son when Omalita Payne sent word through her editor: maybe she ought to check on her mother, Madeline Green. Jylene had sworn she'd never set foot in Steeplewood again, yet here she was, gripping the wheel and craving a cigarette that she hadn't smoked in nineteen years. But she was here now, so she might as well make the most of it. Some research was best done with boots on the ground, and her publisher was already asking for another manuscript.

Before she could change her mind, Jylene cut the engine, shoved the door open, and sprinted to the porch. She pounded against the cracked wood with her fist. Maybe Maddie wasn't home. Maybe she could return to Nashville today. Omalita said Madeline disappeared for days at a time without explanation.

The front door jerked open, its glass panes dull and fractured.

"Oh, hell. You gotta be kiddin' me," Madeline Green said.

"Good to see you too, Mother."

Maddie hiked her oversized beach bag higher on her shoulder and fished out a sleek, expensive cell phone. With just one press of a button, she had someone on the line. "It's me. I can't go. My long-lost daughter just fell out of the sky onto my porch." A pause. "Course it's her. She's the only one I got."

Inside Ben Williams' office on Main Street, Winston Payne donned a pair of blue exam gloves. He pulled the priority mail envelope from underneath his rain-speckled uniform shirt before sitting in the leather chair next to Reece Williams. He looked uncomfortable as Ben, already wearing gloves, examined the item in question, addressed to Robert Badcock from the U.S. Department of State.

"No doubt about it. This is a passport," Ben said, passing the envelope to Reece, who was also wearing gloves.

"I concur." Reece handed the item back to Winston.

"I can't delay the delivery any longer," Winston said, eyes narrowed, head cocked to one side. "It can be traced to the post office here in Steeplewood and should be delivered today. The most I feel comfortable in stalling is tomorrow."

"Gentlemen, I know you have further business to

discuss, and I have an off-site appointment this afternoon, so if you will both excuse me." Reece left the room, removing the gloves and sliding them into his pocket. He passed by Adele with a strong side glance as he walked out of the building. She discreetly smiled and kept typing at her computer before answering an incoming call. It was part of her job to keep an eye and ear on what was happening in the office at all times.

Judge Nelson Pedigo turned off the main highway a little too fast, gravel spitting from his tires as *Molly Hatchet* thundered through the truck's speakers. He wasn't trying to make an entrance but he usually did.

The Judge's salt-and-pepper hair caught the wind through the open window, sunlight bouncing off his mirrored aviators. He'd meant to get here early, but Sheriff Vechel Locke had caught him on the phone, chewing his ear about the upcoming bass tournament. Vechel had a way of turning five-minute calls into twenty-minute rambles about boat motors and prize money. Nelson didn't give a damn about either.

He turned the music down as he pulled onto the site. The half-built structures rose like skeletons against the Tennessee sky—wood framing, steel, and dust. This was the kind of place where business got done long before contracts were ever signed.

He spotted Reece Williams standing near a bank of portable offices, talking to a foreman. Reece looked sharp as always, the late-afternoon sun catching the clean lines of his pinstriped suit. He had the look of a man who belonged to two worlds—the courtroom and the backroom. Nelson, by contrast, wore denim and boots, a black dress shirt embroidered with the county seal: a handshake deal and a quick decision kind of man.

"What's up, Nelson?" Reece called, raising his voice over the grind of machinery. The foreman disappeared back into one of the buildings. Reece extended a hand, smooth as ever.

Nelson hesitated before taking it, gripping just firmly enough to look cooperative. "Just checking in before I head out of town for a few days," he said. "Wanted to make sure you, Winston, or Robert Badcock don't burn down the county while I'm gone."

Reece's grin came quick, his eyes unreadable. "You wound me, Judge. You know, twenty-five years ago, I never pictured you in politics."

Nelson smirked. "And I never figured you'd make it through law school. Yet, here we are." His voice lost its humor. "You didn't answer my question."

"Touché." Reece slid his hands into his pockets. "Far as I know, no matches waiting to be struck."

Nelson studied him, the air between them heavy with old distrust. "Good. Because my second in command knows only what's on paper, and I'd hate for him to learn something the hard way."

"I appreciate your point," Reece said lightly.

"I sincerely hope so." Nelson shifted, brushing a fleck of dust from his jeans. His longer-than-usual pause caught his associate's attention. "Had a surprise visitor at the office this morning."

Reece's eyebrows lifted. "Does this visitor have anything to do with Robert Badcock?"

"In a manner of speaking." The Judge's tone flattened. "It was Jylene Green."

Reece blinked. "No shit?" He let out a quiet laugh of disbelief. "Never thought this town would see that girl again."

"She said she was here checking on her mama, Madeline," Nelson went on, glancing toward the horizon. "But it didn't take her long to start asking about when Darby was shot at Napier's Farm Store by Calvin Napier."

Reece's gaze sharpened. "Does Robert know she's here?"

"I have no idea." Nelson kicked a small stone toward a dirt trench by his boot. "Jylene was the best thing that ever happened to that man, and he still managed to screw it up. Some things and people don't change."

They stood in companionable silence for a long moment, the sounds of hammers and diesel engines filling the gaps.

Reece's voice broke the tension. "Nice truck, Judge. Went with that new electric blue, I see."

Nelson snorted. "Wife picked the color." He paused, then added dryly, "Thinking about having it painted."

Reece raised an eyebrow. "Why?"

"Because Morgan Badcock, Jr. bought one just like it," he replied with disgust.

"You fucked up again, Robbie," said the voice in the late-day shadows of his living room. "But that's no surprise because you've been fucking up your whole life. All you had to do was keep your mouth shut, follow directions, and you had it made. But, no, you had to go and mouth off to the one person who wasn't afraid to kick your ass."

"You weren't there. You don't know what happened." Robert Badcock's hands gripped the arms of the recliner so tightly that each of his knuckles went white.

"I know that little girl took you down, and then the drunk fool you are, you went to the sheriff's office making threats, and that brought Winston Payne to your door." The voice paused. "But worst of all, your actions brought Ben Williams into the picture. The number one thing you do not want to do in this part of the world is get on the wrong side of a Williams. Now, I need you to get your sorry ass out of that chair and go to Florida."

"I ain't never made a run to Florida. How do I know you ain't settin' me up?"

"You don't, and there is a first time for everything. The usual courier has other plans. This run is going to be a little different. You're going to take a bus to Florida and drive a vehicle back to Tennessee. The information is in here," the voice handed him a heavy manila envelope. "Don't make any mistakes or you'll wind up dead. And for God's sake, keep your mouth shut, or you're dead anyway."

"You threatening me?" Robert fought to control his urge to strangle the other person—a feeling he knew well and had struggled with for a long time.

"Not at all. It's a promise, you sack of shit."

Once Badcock had left the Steeplewood city limits, it hadn't taken long for Hunter North to catch up, driving a common-looking gray pickup truck—a vehicle designed to blend effortlessly into the flow of traffic. He followed Robert to a parking lot near the bus station in Nashville, where Badcock boarded a bus headed south.

A well-placed $100 bill soon revealed the destination: Ocala, Florida. Hours later, Hunter followed a taxi to a Florida hospital, where Badcock entered an unlocked vehicle with an interior heavily modified to support a substantial payload. Without delay, he began the drive north on Interstate 75. Eight hours later, Robert parked the unmarked SUV, now bearing stolen plates, in the same Nashville bus station lot. He returned to his own vehicle and headed back to Steeplewood with Hunter tracking silently behind him.

From across the parking lot, Boyd watched as, fifteen minutes later, a slender individual dressed in dark clothing slipped into the abandoned SUV and headed in the opposite direction. Experience told him the driver was either female or adolescent—possibly both. He shadowed the vehicle until it eventually veered onto I-40 West. Boyd bypassed the exit and turned back toward Steeplewood; he knew the DEA was picking up the tail now, and he couldn't have cared less.

Returning to his home, Robert Badcock checked his street-side mailbox. Finding it empty, he punched it hard, leaving a jagged dent in the metal and fresh blood on his knuckles. He stormed into the house and slammed the door behind him. The partial bottle of expensive gin he had left for himself was waiting, and he welcomed its presence like an old friend.

CHAPTER 19

Blake arrived home to an empty house. He didn't like it; he never had since marrying Darby. It was similar to the hollow feeling he'd get when reaching for her during the night and finding her side of the bed vacant. Thankfully, those occasions had been rare.

He'd had time to change into his favorite pair of gray cargo shorts before the front door finally opened and she walked in. "There's my girl." He crossed the room to deliver a tender kiss to her cheek.

"Hey, cowboy. I thought you'd be at the gym this afternoon." She set her purse down on the table-shelving unit Blake had designed for that purpose. He'd been extremely proud of the piece, especially after she had bragged about his craftsmanship to anyone who would listen.

"No gym for me today. Besides, you're late," he pointed out.

"Adam insisted on walking me to my car, and I had to wait until he was off the phone," she said. Blake followed as she headed toward the kitchen.

He opened the refrigerator and bent to peer inside. Her slender hand patted him on the behind, and he felt his dick twitch at her touch. He glanced back over his shoulder, his soft, crooked grin making her knees weak, before he removed a recorked bottle of wine and placed it on the counter.

"Glass?" She moved to open a cabinet.

"Nah, let's drink out of the bottle." He motioned toward the living area with a tilt of his head.

"Okay." She closed the cabinet and let her eyes caress him again before moving toward the sofa. "Well, work is only for six to eight more weeks while Carolyn is out for surgery. The new manager is doing great. Then we'll see. I felt somewhat obligated when Richard Nealy asked me to fill in. I mean, TNT gave me a job when it came in handy." She followed him, admiring his stride.

"We've got plenty of leftovers, cowgirl. Let's relax." He handed her the bottle, and she took a drink before handing it back. He fought the urge to ask if Greg Turner was hanging around, looking down her blouse again, but thought better of it. He knew the other partners were fully aware of the situation and most definitely did not want to lose the Williams family business.

"I'll go change." She walked away toward the bedroom.

He sat on the sofa and took another long drink before setting the bottle on the designated coaster. He picked up the remote, only to put it back down. "You know, Darby, I was thinking today that now might be a good time for you to get a PhD," he called over his shoulder.

"Really?" she answered from the bedroom. "I thought

we were going to try again for a baby. Not sure I'd want to be staring down the barrel of a doctorate with a newborn to care for. Besides, are you sure you could deal with the whole title thing?"

"What title thing?" he asked, taking another swallow of wine.

"You know, Mr. and Dr."

"Hilarious, sassy girl." He stood and started toward the bedroom. "Besides, it would be Attorney and doct—" His voice cut off mid-word.

She was bent over at the dresser, digging through the lowest drawer. The curve of her hips, the long line of her legs, her full and firm breasts—every detail arrested him. Heat coiled low in his chest and radiated downward, scattering the rest of his thoughts.

She glanced over her shoulder, caught by his silence, and straightened slowly. "You startled me. I didn't realize you came in." Her tone was light, but the flush on her chest betrayed that she knew exactly what he was staring at.

He dragged his eyes back to hers, though it took effort. "Darling… if I'd known this was waiting in here," his hand made a sweeping motion in her direction, "I wouldn't have wasted time talking."

He approached like a panther moving in on its prey. He pulled her utilitarian panties down to her ankles and leaned forward, delivering a deep kiss to her mouth while his hand gently cupped her heat, stroking softly.

"Blake…" she whispered, her face flushing pink. He felt her tremble as he breathed in her scent like a wild beast. Then he lifted her and tossed her onto the bed, the white cotton panties flying into the air before dropping out of sight. Darby collapsed into a fit of giggles.

"Hey." He climbed on top of her, playfully pinning her wrists against the mattress above her head as she continued to giggle. "What gives, pretty girl?" He had the confident smile of a man used to getting his way. "I'm throwing down some smooth moves here, and you're laughing at me?"

"Cowboy, you don't do the *toss the girl on the bed* move often, but it's always thrilling when you do."

"It's supposed to be seductive." He nuzzled her neck.

"I'm still here, aren't I?" Her grin was playful, inviting.

"Damn right you are." His breath touched her throat. Blake released her wrists and wove his fingers through her hair, catching that faint scent of jasmine. He brushed his lips to hers, his eyes filling with lust.

Her hands slid down his firm body to push at the waistband of his shorts. He repositioned himself with lethal grace and shed the clothing. Darby sat suddenly upright before he could return to her. His knees on either side of her body, his hand went quickly to her throat.

"Where do you think you're going?" His voice was deep, though he did not apply pressure to the grip.

She reached behind her back, undid her bra with a teasing smile, and tossed it to one side. He released his hold and gently guided her back down onto the bed. She twined her legs around his waist and pulled him to her.

"Bully," she purred.

"Hellcat." His breath was ragged in her ear.

Blake took another bite of the cheesecake she was feeding

him while sitting on his lap.

"Darby, I should be taking care of you. Not the other way around." He tried to take the fork from her hand, but she pulled it back with a playful grin.

"I like doing things for you. You're my hottie husband," she teased. "Besides, once we have a family, a moment like this might be hard to capture in the middle of our living room."

"Don't remind me, honey, but I know we'll find time for one another." He accepted another bite before his cell phone started buzzing again.

"Dad." Blake rolled his eyes. "Might as well get this over with." He pushed the answer screen. "Yeah, Dad. You're on speaker because we're having dinner." Blake's tone was unusually firm.

"Just calling to see when you're coming to Steeplewood to discuss the land development expansion, Son," Reece said.

"I don't have to go anywhere. Darby will bring the information home with her tomorrow, and I will review it here. If I agree to the conditions, I'll sign and return it to TNT."

"And if you don't?" Reece asked.

"Then you and they will hear from me." Blake was blunt and to the point as he licked a smudge of dessert from her fingers.

"Blake, I know that things didn't go well on your last visit here, but…"

Darby tried to move away from Blake and the conversation, but he gently guided her back to his lap, his hand a steady weight on her hip.

"Dad," Blake interrupted. "I no longer feel comfortable in that environment."

"Blake, we need to talk about the future. Like where we might like to build a new law office inside of phase three."

"You're assuming too much. I currently have no plans to practice law in Steeplewood. If you wish to build a new office there, then by all means proceed according to the necessary parameters."

"Are you saying that you never plan to return and live in Steeplewood?"

"I did not say that."

"What are you saying?"

"Due to recent events, Darby and I are evaluating our future endeavors."

"Look, Blake. I know your grandfather can be overbearing—"

"Overbearing? That's putting it politely. I refuse to be like him, or you, for that matter. I'm good at what I do here in Nashville. Plus, I have an amazing wife. Unlike you and my grandfather, I will put her and our future family first. It may or may not be easy, but we'll always know where we stand and that we'll be together."

"Okay, son. I get it. You want to be your own man."

"No, dad," Blake paused, his voice ringing with absolute certainty. "I *am* my own man."

When Blake ended the call, Darby's cheesecake-flavored lips crashed into his. The sweetness melted into something hungrier, her kiss demanding, tasting of sugar and defiance. His hand slid to the back of her neck, pulling her closer, and she made a soft sound that unraveled him.

"You are an amazing man, Blake Williams. That took so much courage," she whispered against his mouth, her breath mingling with his, before kissing him again—deeper this time, as if she could press her pride into him.

"I hope you still feel that way," he murmured, brushing his thumb across the hollow of her throat, "if our babies end up crawling across the dirt floor of a cabin, Mrs. Williams."

Her lips curved against his, her reply a sigh and a promise all at once. "Blake, if that happens, you can rest assured—you chose the right woman."

"Darling, I chose the right woman, no matter what happens." His words broke against her kiss as he gathered her into his arms, her body flush against his. Her fingers tangled in his hair, tugging just enough to make his pulse race. When she breathed his name, it was half a plea, half a vow, and he knew there was nothing he wouldn't do for her.

Reece Williams sat alone in the darkness of his office. The only light came in faint slices from the streetlamps outside, casting thin bars across his face and desk. The building was silent except for the occasional hiss of evening traffic on a small town's Main Street.

He pulled the small prescription bottle from his pocket, shook out a pill, and placed it beneath his tongue. It was meant to quiet the tightness in his chest, that leaden squeeze that made him catch his breath at night. But tonight, he doubted it could touch the ache gnawing at him from the inside.

Josephine was at a committee meeting, but he couldn't remember which one. His daughter hadn't called since she'd followed her brother's lead and left the farm weeks ago. Blake had always been Katelyn's hero, and why not? When she was three and terrified of thunderstorms, it was Blake—only five himself—who had crawled under her bed to hold her hand until the storm passed.

And now, the boy who had once shielded his sister from the thunder had given his father an ultimatum. Tonight, his only son and heir to the Williams dynasty had basically told him to *fuck off*. The conversation still echoed, hollow and merciless, louder than the pain in his chest.

Over a tense breakfast, Darby had tears in her eyes. Blake always struggled when that happened. This strong and beautiful woman had endured so much. To see her cry made him want to take on the world to protect her. No one—and he meant no one—was allowed to make his wife cry.

"I'm not sure, Blake. What do you think?" The corners of her pretty pink mouth formed a frown.

"Darby, how you want to respond to Tyler is your decision." Blake took her hand in his and kissed her knuckles. "My job is to support whatever that decision becomes."

"Job?" she challenged.

"Don't overthink this, honey. What do you want to do?"

"I want to avoid the issue." There was now at least half

a smile on her face.

"Do you think that's wise?"

"Probably not, cowboy. I need more time."

"Then, *more time* is a legitimate response, cowgirl." He paused. "The question remains, is that the reply that you want me to deliver to your brother?"

"I don't know." Her chin dropped almost to her chest.

"Darby, I want to understand where you're coming from. Help me," Blake said softly.

"Blake, there were many days in my young life when Tyler Payne felt like my only friend. But when we grew up, and he proposed, I knew that we were on a different plane. I was in love with and missing you. It's a miracle I didn't go to bed with him just to crush a need."

"Thank God that didn't happen," Blake whispered. He was the only man his wife had ever known in the flesh.

"I'm emotionally unsure, Blake. The boy I knew is gone. I was under the impression that he now hated me," she said.

Blake didn't respond. He thought it was better to let her work through this dilemma on her own.

"Will you be beside me, husband, and promise to keep a cool head?"

"Of course I'll stand by you, wife."

"And the cool head?"

"Darby, I am a professional," he said to her. To himself, he thought: *And if Tyler Payne hurts you, I will break him into a million pieces.* "Can I share with you my viewpoint?" he asked.

"Yes, I think that would help me," she replied, dabbing

her tears on the end of her sleeve.

He took a slow, controlled breath. "Meet with him strictly on an adult level, not as the children you once were. Seek to put an end to the animosity, but understand what will be, will be."

"Alright," she reached up and caressed Blake's cheek. "Make the arrangements. You are in control here, cowboy."

"Oh, Darby, I think in reality you've been in control since that first Sunday we sat in the swing on your front porch." He cupped her face and kissed her lips.

"Tyler, before an agreement for a time and location can be reached, you should know that my wife has requested that I stand beside her during this meeting," Blake spoke calmly into his cell phone, as if this were just another negotiation on behalf of a client. But Darby wasn't a client. She was the love of his life.

"Good," Tyler replied. "I want to speak with both of you. As far as a location, the Payne brothers will be in Steeplewood a week from Saturday for a family reunion of sorts. If it's acceptable, we could meet at Dad and Omalita's place."

"That sounds reasonable," Blake agreed.

"Darby and her husband, Blake, are coming to Dad's for the reunion," Tyler shared with Melissa over dinner.

"That's a lot of people for such a private conversation, don't you think?"

Tyler's eyes narrowed, and his jaw clenched. "You

instigated this event, Mel." He rubbed his forehead, wishing he could be somewhere else.

"I think it's important for the future of our family that you're over her, Tyler."

"I would never have married you if I weren't over Darby." He threw his hands up in an *I-give-up* gesture. "Besides, no one knows how stressful being with the Payne family is going to be for both Blake and Darby. It hasn't been that long since they lost their baby, and they'll be in the presence of Colt's son and two pregnant women. I clearly wasn't thinking when I set the time and place."

"Well, who steps out in front of a van anyway, Tyler?" Melissa's tone was unusually sarcastic.

Tyler's glare was frightening, and the volume of his voice rose significantly before he could stop himself. "The van hit Darby on purpose. It wasn't her fault. Whoever was driving that vehicle meant to do more than terminate a pregnancy. They meant to terminate my sister. The police still don't know who it was or why."

"Oh," Melissa said, her tone softening instantly.

"Yeah, *oh* is right." He leaned in across the narrow table. "You and I will soon have a healthy baby girl, and they had to bury their child. Dad's grandson. Our nephew. And they have to live with that fact every day. The only reason I'm meeting with them at this time is because of you. So, try to have a little compassion, Mel."

"I'm sorry, Tyler. That would be awful. I don't know if I could stand it." She caressed her protruding stomach.

"Exactly." Tyler stood and walked away. He would hug her later, but right now, he felt like a little distance would be a good thing. In his mind, if Darby happened to have a chip on her shoulder, she had earned it ten times over. But he knew he had been the one with the chip in their relationship, previously taking out his anger on the one person who had never deserved his ire.

The crowd at Garcia's adored Eduardo. Even on a rainy Wednesday night, with the rhythmic drumming of a Nashville downpour against the windows, he played to them as if the cameras were rolling, waving, bowing, and blowing theatrical kisses before he finally reached the Chef's table. When he did, he clapped Blake on the back with his usual warmth and flair, the smell of expensive cologne and woodsmoke clinging to his jacket.

"*Hola*," he said, sliding into the seat beside his friend and attorney. "You're amazing, brother—another movie, a bigger role, better pay. I owe you everything. Dinner's on me tonight."

Blake laughed, shaking his head at Eduardo's infectious energy. "Eduardo, I'm serious—we need to find you a real agent. My law practice is taking enough of my time without me moonlighting as a talent scout."

"No, mijo." Eduardo leaned back, signaled the waiter for a bottle of their best red, and lowered his voice. "You are family. Some agent in California or New York won't know me, won't know the soul I put into my work. They won't understand how much my family loves one another. But you and *mi hermana*—you, I can trust with my life and my career."

At the far end of the table, Darby was laughing with

Miguel and his partner, Dr. Steve. The sound of her voice—that bright, easy lilt that carried even through the ambient chatter of the restaurant—tugged at Blake's attention the way it always did. She had a rare gift for softening the sharp edges of any room she entered, for making people forget, if only for an hour, whatever heaviness they had carried through the door.

Eduardo leaned forward, his expression turning uncharacteristically somber. "Look, Blake. There's something else I need to discuss. Something… personal."

Blake straightened slightly, his professional instincts kicking in. "Lay it on me, brother."

"Tyler Payne has a reservation for brunch on Sunday. He said he'd be in town and wanted us to meet his wife. They're expecting their first child." Eduardo paused, gauging Blake's reaction. "Miguel remembers him fondly and said that Tyler never judged him, even back then when things were difficult. None of us have seen him since the forklift accident. I don't know the details, nor am I asking to, but I realize things haven't been good between him and your family. You say the word, and we'll cancel. No questions asked."

For a moment, Blake said nothing. The name *Tyler* stirred something old and unpleasant—not the hot anger of a few months ago, but a cold, lingering memory of betrayal. He turned his wineglass in his hand, watching the rain slide down the restaurant window in thin, restless lines that mimicked his own thoughts.

"You don't need my permission, Eduardo," he said at last, his voice level. "Tyler's had a rough few years. He's said and done things, Darby, and I didn't appreciate—things that are hard to move past—but if he's found peace and a family of his own, good for him. Whether we ever see him again is our decision. It shouldn't affect your business or your tables."

Eduardo nodded, a visible weight lifting from his shoulders. "Gracias, brother. It is good of you to take the high road. Few men would."

Darby caught Blake's eye from down the table, a tiny question flickering behind her smile. He gave the slightest, almost imperceptible nod, and whatever she saw in the steadiness of his gaze made her expression ease instantly.

That night, back at the condo, the house's quiet felt like a heavy silk blanket after the chaos of the city's rain. Blake lay in bed, the glow of his phone illuminating his face as he scanned the day's last emails, when Darby rolled onto her side and propped her head in her hand, watching him.

"There was a lot of whispering between you, Miguel, and Dr. Steve tonight," he said, setting the phone aside.

Her grin was immediate and conspiratorial. "Will you keep a secret?"

He looked over at her, amused by the sparkle in her eyes. "You're dying to tell me anyway. Go on. Spill the tea, darling."

"Okay, fine." She bounced onto her knees, her hair falling forward in a dark curtain as she leaned over him. "Miguel and Steve are thinking about getting married. For real this time."

Blake blinked, then a slow smile spread across his face. "That's great, babe." His hands slid to her waist, steadying her. "I take it this is a top-tier secret?"

"Yes—there's a lot for them to navigate. Mr. Garcia still acts like Miguel's life is just a long phase, like he'll wake up one morning and fall for *a nice girl from church*. And honestly, this is the first time either of them has really talked about forever."

"It could work," Blake said, his thumb tracing the soft skin of her side. "You and I only had one serious relationship, and I'd say we're holding up pretty well."

"You bet we are." She leaned down to kiss him, a quick, lingering spark of affection. "But they're already debating the logistics. They both own property and are discussing whether to adopt or hire a surrogate. The list of *what-ifs* is a mile long."

He paused, his mind quickly connecting the dots. "Wait—if they move in together, are you saying Miguel's house might come on the market? It's only a couple of miles from here, right?"

"It's possible," she said, her voice dropping to a whisper. "It's a beautiful place—two stories, a real basement, that big garage he loves. Miguel got a steal when he bought it, but he's put so much heart into the renovations."

Blake's pulse kicked up a notch. He knew that house; he'd spent more than one weekend there with a hammer in his hand. "You and I spent a lot of time helping him out. I know that foundation and the wiring better than I know some of my own case files."

Darby tilted her head, recognizing the look of a man making a closing argument. "What are you thinking,

Blake?"

"That we should buy it. That we should buy Miguel's house and make it ours."

She laughed—that bright, delighted sound that had been the soundtrack to his recovery and his life. "You're impossible, cowboy. It hasn't even been listed."

"Or I'm brilliant," he countered, pulling her forward until her laughter was muffled against his chest. "Private sales happen every day."

Darby pressed her face into the hollow of his neck, her breathing slowing as she let the idea take root. The thought of a new home—a place with room to grow, away from the shadows of the past year—hovered between them like the promise of a clear, sun-drenched morning.

CHAPTER 20

Wyatt Payne spotted her graceful lines and long red hair cascading down her back as she sat alone at the bar. Shapely legs crossed. Head tilted at the right angle to invite intrigue. Everything about her exuded a whisper of elegance and quiet power. The young bartender was obviously smitten with his only customer, as the restaurant had just opened for the evening. Wyatt was sure he knew who she was, and his intuition told him his life was about to change.

He usually kept a low profile when in town, but his stepmother, Omalita, didn't like *hard liquor,* as she called it, being brought into her house. With all the asses he'd had to kiss to get the time off to be here for the mini family reunion, Wyatt needed something more substantial than beer or wine to wash the taste of politics out of his mouth.

He was positive that the redhead had made him the minute he'd walked in the door. He'd taken too long to approach. He opted out of the pickup-line maneuver of the bar stool directly beside her, leaving one vacant between them—a tactical buffer. No way was he going to sit at the opposite end of the bar this evening. Wyatt nodded in her direction and focused on the bartender, who looked annoyed that his play for this beautiful woman had been interrupted by another male presence.

"Shot of *Jack*. Neat," Wyatt said, pretending not to notice her subtle grin reflected in the smoke-hued mirror behind the bar. He was a goner, and she had yet to say a word. "Wyatt Payne," he introduced himself, sticking his hand out in her direction like she was a male counterpart. She ignored the attempt at a handshake, and he dropped his hand back onto the bar to pick up the newly delivered shot glass, downing half the contents. If he hadn't known before, he now knew full well that she was out of his league.

"You can drop the *Casablanca* attitude, Payne. I know who you are, and I suspect you already know who I am," she said, her teeth too white, her voice smooth and polished like sea glass.

"All right. Let's play this out to some conclusion, shall we?" He moved onto the seat next to her, taking his drink with him. "How in the hell does Jylene Green know who I am?" He threw back the rest of his drink to the melodious sounds of her laughter, a sound that caused heads to turn in their direction.

"I was hoping to track you down, but I had no clue you'd walk in here tonight," she said. "Sometimes opportunity lands in one's lap."

His eyes glanced down at her lap, lingering a little too long on purpose, and then back up to her eyes. The lack of subtlety wasn't lost on her. "Opportunity? Is that what you call this? Not something more poetic like kismet?" Wyatt pointed to his glass, then to hers, and finally to the bartender for another round.

"I know you're the man who put a bullet into the brain of John Holder. The mercenary that Luis Hart hired to kill Darby Hart, now Darby Williams. A woman who is your illegitimate half-sister and is married to the much sought-after Nashville entertainment attorney, Blake Williams. I want to interview you, Payne. Get your professional take on what happened. Not some sanitized, weak federal report." Jylene whirled the watered-down contents of her glass and downed it before setting the empty glass onto the bar and picking up the fresh drink he bought for her.

Wyatt's disappointment showed across his face faster than he would have liked. She wasn't interested in him; he was just a character in a story she was writing—a primary source for a manuscript. "Sorry to disappoint you, Ms. Green. You may no longer be employed by the federal government, but I am." Wyatt leaned in slightly, his voice dropping an octave. "Be careful, Jylene. Truth gets people killed in this town. Especially truths that involve the Badcocks."

"That's a risk I understand," she said. He believed her—every word.

Their words hung there, quiet but charged. Around them, the restaurant hummed to life—servers setting tables, a distant laugh, the clink of silverware—but it all felt secondary, muffled by the gravity of their conversation. The world had narrowed to the two of them and whatever lingered between their conflicting worlds.

Then something shifted in her posture. Subtle, but unmistakable. Her gaze flicked toward the mirrored back bar—not at him, but just past his shoulder. For an instant, her expression tightened, the mask of the elegant novelist slipping to reveal the operative underneath.

Wyatt didn't turn right away. He let his hand drift casually to his drink, eyes on the mirror. In the reflection, a man sat alone in the far corner booth, a newspaper open but untouched. No food, no drink. Just a steady, heavy presence pretending to blend in.

"Friend of yours?" he asked casually.

"Not yet," she murmured.

"Then you should make sure he stays that way. Jylene, there's a storm brewing. Now might not be a good time for a casual visit to Steeplewood, if that's your only mission here."

She gave a slow nod, the kind that meant *message received.* He took a deliberate sip of whiskey, masking the quick pulse at his throat. Whoever the watcher was, he'd picked the wrong pair to tail, but Wyatt was reasonably sure the shadow was for Jylene. He knew what was coming; he just didn't know the zero hour.

A deep dive into Darby's lead had revealed that the owner of a Georgia rental agency had made a high-dollar, off-the-books deal with a female for the use of a van. The same van that ran down his sister. The man working the counter had a record and didn't want to go back to jail, but his description of her had been vague: a long blonde wig and tight clothes on a nice body—classic distraction. She had worked quietly with the owner while the counter man had been sent to the back, where he had covertly watched. When she took off her dark sunglasses and laid a stack of cash on the counter, the owner slid the keys to her. But the damning piece of evidence was the red hoodie casually draped across her arm. The employee had captured it all on grainy video. A month later, and after a visit from Hunter North, that employee had wisely moved on to a better job in Savannah before the feds had found him.

As the last slant of sunlight bled from the bar's windows, Jylene Green smiled—just slightly, the smile of a woman who'd played this game before and had no intention of losing. She swirled the last of her drink, watching the amber liquid catch the light. Jylene didn't need to turn to know the man in the booth hadn't moved. Men like that never did. They wanted to be noticed just enough—a threat that pretended not to be one.

She had seen it before in surveillance rooms and back alleys where the air hummed with danger. The stillness wasn't patience—it was control. Her fingers tapped the glass once. "He's not local," she said quietly.

Wyatt's brow lifted. "I agree. What's your assessment?"

"Shoes," she said. "Polished. Wrong cut of jacket for this town, too. The paper's a prop. He's military or ex-agency, but not freelance. Too disciplined."

"You've done this before," Wyatt said.

"I've *survived* this before," she corrected.

She shifted her gaze to her reflection in the mirror, careful to look past herself to the man behind her. He didn't flinch when she met his eyes in the glass. That told her everything. Whoever sent him didn't care if she saw him—they wanted her to know she was being watched.

A low hum started in her chest, a rhythm she recognized. The old instincts were kicking in, her pulse slowing instead of quickening as her thoughts sharpened into a blade. She smiled, slid a bill beneath her glass, and stood. "Well," she said lightly, "it's been nice chatting, Mr. Payne. Maybe I'll see you again before I leave town."

Wyatt started to speak, but she gave a slight shake of her head. "Don't. Finish your drink before you leave."

Her heels clicked softly on the tile as she crossed the room. She didn't glance back, but she could feel the eyes from the booth tracking her every step. She reached the door, paused long enough to fix her lipstick in the small reflection of the glass—using the faint gleam to confirm the man had folded his paper and was standing now, preparing to follow her into the damp Tennessee night.

Outside, twilight had settled over the parking lot. The neon from the restaurant sign flickered once, twice, throwing the world into pulses of pink and shadow. Jylene slipped her keys into her hand so that one long edge pressed between her fingers—a habit from another life— and smiled faintly to herself.

Wyatt would have walked her to her car as a shield, but she had made it clear she wasn't interested in being protected. *Oh well*, he thought. She had been warned. As soon as the stranger followed her out the door, Wyatt threw another bill on the counter and casually made for the exit. But by the time he reached the parking lot, the humid air was still; neither Jylene nor the man with the polished shoes was anywhere to be found.

It was time for him to head in the opposite direction and forget all about her. On the other hand, Jylene Green was a beautiful woman with a silhouette that could distract a saint, and a behind—as the old-timers said—you could bounce a quarter off of, though he couldn't personally attest to that specific idiom. Her presence lingered like a persistent ghost in his subconscious.

The local gossip mill was already churning by the next morning, chatting about Wyatt Payne being seen *cozying up* to the famous Jylene Green at the bar. It was the last thing either of them needed, but such was the relentless nature of life in a small town.

"Maybe now isn't the time to be getting close to someone with ties to Robert Badcock, Wyatt," Winston said over breakfast. The clink of a fork against a plate punctuated his disapproval.

"Dad," Wyatt's tone was casual, yet firm. "I've been taking care of myself for a few years now. Been all over the world. Met a lot of people, some of them women. I believe I've earned the right to mind my own business. Besides, I seriously doubt that Jylene Green is *close* with Robert Badcock." He drank liberally from his coffee cup. Not only was Omalita an excellent cook, but she also made an exceptional cup of coffee—strong enough to wake the dead.

His older brother, Colt, chuckled at the exchange, only to choke on his eggs when his wife, Laura, slapped him on the back of the head.

"Well, close or not," Winston refused to let the subject

drop, "the rumor is she's got a grown son who looks a whole lot like a young Badcock. That would make her a fair bit older than you, Wyatt."

"I don't see how that matters, Dad," Colt chimed in, recovering his breath and reaching for another biscuit dripping in butter. "You're a lot older than Omalita."

"We're not talking about me," Winston said, pointing his fork in Colt's direction like a weapon. "We are talking about your brother. My relationship with Omalita occurred under a whole different set of circumstances." He turned his focus back to Wyatt. "And according to Howard Napier down at the Farm Store, Jylene has been all over town asking pointed questions about your sister, Darby."

"She wanted to talk to me about the same subject matter. I turned her down." Wyatt had yet to put any food on his plate. Omalita noticed but decided to remain silent. The boy was right, she thought; he was a grown man capable of making his own decisions, and he certainly knew whether he was hungry or not.

"Well, Wyatt," Omalita finally spoke, her voice cutting through the tension with a quiet grace. "If you run into Jylene again, you should invite her here for a meal. I'd be honored to have her. Whatever happens after that is between you and her." She reached over to pat the back of Wyatt's hand. "We don't hold things like a person's parentage against them in this house."

Both brothers had to force themselves to refrain from laughter, their eyes meeting over their plates. Omalita's words were a not-so-gentle reminder that Darby Hart Williams was their father's illegitimate daughter and their half-sister. The room went quiet, the weight of that truth settling over the breakfast table like the morning mist over the Tennessee hills.

Wyatt entered the restaurant again the following afternoon, unable to talk himself out of it. He had spent the morning hoping she had heeded his warning and caught the first flight out of Nashville, but there she was. He wondered, with a wry twist of his mouth, if Jylene had chosen today's particular bar stool because the overhead mini spotlight perfectly highlighted the natural fire in her red hair. He'd never been with a redhead, but he had always wondered if the rumors about their temperament were true.

Wyatt had thought about Jylene Green all day, especially last night, when the memory of her polished voice competed with the data he had pulled from the secure servers. He had done his homework, digging into her past as an operative. Learning her prior code name had caused him a moment of genuine concern, a cold prickle at the base of his spine that he'd tried to brush off. *Black Widow* only sounded like a comic book trope until his contact had provided the list of deceased males in her wake—a trail of bodies that started when she'd been sixteen years old and living right here in Steeplewood. But even that classified ledger of loss hadn't stopped him from showing up at the bar again this evening.

"Good evening, Payne. Fancy meeting you here again." She looked toward Andrew, the bartender, her expression unreadable but welcoming. "I believe I owe Mr. Payne a drink, Andrew. That would be *Jack*. Neat."

The young bartender didn't question the order or the woman's sharp memory. He simply poured the shot and placed it in front of Wyatt as the younger Payne settled onto the stool next to her, the air between them immediately tightening with the same electric hum as the night before.

"I appreciate your generosity, Green." Wyatt threw back the shot in one sharp gulp, the burn of the whiskey grounding him. "Hit me again, Andy, but this time it's on me." He tossed enough cash on the counter to make the young man on the other side smile broadly, then downed his second straight shot of *Jack Daniels* before sliding off the barstool and turning his back on the infuriating woman.

"Wyatt." She reached out, her hand clasping his arm with surprising strength. "I thought you were tougher than this."

He looked down at her fingers and then back up into her eyes, his expression hardening. "I see you survived your admirer last evening." He gave her his best *007* smile, then firmly removed her grasp with his other hand.

"He followed me back to my mother's house and was then on his way. A different car showed up and parked across the street, but was gone before daylight. Anything else you want to tell me, Wyatt?"

"Sorry to disappoint you, Ma'am, but my attention is expected elsewhere this evening."

"Wyatt, wait," she said, following him as he strode toward the exit. "I still want to interview you."

Wyatt parked the rental car in the driveway of Omalita's prized Victorian home. He had woken up in the motel room to find her gone, a hollow space where she had been. After the most amazing night of sex in his life, he'd fallen into a heavy, dead sleep with her red hair cascading across his chest, but he had no clue as to when she'd slipped away. For a man in his line of work, that kind of lapse could be fatal. But he had other responsibilities today. He needed to share information with his sister—and with no one else— and she would be arriving soon.

"Morning, slut," Colt said from the porch, leaning back in an Amish rocker with a smug grin.

"Fuck you," Wyatt replied as he passed by his brothers.

"Wyatt." Tyler nodded in his direction with a note of cynical amusement.

"Tyler," he muttered, passing through the front door and sprinting up to the second floor.

Fifteen minutes later, shaven and wearing clean clothes, Wyatt heard her voice just as he started back down the antique wooden staircase.

"Hello, I'm Jylene Green. Wyatt invited me to lunch." Her voice floated upward, smooth and polished, as Omalita greeted her.

Wyatt froze for a split second. He remembered asking her if she had ever been to Paris. She had. But he had completely forgotten about the lunch invitation.

"Jylene," Omalita said. "I'd know you anywhere. Come in and meet the rest of my family. How's your mamma doing? She missed the last Ladies Auxiliary meeting." She ushered her guest into the foyer with practiced southern hospitality.

"She's doing fine, Omalita. Thank you for asking. She's just a little bored. I told her she should volunteer at the library."

Wyatt placed his hand over his mouth to keep from laughing out loud. Having Madeline Green underfoot at the public library would serve Omalita right for being nosy. He was, however, sure that Maddie would soon be spending her time elsewhere. He hurried his pace down the steps.

"Oh, Wyatt, your guest is here," Omalita said as he joined the two women. "Can I get you two a glass of tea?"

"I could use one of your amazing cups of coffee, Omalita," he said, trying to find his footing. "Jylene?"

"I'm fine, but thank you," Jylene said. She looked impeccable. There was nothing about her appearance—the crisp lines of her outfit, the perfect composure—to suggest they'd spent most of the night talking and tangled together in a local motel room. Instead, she looked like she'd stepped directly off the dust jacket of one of her best-selling novels.

"You two make yourselves comfortable wherever. I'll find you with that coffee." As Omalita smiled and walked away, Wyatt leaned forward and kissed the corner of Jylene's mouth before he could think to stop himself.

CHAPTER 21

Robert Badcock eyed the passport with something close to reverence, a cracked smile tugging at his unshaven face. The document was already smudged with gin and fingerprints, but to him, it looked like salvation. His ticket out. *Ubiquitous freedom*, he thought, savoring the way the syllables felt in his mind. The gin burned like acid down his throat, but it was the good kind of burn—the kind that reminded him he was still alive, for now.

He sat in his father's old recliner, its arms polished smooth from decades of nervous rubbing. The smell of mildew clung to the chair like a second skin. Around him, the room was a chaotic archive of bad choices—half-empty bottles, old envelopes with overdue stamps, and a muted television frozen on static because he'd never gotten around to paying the bill.

It was all temporary, he told himself. One last drink in this godforsaken town, and then he'd disappear for good. Let them gossip. Let them wonder. He'd be nothing more than another local ghost story told over cheap beer.

He might've made it, too—if not for her.

He hadn't recognized it for what it was at the time: an omen. A curse in lipstick and long red hair. Jylene Green.

He'd seen her from a distance that afternoon, standing outside the drugstore, phone in hand, that fiery hair catching the light like it was spun from vengeance itself. She hadn't looked his way. Why would she? But he felt the sight of her like a knife under the ribs. The mother of his only child.

His son.

He took another swallow, his eyes watering as the alcohol hit. The liquor always got meaner when he thought about the boy.

Jylene had been too good for him even back then—college degree, perfect diction, and that sharp little mind that could cut a man down with a single sentence. He'd come back from the Army with little more than a duffel bag and bad habits, and when she'd told him she was pregnant, he'd said the worst words a man could ever say to a woman who loved him. *Get rid of it.*

He regretted it the minute the words left his mouth, but by then the gin had made him proud and stupid. Regret was a luxury for sober men, and Robert Badcock hadn't been sober in a long time.

Now, all these years later, the consequences of that pride had grown up into a man with a guitar and a stage name: Jackson Green. Nashville. Robert had looked the kid up recently, late at night when the house was too quiet. The smile, the chin—too much of Jylene, not enough of him. Probably a blessing for the boy.

The kid had reached out twice over the years, polite little messages sent like olive branches. Robert hadn't answered either one. He'd convinced himself it was an act of mercy; the Badcock name came with too many negative demands and a legacy of rot.

He stared at the passport again. His name—**BADCOCK, ROBERT ALLEN**—was printed in sharp, official black letters that looked foreign to him. With this in his hand, he could burn it all behind him—the name, the failed relationships, the caves, and the town.

But seeing Jylene had lit something dangerous in him. Restlessness. Guilt. Memory.

She'd done everything right—officer, agent, screenwriter, novelist. Hell, she probably owned a house in California with white shutters and a dog that didn't bark. She was a success story. And him? He was a punchline with a bottle. He dragged a dirty hand down his face and across his red hoodie, chuckling without humor.

"Hell, Jylene," he muttered, his voice rough as gravel. "You win."

But the thing about Robert Badcock was that even broken men had a threshold.

He re-inspected the two gym bags. One was stuffed with clothing for the first leg of his road trip. Mostly clean underwear. He would make his routine deliveries so that no one would get suspicious. Except this time, when he finished in Georgia, instead of returning to Tennessee, he'd head for Jacksonville and the first flight out to the Caymans. The second bag was stuffed with cash—enough to disappear. There would be plenty more waiting for him once he hit the islands. From there, who knew? He'd always wanted to see Australia. Maybe he'd take his chances in the outback.

Robert didn't bother to lock the door as he left his ancestral home, throwing both heavy bags onto the back floorboard. This journey had taken years to plan, and Jylene's return to Steeplewood only confirmed his need to move on. Backing his long-deceased father's Mercedes out of the garage, Robert's mood was particularly diabolical. He had always driven his old Chevy for deliveries to avoid drawing attention, but his last drug run deserved a little more class. He planned to leave the antique vehicle at the airport in Jacksonville, doors unlocked and keys in the ignition—a final gift to whoever found it.

He did, however, plan to drive by her mother's house before leaving town. He'd seen Jylene from a distance and knew time had been good to her. Her naturally long red hair cascaded down her back, accentuating her slender waist and the high rear end he remembered all too well. She had done well for herself and their son. In his twisted logic, he'd done her a favor by not offering to marry her.

Robert waved to a neighbor as he drove down the street in the dusty vehicle. He wasn't going to waste energy or money washing a piece of machinery that had meant more to his father than he ever had. He laughed out loud in the empty car, the sound echoing off the leather. His old man was probably shitting bricks right now down in the Methodist cemetery. Just for fun, Robert ran a finger up his nose and flicked a booger onto the leather dash, then turned the radio volume up so high it hurt his ears before pointing the car toward the wrong side of town.

Blake eased the aging BMW to the curb; the driveway was already full. The old Victorian house looked scrubbed clean—new roof, fresh paint, the kind of improvements Omalita had insisted on after marrying Winston Payne, just a few years after the boys' mother had succumbed to cancer.

He stepped out and walked around to open Darby's door. She looked strong, put-together—hair perfect, eyes alert, but he could feel the flicker of hesitation she tried to hide behind a polite mask. Blake didn't mention it. Instead, he said quietly, "You look beautiful, honey."

Her answering smile—bright and genuine—still made something in his chest loosen, even after all they'd been through.

From the porch, Colt Payne appeared, his posture as stiff as a sentry's. "Well, hello there. Good to see you both this morning." He swept Darby into a hug that looked more like a defensive hold before extending a hand to Blake. "Can't wait to catch up, got plenty to share."

Before Blake could answer, Colt's wife, Laura, came rushing from the house with young Henry balanced on one hip and a baby bump just starting to show. "Darby! It's so good to see you again. And you must be the infamous husband." She extended a freckled hand toward Blake. "I read an article about you—something about *black belts and courtroom composure?*"

"Husband, most assuredly," Darby said with a grin. "Infamous… jury's still out." She reached for Blake's hand

and laced her fingers through his, anchoring herself.

"A pleasure," Blake said, shaking Laura's hand briefly. The contact was polite but fleeting, and Laura, sharp as a tack, noticed the distance in his eyes.

On the porch, Wyatt stood beside yet another red-haired woman, looking oddly pleased with himself. Darby blinked, unsure who the stranger was. *Wyatt and Colt,* she thought, *definitely share a type.*

Wyatt came down the steps first, his companion a careful step behind him. Blake's expression didn't change, but Darby saw the subtle tension in his shoulders that meant he was already calculating the exits.

"Blake Williams," he said, extending his hand past Wyatt to the redhead.

"Jylene Green." She took it without hesitation, her grip firm and professional.

"I'm confident you're related to Jackson Green," Blake said evenly.

"Jackson is my son."

Wyatt frowned, his gaze darting between them. "You two know each other?"

"We don't," Blake said, his voice dropping into the low, calm register he used for hostile depositions. "But her son's been trying to hire my firm. He's left… quite a few messages for me. Because of that, we won't be discussing anything further with her present."

The tension hit like static in humid air. Blake shifted, subtly moving so Darby stood half a step behind his shoulder—the classic protective stance of a man who knew exactly where the threats were.

"My wife and I are here for a scheduled meeting with Tyler," he said, his tone clipped and cold, "and then we'll be on our way."

Colt looked between them, caught off guard by the sudden frost. "We had no idea—"

"If Tyler's here," Blake interrupted, "please ask him to make his presence known." The weight in his voice made Colt straighten instinctively.

"Get her out of here," Colt said, motioning toward Wyatt and Jylene.

Wyatt grabbed Jylene's arm and steered her toward the side of the house. At that same moment, the cell phone in his pocket began an insistent, rhythmic buzzing—a specific vibration that only he seemed to understand. He quickened their pace, his mind already miles away from the family drama.

"Jylene," he muttered, his voice tight as he opened her car door. "You need to leave town. Now." He glanced at the screen of his phone, his face paling under the Tennessee sun.

"Wyatt, I didn't know Blake Williams would be here— you said only your sister—"

"Forget about Blake for now. Get out of town quick. DO NOT go back to your mother's house. Just drive and don't look back. Hurry."

The words landed hard. Jylene froze, her lips parting to argue, but he'd already slammed the door and was running toward the front lawn. She started the rental car and drove off slowly, her heart hammering against her ribs. Wyatt watched her go, a heaviness filling his chest. Why would a woman like that ever want a man like him—except to use him? But there was no time for self-pity. *It* was going down today. Now.

"Thought you'd already left," Maddie Green scoffed, leaning against a porch post.

"I'll be gone in five minutes," Jylene said, pulling up to the curb. "I just need to grab my bag out of the house."

The sound of obnoxious, bone-rattling music preceded the old Mercedes lumbering down the street. A cloud of toxic black smoke trailed behind the vehicle like a funeral shroud.

"What the hell?" Maddie Green stepped off the porch, moving too close to the edge of the highway to get a better view of the approaching car.

Inside the Mercedes, Robert Badcock was losing his grip on reality. He shouldn't have had those microwave tacos, and he definitely shouldn't have had the two long pulls from the gin bottle resting in the passenger seat. The pain in his chest was no longer a dull ache; it was a tightening vise. His left arm began to throb with a rhythmic, sickening heat.

He saw the woman standing in the road at the last possible second—just as his lungs seized and an explosion ripped through his chest.

The car veered violently, careening over Maddie Green. There would be no more trips to Florida for the former mistress of Morgan Badcock Senior. She was dead before the car even stopped. The Mercedes only came to a halt when it slammed into the front porch of her dilapidated house. The rotting roof groaned and collapsed onto the hood, spiderwebbing the windshield.

The roar of the impact and the continuous, dying wail of the car horn alerted the neighbors long before Jylene's scream pierced the air as she was buried beneath the porch rubble.

Three vehicles descended on the property like vultures. Detective Jenkins jumped out of the lead unmarked car, his weapon drawn, scanning the wreckage.

"Help me." Jylene's voice cut through the chaos, muffled by wood and dust. "Somebody, please help me."

"Hey, folks." Tyler stepped out of the Payne house and started across the yard, only to stop short at the sight of the standoff. "Is something wrong?"

Colt rubbed the back of his neck, glancing at Blake. "Ah, Tyler… looks like Jylene Green might've been waiting to corner Blake about her son's career. Wyatt's already seen her off."

Tyler frowned. "I had no idea she was even here. I'm sorry about that."

Blake stood with one arm loosely draped over Darby's shoulders. He looked calm—almost relaxed—but there was a predatory stillness to him. Darby, however, was wound tight, her breath coming in shallow hitches.

"Let's just focus on why you asked us here today," she said, her voice like a snapping twig.

Tyler drew in a breath and squared his shoulders. "I was hoping to do this in private," he said, looking straight at Darby. "I was angry for a long time. I took it out on you. I made you a target." His voice cracked. "I regret that more than anything. I've got a good wife now, and a baby on the way. I just… want to put the past behind me. I'm asking both you and Blake to forgive me."

The air hung still. Darby's eyes shimmered—not with tears, but with a sharp, cold clarity. "I'll think about it," she said, turning toward the BMW.

"Darby, wait." Wyatt caught up with them, embracing his sister and whispering fiercely in her ear. "You were right about everything. The bust is going down *now*. Get to Williams Farm or back to Nashville, but stay away from the Badcocks. Love you, Babygirl. Our secret."

"I remember. Love you too, brother," she whispered back, beginning to tremble.

Wyatt backed away and shook Blake's hand stoically. Darby addressed the remaining Paynes, her voice dripping with disdain. "It seems every time I'm around this family, there's unnecessary drama. I'm tired of it. Enjoy your reunion."

"Daughter, wait! Don't leave!" Winston yelled, bounding off the porch toward her.

Darby turned abruptly, her face contorting in a fury that had been building for years. Blake's reaction was lightning-quick; he lunged and caught her by the waistband of her slacks. "Darby, calm down!"

She twisted like a feral cat. "Let me go!" She thrashed, her feet leaving the ground and landing a solid kick against Blake's shins.

"Damn it, Darby, that hurts! Stop it!"

"Put me down!"

"I'll put you down, alright." Blake set her feet hard onto the gravel, catching her off balance. In one fluid motion, he spun her around and delivered a firm swat to her behind.

The silence that followed was deafening. Darby's eyes went wide with shock.

"You are behaving like a child, Darby," Blake said firmly. "The last time you kicked someone's ass, you nearly landed in jail."

"Dude," Colt's breath was long and drawn out as he stepped forward, his fists balled at his sides. "You just hit my sister."

"No," Blake turned her to face their audience, keeping his hands steady on her shoulders. "I spanked your sister to get her attention. I'd never hit her. Never have. Never will."

"Sure looked like a hit to me," Colt growled, his brothers closing in behind him.

Blake immediately recognized the shift in the atmosphere. He had just disciplined a Payne woman in front of her father and three brothers. The *unscripted play* had just turned into a fight, and the Payne clan wasn't about to let it pass.

"Take your hands off my daughter." Winston Payne was at least five inches shorter and twenty pounds heavier than the lean and muscular Blake Williams, but the man had three sons to back him up—and Blake was certain that at least one of them was packing heat.

With one fluid motion, Blake maneuvered his wife behind him, using his body as a human shield. He fished a key chain from his pocket and passed it backward to her without breaking eye contact with Winston. "Darby," his voice was a calm, low vibration that brooked no argument, "Get in the car and drive. Do not stop until you reach the bunkhouse at the farm. Tell whoever is there to look after you until I arrive. Love you, baby. You're mine, and I'm yours. Now go."

"Do as he says, daughter," Winston stepped even closer, his jaw set. It was apparent that Blake was his intended target, the catalyst for decades of buried shame.

"The hell I will!" Darby shoved the keys into the pocket of her jeans as she darted around her husband to stand toe-to-toe with her biological father.

"This is going to be good." Tyler stepped back, motioning for his brothers to do the same. The smile on his face was enormous, a jagged thing born of chaos. On the porch, the women lined the elaborate railing like a worried jury. Laura was frantically gesturing for Colt to join her, but there was no way he was giving up his front-row seat to this.

"Fuck you, Winston Payne!" Darby slapped him so hard his head snapped to the side, and he stumbled back into the grass. "Don't ever call me daughter again. I find it repulsive. You are a liar and a cheat."

The words came out like a flood over a broken dam. "It's hard to believe you couldn't perform the simple math that would have proven who I was. If you truly believed Malina Hart when she said I wasn't yours, then why did you ask her twice? You knew, you son of a bitch. You knew, and you chose to ignore the fact that Luis Hart and your lover abused me for eighteen years. They even tried to have me murdered, and in all that time, you never once notified the authorities? Not even anonymously?"

The quiet that followed was absolute, almost deafening. Winston's head hung low toward his chest, his shoulders slumped under the weight of the truth.

"Divine intervention brought Blake Williams into my world," she continued, her voice trembling with the force of her conviction. "He loves me. He takes care of me. Okay, so he swatted me on the behind today to get my attention. Truth is, I like it." She paused for a breath, and Blake turned his head to hide the sudden, sharp grin of pride. "Trust me, boys, I know what it's really like to be hit and beaten. I still have the scars to prove it. Blake hasn't given me a single one."

The distant echo of an explosion and the faint, rising wail of a siren broke the tension. More emergency vehicles joined in, the sound carrying across the humid Tennessee air.

"Somebody must have run the only red light in town again," Colt muttered, his eyes drifting toward the road.

Wyatt, however, felt a chill of foreboding crawl up his spine. He checked the phone vibrating in his pocket, his eyes briefly catching Darby's. He gave a sharp, subtle nod toward the road—a silent order to leave.

"Please take me home, cowboy." Darby turned and encircled Blake's waist, her fire spent, replaced by a deep, weary need for his strength.

Blake's arms wrapped around her, pulling her flush against him. "Whatever you want, cowgirl." He kissed the top of her head, then turned to open the BMW's door. He held her hand as she slid inside, his expression one of fierce, unyielding pride. He walked around to the driver's side and drove away without a single backward glance.

A helicopter thudded high overhead, moving fast toward the Badcock property, unnoticed by everyone but Wyatt.

Tyler Payne couldn't erase the look of satisfaction from his face. He walked calmly onto the porch and gave his surprised wife a firm swat on the behind. "Happy now?" he asked with a wink before entering the house, letting the screen door slam behind him.

The sound of Colt's laughter abruptly ceased when Laura reached out and slapped the back of his head.

The luxury hotel suite lived up to its promise: all marble, sunlight, and quiet indulgence. Blake leaned against the dresser, watching as Darby slipped into her simple bra and panties. He couldn't decide which he preferred—watching her put them on or being the one to take them off. It felt almost criminal to hide her beauty beneath the pink, knee-length dress she'd chosen for the day.

They were both dressed for the destination wedding of Miguel Garcia and his fiancé, Dr. Steve, wearing vintage designer pieces they had scavenged from the Williams Farm closets. Miguel had been thrilled by the choice, and Darby even more so.

Blake was already dressed in his formal attire, but he paused to draw her gently back against him, the length of her body soft against his. "You think we've got time before we have to be downstairs for the ceremony?" he murmured, his voice dropping into that low, gravelly register of desire.

She laughed and pushed lightly at his hands. "No. You'd

only need to zip your pants, cowboy, but I'd probably need another shower."

He sighed, conceding the point. "You win—for now." Yet he didn't step away. He turned her around in his arms, his tone shifting as concern edged out the playfulness. "You feel all right, honey?"

He studied her face, searching for a sign of fatigue. "I noticed you skipped the wine last night and passed on the coffee this morning. The blend was exceptional, by the way." He hesitated, studying their joined reflection in the mirror. "If I didn't know better, I'd swear you're..." His voice trailed off as the realization took root. "...pregnant," he finished in a whisper.

Darby turned to him fully, her radiant smile already blooming. "Now, Blake, don't go crazy," she teased as he staggered back and landed on the edge of the bed, looking utterly blindsided. "Today is about Miguel and Steve."

"Are you sure?" he managed, his eyes wide with the magnitude of the question.

"As I live and breathe, Blake Williams, you're going to be a daddy."

He blinked, his mind racing to do the math. "Wait—when? How did I miss—"

She stepped into his space, silencing his frantic thoughts with a tender kiss to his cheek. "In about seven and a half months, cowboy."

For a long moment, he simply held her, his face buried in her jasmine-scented hair. The noise of the world outside—the music, the crashing ocean, the distant wedding bells—seemed to fade until there was only the steady rhythm of her heartbeat against his.

"I love you, Darby Williams," he said quietly, the words thick with emotion.

"I love you, Blake Williams," she said, smiling against his chest as he pulled her closer, the promise of their future finally outweighing the shadows of their past.

THE END

CAST OF CHARACTERS

<u>Adam Taylor (boo bear)</u>: Engineer. Partner of TNT Engineering Firm. Husband of Katelyn Williams Taylor

<u>Adele Carter</u>: Office Manager of Williams Law Office and Paralegal.

<u>Andrew</u>: Bartender

<u>Austin Napier</u>: Son of Howard Napier

<u>Benjamin Franklin Williams (Ben, Pops, Gramps)</u>: Attorney/Politician, Patriarch. Primary Owner of Williams Farm and all Williams Corporations. Father of Reese. Grandfather of Blake and Katelyn.

<u>Blake Benjamin Williams</u>: Third-generation attorney. Black Belt. Son of Reese & Josephine Williams. Heir to the Williams Dynasty, Married to Darby Hart Williams.

<u>Boyd</u>: Williams Farm Foreman

<u>Britney Carter</u>: High school friend of Katelyn Williams Taylor

<u>Carolyn</u>: Darby's coworker

<u>Calvin Holder</u>: (Deceased) Brother of John Holder

<u>Chelsea Lambert</u>: Talent Agent

<u>Clara</u>: Owner of Clara's Thrift Shop

<u>Colt Payne</u>: Son of Winston and Michele Payne

<u>Connie Hildebrand</u>: Paralegal at Williams Law Office

<u>Darby Hart Williams (Kitten)</u>: MBA, Interim Office Manager at TNT Engineering Firm. Wife of Blake Williams. Illegitimate daughter of an illicit affair between Winston Payne and Malina Hart.

<u>Detective Jenkins</u>: State police

<u>Dr. Steve</u>: Miguel Garcia's Fiancé/Partner

<u>Eduardo García</u>: Professional Chef

<u>Eric Youngman</u>: Williams Farm Security

<u>Genevia Williams (Grammy)</u>: (Deceased) Second wife of Benjamin Williams. Mother of Reese. Grandmother to Blake and Katelyn.

<u>Greg Turner</u>: Engineer. Partner of TNT Engineering Firm.

<u>Henry Payne</u>: Son of Colt and Laura Payne.

<u>Howard Napier</u>: Owner of Napier Farm Store. Father of <u>Luke</u> Napier, <u>Austin</u> Napier and more.

<u>Hunter North</u>: Williams Farm Security

<u>Jack Butler</u>: Former employee of both Williams Farm and Badcock Farm

<u>Jackson Green</u>: Musician. Illegitimate son of Jylene Green and Robert Badcock.

<u>Janiece Badcock</u>: (Deceased) Wife of Morgan Badcock, Sr. Mother of Morgan, Jr, Robert & Terry Badcock.

<u>John Holder</u>: (Deceased) Mercenary. Brother of <u>Calvin</u> Holder (Deceased).

<u>Johnathan Q. Hawkins (Hawk)</u>: Williams Farm Security

<u>Josephine Williams (JoJo)</u>: Wife of Reese. Mother of

Blake and Katelyn.

<u>Jylene Green</u>: (Former Officer, Agent) Screenwriter, Novelist. Daughter of Madeline and Nate Green

<u>Katelyn Williams Taylor (Kate, Katie, Baby Sis)</u>: Nurse Practitioner. Daughter of Reese and Josephine Williams. Younger sister of Blake. Married to Adam Taylor, Engineer.

<u>Laura Payne</u>: Nurse. Wife of Colt Payne. Mother of their son, <u>Henry</u>.

<u>Luis Hart</u>: (Deceased), former schoolteacher, Father of Wade Hart and Jade Hart. Husband of Malina Hart

<u>Luke Napier</u>: Son of Howard Napier.

<u>Madeline Green (Maddie)</u>: Mother of Jylene Green, Wife of <u>Nate</u> Green (deceased)

<u>Maedean Buley</u>: Owner of The City Diner

<u>Malina Hart</u>: (In prison), former schoolteacher, Mother of <u>Wade</u> Hart, <u>Jade</u> Hart, and Darby Hart Williams

<u>Melissa Algood Payne (Mel)</u>: Physical Therapist. Wife of Tyler

<u>Michelle Payne: (Deceased)</u> First wife of Winston and mother of his three sons. Died from cancer.

<u>Miguel García</u>: Nurse Administrator

<u>Mindy</u>: ICU Nurse

<u>Morgan Badcock, Sr</u>: (Deceased) Owner of Babcock Farm and Badcock Insurance Agency. Married to <u>Janiece</u> Miller Badcock (Deceased). Father of <u>Morgan</u> Badcock Jr, <u>Robert</u> Badcock (Robbie, Rob), and <u>Terry</u> Badcock.

<u>Morgan Badcock, Jr</u>: Son of Morgan Badcock, Sr.

<u>Mr. Garcia</u>: Owner and Head Chef of Garcia's

Restaurant. Father of Miguel, Eduardo, Carmen, and more.

Nate Green: (Deceased) Husband of Madeline Green. Father of Jylene Green

Nelson Pedigo (Nels): County Judge Executive

Omalita Hanes Payne: Second wife of Winston Payne

Paul Johnson: Woodwright, Former employee of Williams Farm

Rachel O'Rourke: Legal Secretary/Assistant to Blake Williams

Reese Williams: Attorney, Owner of William Law. Only child of Benjamin & Genevia Williams. Married to Josephine. Father of Blake and Katelyn.

Richard Nealy: Engineer. Partner of TNT Engineering Firm

Robert Badcork (Robbie, Rob): Son of Morgan Badcock, Sr.

Royce Sullivan: Government Agent

Shiloh and Winnie: Horses on Williams Farm

Terry Badcock: Daughter of Morgan Badcock, Sr.

TNT = Turner, Nealy & Taylor Engineering Firm: Owners Greg Turner, Richard Nealy & Adam Taylor

Tyler Payne: Son of Winston and Michelle Payne

Vechel Locke: Sheriff

Winston Payne: Postmaster. Married to second wife Omalita Hanes Payne. Father of Colt Payne (Physician), Wyatt Payne (Government Agent), Tyler Payne (Engineer), and Darby Hart Williams.

Wyatt Payne: (Government Agent), Son of Winston and Michelle Payne

ACKNOWLEDGEMENTS

Shout out to Kim, Michael, Elizabeth, and Don -- my Nashville connection. Laura, Clara, and Lannie, you are the best of my deeply rooted memories of the fictitious Steeplewood. To my gym mates, thank you for your support and friendship throughout my long and arduous journey. To my family and friends, I love you all.

Finally, to **Dr. Robert Urban,** thank you for metaphorically holding my hand and genuinely believing in me.

About the Author

Raised in the heart of rural Tennessee, Elizabeth grew up surrounded by porch talks, rolling hills, and the kind of silences that spark imagination. Her writing draws on that sense of place—infused with grit, grace, and the complexities of everyday life.

After earning her Bachelor of Science degree from Tennessee Technological University, Elizabeth spent over a decade in healthcare administration, where she witnessed both the fragility and resilience of the human spirit. That experience continues to shape the way she approaches storytelling—with empathy, nuance, and an unwavering interest in the personal truths that define us.

Today, she writes full-time, crafting fiction and short stories that explore themes of identity, family, memory, and change. Her voice is rooted in the Southern tradition but speaks to universal experiences—always with an eye for detail and a heart for characters who feel deeply real.

COMING SOON

SILENT BETRAYAL
Book III of The Steeplewood Series

The deadliest lies are the ones told closest to home.

When authorities uncover shocking evidence linking Blake William's powerful family to a series of crimes, loyalty becomes a dangerous game. Darby's attorney husband demands her silence.

Her half-brother tempts her with a truth she doesn't want to face.

As enemies close in, Blake and Darby cling to one another and must navigate a maze of deception where every betrayal cuts deeper than the last—and one wrong move could have devastating consequences.

9 789899 477452 6